DEVIL
in the
DUST

by

CARA LUECHT

DEVIL IN THE DUST BY CARA LUECHT
Published by Heritage Beacon Fiction
an imprint of Lighthouse Publishing of the Carolinas
2333 Barton Oaks Dr., Raleigh, NC, 27614

ISBN: 978-1-946016-07-2
Copyright © 2017 by Cara Luecht
Cover design by Elaina Lee
Interior design by AtriTex Technologies P Ltd

Available in print from your local bookstore, online, or from the publisher at: lpcbooks.com

For more information on this book and the author visit: caraluecht.com

All rights reserved. Non-commercial interests may reproduce portions of this book without the express written permission of Lighthouse Publishing of the Carolinas, provided the text does not exceed 500 words. When reproducing text from this book, include the following credit line: "*Devil in the Dust* by Cara Luecht published by Heritage Beacon Fiction. Used by permission."

Commercial interests: No part of this publication may be reproduced in any form, stored in a retrieval system, or transmitted in any form by any means—electronic, photocopy, recording, or otherwise—without prior written permission of the publisher, except as provided by the United States of America copyright law.

This is a work of fiction. Names, characters, and incidents are all products of the author's imagination or are used for fictional purposes. Any mentioned brand names, places, and trademarks remain the property of their respective owners, bear no association with the author or the publisher, and are used for fictional purposes only.

Brought to you by the creative team at Lighthouse Publishing of the Carolinas:
Eddie Jones, Ann Tatlock, Marisa Deshaies, Shonda Savage, Brian Cross, Elaina Lee

Library of Congress Cataloging-in-Publication Data
Luecht, Cara.
Devil in the Dust / Cara Luecht 1st ed.

Printed in the United States of America

With love and appreciation, this book is dedicated to my father,
Pastor Tom Edwards.

CHAPTER ONE

June 1933

The wind stopped. The house grew quiet. Lillian kicked the oil rag out of the way and eased the kitchen door open to listen, to see if it was safe.

A single drop of rain splashed down on the rickety porch, and for a brief second Lillian could remember what the wood once looked like. But too soon the drop remembered where it was, that it had no place in the Oklahoma Panhandle, and it rolled, following a parched crack in the ever-present layer of dirt. And then it disappeared into the ground.

Lillian took a step out of the house and stretched her bare toes against the hot, soft dust. The screen door no longer hung in the way, and with a diminished need for the protective layer, no one felt the urge to retrieve it. The frail door had made it through the first summer. But the second summer, when the drought refused to loosen its hold, the winds had ripped it from its hinges, stretched the frail metal spring to the breaking point, and set the door down against the fence. There it rested, with one board broken and a ripped screen, leaning on a fence post that once marked the entrance to the garden.

Now the fence marked nothing. An entrance to nowhere.

When the dust settled, she could see for miles from her kitchen door. Miles that once cradled golden fields of wheat, dew-covered footpaths, acres of grasses, and the occasional neighbor walking through to visit. Lillian took another hesitant step, careful not to stir the persistent cloud of soot that coated everything. In years past, the dirt—the rich topsoil of the Oklahoma territories—had been the source of life. Now that hope, the black wealth the old settlers had risked their lives for, smothered the city. It seeped into every crevice, into every building, into their lungs and ears. Their most valuable asset, once under their feet, now smothered their tiny town.

Lillian reached up to shade her eyes from the sun, looking for the stray cloud that had mistakenly dropped its burden.

Another drop fell. And then, another.

Lillian shuffled out of the shadow of the small farmhouse and up the side to what had been their front yard. Now dominated by rippling drifts of fine dirt, there wasn't much left of the grass that used to dampen the toes of her shoes or her flowers with their heavy velvet petals.

But a neighbor still lived across the street.

Her listless children, long since worn free of the desire to run and carry on with sticks and games, stood in the yard looking up. They'd seen it too.

The sun burned against Lillian's blonde hair. At least, it used to be blonde. The layer of dust covered everything, including people, and where there had once been defining characteristics, now there was likeness. The Negro man on the old shanty claim just outside of town was the same color as the horde of white children across the street. The dirt made sure of that. It was, if nothing else, an equalizer.

Lillian watched the shoeless children. There were five, and no one left in town thought it strange that they traipsed down the street without shoes. Shoes filled up with the soot. Add to it the summer heat, and the ensuing paste meant the freedom of bare feet outweighed the humiliation of it. At least for the children.

Lillian looked up at the lumbering brown cloud overhead.

"Here, over here!" A young boy jumped up at the sky, waving his arms and stamping around as if performing some kind of rain dance. The others joined in, hooting and calling to the meandering cloud. Another drop fell, and then another, and for a brief second they watched each other from across the street while the rain crashed against the dirt in impossibly huge drops and a cloud of dust rose and fell from the miniature impacts.

Rivulets of water ran down Lillian's arms, streaking through the dust. She glanced across the street where the mother of the children stood in the middle of their undignified splashing dance. Lillian lifted up to her tiptoes and waved to the woman.

And then, her arm still in the air, the rain stopped.

The cloud moved on, almost as if it had been a mistake. Where it had blocked the sun, suddenly it didn't, and it took only a matter of seconds for the hot rays to undo the rain's damage. Lillian looked down at the unchanged earth and then back up to Mrs. Owen and her children, but she had already retreated into the house.

***

Sidney watched the cloud from his shanty on the skirts of what used to be his town. He sat on a spot of land his grandfather had bought and paid for with his hard work. He'd managed to keep it without a mortgage—a rarity, and one a few of the white folks didn't much like.

There'd been droughts before. There'd be droughts again.

He had no wife and no children. A man could live on very little with no other mouths to feed. Corn bread and dried beef. A man could live a long time on corn bread and dried beef.

Sidney leaned back in his rocking chair. Like most other furniture, this one had been blasted free of its paint. The remaining gray wood creaked under his weight. He moved slowly, so as not to kick up the dust, and lifted his bare feet to rest on a stack of dry wood. He couldn't remember why the stack of wood sat there next to his door. He supposed he'd had a reason at one point, a plan. Drought had a way of erasing intentions, and what wasn't forgotten due to the lack of rain was blown away by the relentless wind that usually battered the town.

There was little to the house. The windows had never had glass. Shutters used to keep the rain out. And the bugs, well, sometimes they were bad. Sometimes not. But the dust and sand. That kept Sidney busy keeping care of those shutters. Best-tended hinges around. Sidney smiled. A man had to take pride in something.

The cloud that had paused over the town had moved on and now teased the fields. Its shadow dragged across the ruts he'd plowed last spring. Of course, nothing had grown. Now the ruts were drifted almost level in some places, with occasional sticks to remind anyone who passed that it had at one time been planted.

Sidney listened to the sound of an approaching old Ford coming by way of town. He dropped his feet to the dirt and stood, leaning on the post that supported the bit of a roof that hung over the front door of his shanty. It sounded like the Drapers' old truck.

He could see the cloud of dust it kicked up before the truck came into view. And when it did, the furniture and belongings stacked and tied like bundles of kindling made it obvious they were leaving.

He'd lost count of how many families had left. It was easier to count the ones still there.

Sidney scratched his shoulder and crossed one leg over the other. He waited until the truck neared before standing straight and walking to his broken-down front gate.

"Y'all's leavin'?" He waved them down.

Mr. Draper pulled the brake back, and the truck shuddered to a standstill. He lifted his hat off his brow and wiped the sweat out of his eyes. "No sense a-stayin' here anymore."

His wife, seated next to him, frowned. "How long you gonna hold out?"

"Long as it takes." Sidney crossed his arms over his chest. He wore denim overalls, the same kind his father had dressed in, but his father had had a wife to wash and iron. In this dirt, Sidney had given up on the idea of clean clothes.

"You're either brave or stupid." Mr. Draper frowned, then punctuated the statement with a friendly attempt at a laugh.

"Probably a bit of both." Sidney touched the brim of his hat. "Good luck to y'alls."

"Appreciate it. Headed California way. Same as most."

Two of their three children fidgeted on a shared seat in the back. Mrs. Draper sent them a narrow-eyed warning. They settled back against the few items of furniture deemed worth the discomfort. The third child sat on Mrs. Draper's lap. They all lunged forward when Mr. Draper released the brake. The rickety vehicle shook with the effort, but eventually it worked up the momentum to rattle on down the road.

Sidney returned, passing his chair and moving to the right of the shanty, to where the water pump and windmill sat near an old dead tree. His grandfather had proudly sunk the deepest well in town. Sidney pulled his hat off and gave the pump a good effort. The water ran clear into the waiting bucket. He ducked his head underneath the flow and sucked in a shallow breath against the cold. The water ran over the back of his head and covered his face. He stood up and let the drips run underneath his overalls, down his back and chest. And then he found his chair again and sat to watch the deserted road.

***

The wind stopped. Emma grabbed her basket off the hook and shoved her feet into her tired leather loafers.

"I'll be back in about an hour. Jessie, you take care of the little ones."

"Yes, ma'am."

Emma looked back at her oldest daughter. She sat in the rocker with the two-year-old, Little Henry, nestled in her lap. He snoozed to the sounds of the familiar hissing of the unreliably broadcast radio story the five of them had waited all week to hear. Waves of dust floated in the sun that streamed through the pinholes in the tightly closed shades.

Emma had waited for the radio broadcast to begin before setting out. It was the only time she could get to the general store without the kids. They'd long since stopped asking for things they couldn't afford, but this time, she was going to have to ask the owner to extend their credit.

The store was only a couple buildings away. They'd never been a big enough town for sidewalks and things like that, but at least no one had ever had to guess where the yards ended and the road began. Emma walked in a diagonal path, avoiding the ruts and ignoring the now imaginary boundaries.

The bell chimed, and she stepped into the deserted store. No one mulled about like they had in years past. No one had money. Or those who did have some money because family had sent it felt guilty, and those who didn't felt jealous. Everyone, though, was ashamed. Ashamed of the dirt smeared across their faces and of the clothes that had long since lost their color. They were ashamed they only could afford preserved meats and ashamed their mouths watered at the busted apples from the government.

The whole town was ashamed. The schoolteacher had left that spring. When the fall learning should start, there would be no one to instruct the children. That, perhaps, was the deepest shame of all. No place, no future for the children. Childhood had become a luxury no one could afford. It was the kind of humiliation that admitted no hope.

Emma strolled down the aisle, past the shelves stacked with faded fabric. Every once in a while, the owner would unroll it, cut off the piece that had been exposed to the dirt, and sell it for scraps, or dresses, depending on how desperate the woman purchasing it felt. Today, the fabric needed to be cut back again.

Small sacks of flour, oats, rice, and sugar waited behind the counter. Sausages and dried meat hung from racks built into the ceiling. Turnstiles with bright buttons sat in the exact same position as the last time she'd been there. No one needed frivolous cheer now. Emma set her basket on the counter and waited quietly. Eventually, he rounded the corner.

"Sorry, Mrs. Owen. Didn't hear you come in. What can I do for you this fine day? We had a bit of rain, we did ... did you see it?"

"Yes, sir, we did."

"Your husband back yet?"

"No, sir, he ain't."

"How long has he been gone?" Mr. Mitchell's brows furrowed. He removed his spectacles and wiped the glass with the corner of his apron.

"Coming up on three weeks now."

"Hope he gets a good price on them cattle. How long did he think it'd take?"

Emma looked at the wide plank floor. At one time it was whitewashed. Now it was the same dull color as the dirt outside.

Mr. Mitchell changed the subject. "Brother's coming to town tomorrow."

"What's bringing him?" Emma breathed out. She hadn't realized she'd been holding it in. Her husband told her he'd be gone a week. There'd been no word.

"He sold his place out east. He's looking to buy in these parts. Says he wants the small-town life."

"I'm sure there's enough folks willing to sell now." Emma shifted, trying to straighten her dress. It always slid to the side, now that she'd lost so much weight.

"That's what he's figuring. So what can I get for you?"

"We need some things, but I wanted to ask you ... well, since my husband's not back ... you see..."

"You need me to extend the credit further?"

Emma felt her face redden, and she blinked back hot tears. "Yes, sir."

Mr. Mitchell slid his ledger book out from underneath the counter and set it on top. He opened the wide book and made a show of turning the pages. Emma knew he wanted her to understand how many customers he issued credit to. "You know, these is tough times."

"Yes, sir." If she knew anything, she knew that. For a month, she'd been feeding her family out of the seeds meant for planting. No hope in farming anyway. Might as well eat them.

He tapped his pencil on the ledger. "Seems to me that your man has kept up pretty well so far. And you say he's gone selling the cattle?"

"Yes, sir. Government's buying the cattle that can't feed because there's no grass."

"And you expect him back soon?"

"Yes." Emma gave a nod that spoke of much more security than she felt.

Mr. Mitchell hummed a bit, wrote a figure in his book, then slapped it shut. "I think I can get you what you need today, but make sure your husband stops by soon after he returns."

"Of course, Mr. Mitchell. Of course he will."

"Good man, your husband. Always liked him. You need the usual?"

Emma nodded, trying not to look as relieved as she felt. She needed the flour bad. And the powdered milk for the baby. She watched as Mr. Mitchell stacked the things on the counter and carefully wrote down each price before settling it into her basket.

"Will this do?"

Emma looked at the items and tried to be thankful. It wasn't enough. It never was. But it would get them by for a while. "Yes, sir." She looked up and met his gaze. He had one brown and one green eye. She was never sure which one to look at. "Thank you. We appreciate your patience."

"Of course." He pursed his lips and gave one curt nod. "You have a nice day now."

Emma slid the basket off the counter, walked out of the dusty store into the blazing sun, and glanced down the street. Once proud houses, now with leaning porches and busted-out glass, sagged this way and that. Despairing flower boxes hung lifelessly from bent nails. She took a deep breath of the dry air and stepped back into the lifeless road.

It was June. Crops should be growing. She should be tending to those first young peas in her dew-covered garden. She should be using up the last of the preserves and looking forward to picking blueberries from the patch by the cool stream that ran through the back acreage of their property.

Not only would there be no blueberries, but no stream to wade in, and no reaching, weedy flowers on the bank for the children to collect and lay on her lap, all wilted and damp with clinging roots and tender petals. Emma kicked at a stone and immediately regretted the cloud of dust that clung to her legs and followed her down the road. No. She shifted the basket to her other arm. This would have to do. It had to. He had to come home soon.

CHAPTER TWO

L illian put on her hat with the largest brim and stepped out her front door. The hot, still house stifled differently, but no less suffocating, than when the wind punished their home. She'd listened all day for the truck her husband, Peter—Reverend Woodall to the townsfolk—drove. He was due to return from Woodward with the town's share of government food. The staples President Roosevelt had ordered to be delivered and disbursed by local charities had finally come through.

The children across the street sprawled on their rickety front porch. Lillian smiled at the thought of bringing extra food to the family. The temptation had been huge to spread the word at the last Sunday service, but they'd decided to keep the news to themselves until the gifts were in hand. Disappointment made for a difficult dinner—much more challenging to swallow than the oatmeal some of the families ate twice every day.

Unlike most parishes, their parsonage sat a half mile from the white clapboard church with its wind-battered tower. At one time the bell rang on Sunday mornings, for weddings, or for any other number of special occasions. Last autumn they'd taken it down due to the winds and sand and dust. Maintaining the shine had been impossible, and besides, the brass had given the church coffers enough of a boost to feed a few families through the winter. That money was gone now.

So when the telegram had been delivered to her husband at the church, Peter rushed home, forgetting his hat on the nail in his office, ran up the faded yard, and kissed her. Three days later, Lillian pressed Peter's suit, and he filled up the truck before heading deeper into what had become the desert between their tiny town and the closest small city with a train station.

But the desert he had to travel couldn't brag of the colors she'd seen painted in books: landscapes dominated by orange expanses and violet cliffs. Not the kind of desert the old Indians talked about—the kind that changed color by the minute, or the kind that held reserves of water if only you were smart enough or experienced enough to find them. Their kind of desert, the Oklahoma kind of desert, was made of dirt. Just dirt. And no amount of ingenuity revealed hidden stores of anything but discouragement.

Lillian stepped carefully. The contest: walking without kicking up the hated dust. She'd practiced for the challenge. As a child, she'd walked in lakes and rivers with their soft sand and the deep kind of muck that oozed between her toes. With her siblings, she'd picnicked out behind their home back east, and when the sun grew hot, they'd strip down to their underthings and wade out into the cool ripples. She'd practiced kicking up as little of the rich leaf rot as possible and scolded the younger ones to keep still so they could bag more of the two-inch-long polliwogs than they had the day before. They never actually counted them. There were too many. Instead, they filled rusted cans to the squirming brim and kept count of the total number of cans.

So she'd practiced tiptoeing through dirt that threatened to suffocate and obscure her view. The children across the street likely had similar memories, and like her, they knew how to keep the bulk of the dust down. By not moving any more than necessary. Which wasn't difficult, considering the heat.

A cloud of dust rose in the distance. One of the older children pointed to the threat, and they all held their breath to see if it was a dust devil, a harbinger of wind and days sequestered in an oven of a house, or if the noise of an engine would travel the distance and they could all breathe out, knowing the black clouds didn't threaten.

Lillian adjusted her hat to better shade her eyes and stood, listening for the sound of Peter's truck to rip through the distance. The cloud dissipated.

The children returned to doing nothing. Too much time had passed for the cloud to hold their attention on such a hot day. Lillian shrugged and continued the path through town to the church. Maybe a half dozen city blocks in all.

Their church rested at the edge of town. Lillian passed by the general store, with its quiet, unplugged ice chest. The shuttered cobbler's shop listed to the back corner, and Lillian wondered how long it would take for the dry lumber to eventually collapse.

Engine noise built in the distance. Peter's truck lumbered down the rutted road toward the town. Lillian walked faster past the butcher's store, where little but preserved meats was sold anymore. Avoiding the dust cloud no longer mattered, as the truck kicked up more dust than she ever could.

The cloud swelled behind the vehicle, pushing it on its way to the church. Lillian could see the crates stacked higher than the cab. She took a deep breath in, welcoming the cool relief of knowing there would be food to distribute.

Peter lifted his hat and waved it around a bit. Lillian smiled and hopped up the four wooden steps and through the door that used to be painted green. The dirt had blasted all but a few chips of the rich color away.

The inside of the church was at least a few degrees cooler than standing in the early summer sun. Lillian dropped her hat on the last pew and brushed the dirt off her skirts. The wood in the inside of the sanctuary still glowed with care. It had taken an effort on their part, but furniture polish, wax, and scraping and reapplying varnish more often than they should have to meant the place of worship stayed exactly that. By way of will and work, so far they'd kept the harshness of the town's existence during the drought from encroaching on the one place where people came to forget. Where they should be able to forget. And if they couldn't forget, then at least from the place they came for comfort.

The truck rattled to a stop outside. Lillian swung the door open to a cloud and then slammed it again. She coughed, rubbed the dust out of her eyes, and counted to thirty before inching the door back open.

"Opened it a bit too soon, did you?" Peter stepped into the church, dragging his own cloud.

"I always forget how persistent it is."

Peter chuckled, pulled off his hat, and wiped his brow with a handkerchief that would never again know white. "I got it. More than I'd hoped."

He smiled. An expression of relief, one that Lillian shared.

"Let's get these things into the cellar here, and then tomorrow morning we can begin distributing some of the goods."

"What'd you get?"

"You name it, they sent it."

Lillian followed him out, squinting in the sun, trying to see what gifts the truck held.

"You go around and unlock the cellar. I'll drive the truck out back and start unloading."

She nodded and walked on what used to be a grass path to the back of the church. Where flowers and birds and well-tended graves once brought the townspeople peace and comfort, now dirt piled up against the stones, like some kind of horrible snow. About the only thing she and Peter still did to tend to the plots was keep the drifts low enough to avoid obscuring the names. Lillian pulled the keys from the pocket of her skirt, opened the rusty lock, and heaved the cellar door back just in time for Peter to round the back of the building with a crate of apples.

"Apples?" Lillian couldn't keep the excitement from her voice. Getting meat, opening a new package of flour, pouring rice into a pan, they all looked forward to those things. But apples—honest to goodness apples with juicy flesh and red skin. The pure luxury of fruit brought tears to her eyes. "The children will be so surprised."

"That they will be." Peter climbed up the cellar stairs to get the next box. Lillian followed him back to the truck.

"You can wait for me in the cellar."

"That's all right." Lillian rubbed her hands on her skirt and held her arms out for one of the smaller boxes. "The sooner we get this done, the sooner we can get home."

"Well, I guess I won't argue about help." Peter handed a box down out of the back of the truck. Lillian knew it was one of the lighter of the load, but still, her carrying even the smallest of the burdens meant fewer trips back and forth for him.

In better times, Peter would have planned ahead and had men waiting for him. But these weren't better times, and burdening any man with the location to stores of food when he had hungry mouths at home was unkind. Although their people were good people, hardship and misfortune had a way of exposing their less benevolent side. When the food came to them tomorrow, it would come as a gift. If they had had to help unpack it today, there would have been more concern about who needed what most, and how much each family should receive. Feelings would be hurt, jealousies sparked, and another piece of their humanity chipped away.

For as dehumanizing as it was to receive welfare, it did nothing less than bring out everyone's animal side when they had to fight for the government scraps.

***

Randall Mitchell maneuvered his new Ford down what had to be the worst road of the trip. Oh, well. One didn't buy land for pennies on the dollar when the place looked good.

He checked his pocket watch. His wife's untimely death had been timely indeed. He waited to feel a pang of guilt that he didn't feel bad about her struggle with the illness that had taken over her body, but he didn't. Nothing.

Sure, he'd missed her for the appropriate amount of time. And he'd even worn black longer than considered necessary for a husband in the throes of grief. But the strains of the position he'd held working under her father, and the constant jibes about how he hadn't finished his college training, and the hateful glares from her sisters at dinner time ... none of that did he miss. She'd gone young. A lot of people go young. But he was here, and the deal his father-in-law had made him to leave the city had simply been too good to refuse.

He cranked the window down all the way and spread his fingers to feel the wind speed past. As long as he didn't slow down, the dust cloud that almost filled the horizon behind him couldn't catch up.

His gold cuff link glinted in the sun, and Randall pulled his arm back in. He had money, sure, but not so much that he wouldn't miss a chunk of gold if the wind worked it out of the buttonhole to be lost to the deep Oklahoma dirt. He loosened his silk tie and twisted the top button of his shirt open. It had to have increased temperature by ten degrees in the past twenty miles.

The car could travel faster. On the good open stretch, he was sure he hit forty miles per hour. Not here, though. Not with the roads like they were, and not when he knew he would stop in a town with no repair shops.

He traveled with little more than his trunk strapped into the trundle seat and some miscellaneous things piled behind him. As far as furniture, his brother, Justin, the general store owner, promised he'd find enough to make due out of the things that had been left behind. Anything he couldn't find or buy from the desperate people left in the town, Justin promised to order for him. As far as a house, he'd heard there were a number to choose from. The bank owned most of them, and they were doing all they could to unload the glut of repossessed homes. For the meantime, he'd stay with Justin in one of his spare rooms.

Randall swerved just in time to avoid an axle-snapping rut. For being so dry, figuring how the ruts formed in ground harder than brick stretched the abilities of his imagination. But it would get better. No drought lasted forever, and by the time this one reversed, well, if he had anything to do about it, he'd own half the town.

CHAPTER THREE

Lillian ran the water in the kitchen basin and plunged a rag in. She rang it out, folded it over twice, and wiped off the table. Even with the lack of a breeze the day before, the rag came up crusted with the brown dirt that coated everything. On a windy day, she didn't even try.

"Glad it looks like a still day." Peter shuffled into the kitchen and sat down at the table.

Lillian scooped some oatmeal out of the bubbling pot on the stove and set it in front of him. He drizzled honey over it. "The chickens haven't laid in two days. We may need to eat them."

Peter frowned. "Not enough chickens left in this town. If we're not careful, eggs are going to be as expensive as fresh meat."

"I'll give them a little extra feed and make sure their water is nice and cool before we leave today. We'll see how it goes."

"You sure you want to come with? It's going to be hot and dirty, and we probably won't get back until late."

"Of course I'll go with you. Besides, I'd rather help and maybe speed things up than be stuck here worrying."

Peter swirled the honey around the bowl and then took a big bite as if he just now thought to be in a hurry.

Lillian pulled her chair out and sat across from him. "I don't think Mr. Owen has returned yet." She smoothed her apron over her knees. It covered the fact that the flowers on her dress, the one she wore nearly every day, were faded. Still, she had it better than most in their parish.

"Not sure what to do about that. Can't see him leaving Mrs. Owen and their kids, but the drought has done stranger things to men's minds." Peter drained his coffee cup and slid his chair back. "I'm going to get changed. Are you ready to go?"

Lillian nodded and picked up his empty bowl. "I'll be ready by the time you are." She couldn't wait to get the food delivered, especially to Mrs. Owen across the street.

She dropped the bowl into the basin of water and added a few flakes of soap. Even soap could be counted a blessing right now. Thankfully, Peter's income didn't depend on the prosperity of their congregation. Their post in rural Oklahoma was considered a mission, so they received a monthly stipend from the bigger parishes out east. And her parents still sent money now and then. They weren't happy about her marriage. They'd had bigger dreams for her. Lillian glanced out the window above the sink at the desolate landscape. They'd had bigger dreams, but she was needed here.

She shook out the flour-sack towel and wiped the dishes dry. The water in the basin had taken on the lazy brown hue of everything else in the room, but it wasn't dark enough to toss yet. She could swirl a few more soap flakes and use it for cleaning.

It would have to wait, though. She could hear the slide and grate of Peter's shoes on the wood stairs. They'd had carpet last year. A red runner with gold designs that crawled up the staircase from the front door to the hallway above. After the first dust storm, the one that had lasted three days, they'd ripped it out, rolled it up, and stuffed it into the corner of their garden shed. There was simply no way to clean it, even with a vacuum.

It had only taken a few stairs after that first big storm to burn out the new machine they'd received as a wedding gift from her sister. Peter had done his best to order new parts. He'd even installed them and tinkered with the machine for weeks. It would work for a while, but then they'd smell a familiar burning. A loud squeal and a puff of dirt, and a few seconds later the belts had seized again. The final consensus concluded that it simply couldn't handle the fine dust that infiltrated every tiny space. So they'd ripped the carpet up and went with a broom.

A broom was quieter, anyway.

Peter ducked into the kitchen. "Ready?"

"Let's go." Lillian untied her apron and slid her feet into her good shoes, which weren't really good anymore. The effort had to count for something, though. She could already feel the sand collecting through the fine weave of her stockings, but she couldn't go visiting without her legs covered and decent shoes.

Besides, maybe if she tried hard enough with the shoes, no one would notice the sad affair of a hat that perched and wilted on her head.

* * *

Emma scratched out the exact measure of everything in her cupboards on a scrap of paper. She sucked her lips in and counted again.

For the six of them, with careful portioning, they could get by another two weeks. Almost. Henry simply had to come home.

He'd taken their broken-down vehicle. It could be that he was walking the rest of the way home because the truck had stalled on the side of the road and he'd had no way to fix it. Or it could be that he'd failed at securing a decent price for the rest of the cattle and had to sell the vehicle. But she doubted anyone would want that old Ford; they'd always had to stop to add water to cool it off every ten miles or so. Emma rubbed her face hard.

Or he might not come back at all.

Some men did that. They couldn't face the hungry mouths, couldn't face losing the farm to the bank, couldn't face watching their families suffer, and they left. Just left.

Henry wasn't like that, though. But who ever thought their husband was?

"Everything okay?" Jessie set Little Henry down and patted his rear in the direction of the front porch. "Go on out and play with the others."

He toddled through the open door and down the steps.

"Everything will be fine." Emma plastered on the smile she'd forced since Henry had left and met her oldest daughter's gaze.

"What if he doesn't come back?" Jessie looked at the dirty floor. "What if he decides to stay in town?"

Emma stood quickly and turned away so Jessie couldn't see the tears that had suddenly sprung to the surface. "You know your father. He loves us all. He wouldn't do that." She'd forgotten how old Jessie was, how perceptive she'd grown.

"How much food do we have?"

Emma closed the cupboards and wrestled her expression into a carefree lie. "Don't you worry about that. You know things will be fine. Go mind the little ones while I start the laundry." She turned away from Jessie. "I'll need help in a bit, so go play while you can."

Jessie turned and left the room quietly.

While you can, little girl. While you can. Emma chanted the words in her mind. Because life was hard, and soon enough Jessie might have to know just how hard it could be.

★★★

Lillian and Peter bounced down the road under the midday sun. Any other time of day might have been better, but the food needed to be delivered before it cooked in the heat or rotted in the cellar.

Their older truck had a fold-down windshield that did little to protect them from the wind. They kept it up anyway, and the dust swirled in evil little tenacious clouds that drifted to fill up the floor of the vehicle.

Two sealed jugs of water rested between them. To drink, first, but also to pour over the rags they held over their faces to try to keep the dirt out of their lungs. Their eyes had to fend for themselves. Lillian blinked, and dirty tears streamed down her cheeks.

"We're almost there," Peter shouted over the rattle of the engine.

Lillian nodded her understanding.

The farm, or what was left of the farm, rose in the distance. The lack of crops, the dust piled against each fence post, and the leafless trees here and there were not a surprise. The surprise came with the deserted look of the place.

Peter furrowed his brow and pressed the brake. They came to a halt in front of the gaping front door.

Lillian covered her face completely with the wet rag, and Peter followed suit. They had to wait for the cloud that had stalked them for miles to catch up and then slowly sink. The truck shuddered twice and then absolute silence took over the landscape.

Lillian lowered the dirty rag. "Where do you think they went? Do they have a vehicle?"

"I'm not sure. I mean, I know they had an old truck they used around the farm, but I don't know where they went."

She cranked the door handle and nearly fell out of the vehicle. Her dress clung to her back, and her stockings felt as heavy as winter weight. The dirt that had made its way into her shoes felt like a paste between her toes. She pulled her hat off her head and shook it out before flopping it back on.

She looked at Peter, raised an eyebrow, and shrugged. Peter smiled in response, jumped out of the truck, and took his own hat off. At least something had stayed clean. Unfortunately, that something was a white line drawn across his forehead, the only place protected by his hat.

Lillian shook her head. "You should put that back on."

Peter chuckled. "We'll look a lot worse by the end of the day. If your mother could see you now, she'd skin me for sure."

"You're probably right." Lillian wiped the sweat from her forehead with her sleeve and refused to look at the resulting streak of dirt. "Let's have a look around and see if we can find anything. I'll look in the house. You want to check the barns?"

Peter nodded and Lillian stomped up the front stairs, hoping if anyone still lived there she'd not scare them to death.

No one responded.

"Anyone home?" Lillian called at the front door. She didn't wait to step in. She could see from where she stood that the farm had been deserted.

The cupboards gaped open on frail hinges. Most of the windows lacked glass, and the dust filled the corners of the two-room home. The beds were left naked of their covers, and a single rocking chair stood absolutely still in the corner next to the fireplace.

"Nothing in the barn. Well, at least nothing alive. There are a couple of dead birds and some farm tools, but I'd say they've been gone for a while."

"Wonder why they left without telling anyone?"

Peter shrugged. "No one wants to announce the bank is going to take their place. Let's walk around back. I wonder if their well failed."

Lillian followed her husband around to the back of the house. The pump still stood in a patch of dry dirt that used to be a kitchen garden filled with flowers and herbs and vegetables. With some effort, water gurgled to the surface. "Well is fine."

Lillian shaded her eyes and scanned the yard. Under a dead tree, two makeshift crosses marked two small mounds of dirt. "Peter." She tugged at his sleeve.

He turned from the pump and clapped his hands together to knock off some of the dirt.

"Do you think?" Lillian asked.

Peter sucked in a deep breath. Lillian took his arm, and they walked over to the two small graves.

Carved into the crosses were their dates of birth and death.

"They lost the twins." Lillian almost choked on the words. "They didn't tell anyone. They just left."

"The last storm must have gotten them. Maybe they got caught in it."

Lillian lifted her hand to cover her mouth. Both babes. They'd lost them both at the same time. "They weren't hardly three years old, Peter."

"I know." Peter blinked back tears of his own. "We'd better get going to the next place. Food's gonna go bad in this heat."

CHAPTER FOUR

R andall pulled up to his brother's store as smoothly as the road would allow. He already knew he'd impress with the new car: one swipe of the dusty surface and the painted black shiny metal would glint in the relentless sunlight. He wanted to arouse curiosity, though, so he pulled through town slowly, waiting to see the children peek out from open doorways or women pull back yellowed curtains, and timed it so he could get out just as Justin opened the door to the store.

He wanted people to see his welcome, to trust his presence as one who would be good for the town.

Justin did as Randall had expected. He swung the chipped and whitewashed door wide, leaned his broom against the side of the building, and eased his way down the steps. Randall waited for Justin to make it down before he walked around his new car to greet him. His brother had aged.

"Glad to see you made it." Justin clapped him on the back and pumped his hand up and down like a long-lost school chum. "You can leave the car out here if you like, or you can pull round back."

"Good to see you too." Randall smiled. His brother had begun to bald. He hoped it didn't run in the family. Neither of them could remember their fathers, so only time would tell. "I think I'll leave it out here. Kids will leave it alone, you reckon?"

"Kids round these parts ain't no bother." Justin turned back to the store. "Come on in. I'll get us some tea, and we can sit a spell. You can tell me what's new with you." The bell at the door chimed.

"Sounds good. That's a darn thirsty ride coming from the city. Took longer than I expected, too, with all the ruts. Not good for the new car."

"I expect not. Nothing anyone can do about it now, though. We're just riding out the drought, trying to stay ahead of the dust storms." He glanced back. "Nice car, though."

"So, what's the population around here anyway?"

"No telling." Justin closed the front door and motioned for Randall to follow him through the curtain at the back of the store. "Suppose about a hundred. Maybe more. Could be less. Not sure with all the farms."

"A lot of families leave? That's what the newspapers have been reporting back east, that families are packing up and leaving their farms deserted for the banks to take back."

"Yep. Not much for better choices when you own a farm and can't grow a single thing. Ground is cursed right now." Justin sat at a small kitchen table and pointed to the chair directly across from him. "That makes me wonder what you are hoping to accomplish here."

"I'm intending to buy up some land cheap. That way, when the drought does end, I'm sitting on prime farming land and grazing grassland."

"That could be years. We've no idea when the rain will come back, if ever."

Randall nodded and sat back in the chair with his arms crossed over his chest. "I have money from when Betty died. Insurance money." He coughed a little at his own lie, but Justin had no way of knowing. He sat up, took a sip of tea, and leaned back again before continuing. He wanted to give Justin time to absorb the information that he had money in his pocket.

When they were kids, Justin had always been the favorite, the one to get the best of the jobs, the one to get the biggest pieces of pie, but now, finally, they were equals. Maybe even Randall had the advantage. He fought to keep his smile from becoming too foolish. "I think I can help out here, maybe buy some farmers out who want to move on, and maybe start over myself."

"It had to be hard to lose Betty. I was sorry to hear about it."

Randall stood. "That it was. Listen. I'd like to get my bags in and get settled. You still have that spare room available?"

Justin took a deep breath in and stood back up. "Sure thing. Just up the stairs. First door on the left."

"Thanks, brother. It's good to see you again." Randall hurried back out into the sun.

***

They rode in silence back toward town. They'd made four stops so far, and only the first had surprised them. The rest were living as wretchedly as they'd all grown used to.

"Where do you think they went?" Lillian didn't have to explain that her mind had drifted back to that first family, the farmers with the twins in the ground.

"Probably California. That's where pretty much everyone is headed. Have to go a long way east before things get better that way, and since most folks come from the east anyway, it's harder to go back after having lost the farm. Sometimes starting new is better than trying to make something old work." Peter almost yelled his answer.

Discussion wasn't easy with all the bouncing and the wind and dust, but it was better than sitting there in the quiet, with only the heat and the grit of dirt in your teeth as a distraction. "I suppose." Lillian watched the simple landscape speed by. "I wonder if they'll ever come back."

Peter shrugged and adjusted his grip on the steering wheel. "I hope not. I mean, I'd like to see them again, but I hope things are so good where they're going that they can forget this place altogether."

"They'll never do that. Their children are buried here."

"Wish I knew for sure how they died."

Lillian nodded and kept watch on the ruts in the road ahead. "Who's next?"

"Mr. Layton." Peter smiled. "Always like to visit him. He's not going anywhere, and I can't tell if he's even put out by the lack of water."

Lillian held her hat for the next bump. Once over, she leaned a bit closer. "He's got the deepest well in town, you know."

"Ha!" Peter laughed. "Don't we all know! He'll never let anyone forget it."

They jostled down the road until the shanty came into view. Sidney was already at the end of the path, leaning against the fence post with his huge bare arms crossed over his chest.

They slowed to a stop, and Sidney reached to open Lillian's door. "Good to see you, Mrs. Woodall."

"Good to see you too, Mr. Layton."

Peter walked around to the back of the truck and shuffled a few things here and there, collecting the goods for Sidney in one crate. "President Roosevelt called for a distribution of some food to communities suffering from the drought. Thought you may be able to use some of this."

"What is it?" Mr. Layton craned his neck to see the boxes stacked in the back of the truck.

"There's some beans, canned meat, some dry goods. Oh, and here's some apples."

Mr. Layton frowned. "You know, it's just me. I don't figure on needing much. Don't see myself takin' no handouts. Haven't so far and don't really plan to."

Peter stopped. "That's right fine of you, Mr. Layton, but this is free. No one has to know."

"Except me."

"I suppose."

"There's families around with little ones. Give it to them. They needs it most."

"Do you mind, though, we've a ton of apples, and they won't keep much longer in this heat. Can we leave some for you?" Lillian lifted a small box of the red fruits.

"Been a long time since I seen color like that."

Lillian nodded.

"I suppose if'n it'll help. Wouldn't want nothin' goin' to waste." Sidney uncrossed his arms and took the small box from Lillian. "You folks want any?" he asked before pulling the box to his chest.

"No, we're fine. We took a share like all the other folks," Peter said.

"Good." Sidney lifted the box closer to his face. "I think I can feel the water in these apples." He shook his head. "You suppose that's possible? For it to be so dry, that a man can feel the water?"

"I think it's more than possible. I think I can too."

Lillian stepped back up into the truck. "Now if you're sure you don't want anything else..." She let the sentence die off.

"I'm sure, ma'am. You give the rest to those families in town. The ones with kids. They needs it worse than me. It's hard to be hungry when you're little."

Lillian nodded and waved out the window as Peter put the truck into gear. At one time, the Kentucky Red on the Laytons' land had stood waist high.

Now even the strongest tractor would have quite a time if a farmer wanted to plow up the rock-hard soil to plant the fast-growing wheat.

But no one had even considered planting this year. No one had anything left to plant.

"Where to next?" Lillian asked.

"On to the Connors' old place."

Lillian looked at Peter.

"I know. But we have to try."

They could try for the rest of their lives. That man, Mark Connor, would likely watch his children starve before accepting any help.

And if he didn't learn to accept help soon, they might just do that.

★★★

Jessie watched her mother from where she sat under the dead tree. If she shrank small enough, she could catch at least a trunk's width of shade.

Her two younger sisters and one younger brother played halfheartedly in the front yard. Well, it used to be a yard. They played on the hard-packed dirt and did their best to avoid the loose areas of dust. The oldest, next to her, worked at sticking a piece of wood into the earth. He dug at it for a while then tossed the stick across the yard to bake in the sun.

Twigs, dead weeds to be exact, still stuck out from underneath their house. The weeds were the last to die off and the last left standing as a reminder of their existence. It had been years since they'd seen the land rich and green with rolling wheat. The smallest children wouldn't remember green at all. Jessie looked up at the cloudless sky. Her parents had thought this plot had been the land of promise, with dirt as deep and black as anyone had ever seen. But it had been a lie. It had all been a lie.

And now her father had run off, maybe, and her mother couldn't face it.

She wracked her fifteen years of memories, searching for some kind of answer to what would happen to them if he didn't return.

She pushed back a stray strand of hair and looked down the road like she'd done every few minutes for the past two weeks. He should have been back. The pastor left and returned the next day. And if he could do it, her father should have been able to do it too.

She stretched her legs straight out in front and examined her dirty toes. She hadn't worn shoes since school ended, and even then, they hadn't been hers. Her mother had shared them so Jessie could get to school. That left her mother to layer thick socks against the cold to go and feed the chickens and tend to the laundry that never seemed any cleaner for her efforts.

Her feet wouldn't stop growing, though, and Jessie grew sick with the knowledge that her mother's shoes probably wouldn't fit her this fall. That's if a teacher could even be found. But who would come here?

She glanced down the road again, and the glint of something shiny caught her eye. She pulled her legs in and stood up easily, trying not to disturb the little ones who, for once, played without begging for her to join in. They didn't realize she was too old to play their games.

Whatever she saw reflected the sun in a multitude of directions. Jessie glanced back at her distracted mother before making her way to the street.

A new car sat at the edge of the road in front of the store. Jessie looked from her siblings playing to where Little Henry sat in a pile of dirt, stacking rocks in a heap, and stepped out of the yard. She wanted to see the new car and see who, in this town, could afford such a thing. No one had money like that. Granted, some were not as poor as Jessie's family, but no one just went to the city and came home with a new car.

A man with dark hair ducked out of the store and met her gaze too quickly for her to pretend she'd not been interested, or at least not been moving in the general direction. Jessie continued on the road, slower, hoping the man would go away before it became obvious she walked to nowhere. But he didn't.

"Miss." He tipped his hat. "You live around here?"

His hair stuck to his head in perfect waves, and Jessie could feel his brown eyes travel from her head to her bare feet.

Jessie burned with the humiliation.

Here was a stranger. Someone with money. Someone she'd never seen, and she stood like a beggar child with bare feet and a floppy dress caked in dirt. She considered running into the store, but he'd just stepped out. She could run home, to the babies, to her mother... But the way this man looked at her—not like she was a child, but like she was a person, someone who might have something to say—no one had ever done that.

She curled her toes up as if she could shrink her feet into nonexistence.

"Name's Randall Mitchell." He held out his hand.

Jessie took a step nearer. "Nice to meet you, Mr. Mitchell."

"May I ask your name?"

"Sure ... Jessie. I'm Jessie Owen."

"Well, Miss Owen. I'm pleased to make your acquaintance. I'm moving to town. Will I see you again?"

"Yes ... I expect you will."

"Good. It's nice to know I have such a pretty face to look forward to."

Jessie watched him walk to his car and untie the trunk from the trundle seat. He wasn't tall, but he was handsome in an older kind of way. When he looked away, Jessie fled to her yard and around to the back of the house. She didn't want him knowing where she lived or have him see the gaggle of children who shared her room.

She could still see her mother through the window. Jessie brushed off and made her way into the kitchen. She should help prepare their supper. There was nothing difficult about corn bread and milk, but still, her mother stood alone in the room. She had for the past two weeks. And the tiny house was growing enormously empty.

CHAPTER FIVE

Lillian watched the barren afternoon landscape waver with the heat of it all. "How many more?"

They'd stopped at the Connor place. Old man Connor welcomed them by leaning against the house with a shotgun pointed in their direction.

Peter had hollered through the distance, tried to reason with him, tried to explain that everyone was to have their fair share, but old man Connor would have none of it.

There were children there, though, lots of them. So before backing out of their yard, Peter took the risk and dropped their portion of the supplies right there next to the road. Then they drove off and left the stubborn man to wrestle with his equally stubborn, but quieter, wife and their hungry brood.

"Just a few in town. The Owens will be next."

A dust devil kicked up in the distance, swirled into a tower reaching into the blue, and then died off as quickly as it had started. Lillian let out the breath she'd held, then watched for the cloud to re-form as they bounced into town.

Peter pulled the truck into the gas station.

The owner, an ancient man who went by the name of Steel, kicked his chair back from the two-legged lean against the tiny shack of a building. "Need gas?"

"Sure do." Peter tapped the outside of the door as if patting the neck of a horse waiting for its oats. "Fill 'er up."

"Gladly." The man struggled to a standing position, allowing time for his back to get used to the changing demands. "Not so young anymore."

Lillian smiled. "Anything interesting happen lately?" She leaned over and called out Peter's window as Steel neared.

"Besides that strange bit of rain, nothing. 'Cept Mr. Mitchell's brother came to town. Fancy new Ford ... one of the shiny ones with the trundle in the back. Goes pretty fast, I reckon. Word is he's stayin' a while."

"When did he pull in?"

Steel picked up the handle of the pump and flipped the switch. "This afternoon." He plugged the nozzle into the truck, gave it a quick shake, and listened for the gas to start flowing. The bells began chiming at regular intervals. Steel smiled a quick, largely toothless smile. "Not much before you. He didn't stop for gas, though. I guess I'll be seeing him soon."

"Most likely," Peter agreed then leaned out the window to continue the conversation. "We've got some things for you in the back."

"You don't say."

"Government sent supplies for the families here, and we've been distributing them all day. Got a box for you."

"What kind of supplies?" Steel checked the numbers on the pump to be sure they stopped at an even dollar, then replaced the nozzle.

Peter jumped from the truck and reached into the side for a box. "You've got some canned food and some other things. Oh, and some apples."

"Been a while since I had me an apple. Bit tough without no teeth, but I figure I'll eat it anyway."

Peter laughed. Lillian watched the men from her place in the passenger's seat. Steel stood at least a head taller than her husband, and even with his age, he had to be almost twice Peter's weight. He took the box from Peter and nodded his thanks.

"You'll put that gas on my bill for this month?" Peter climbed back into the truck.

"Sure thing, Reverend."

Peter turned the ignition, and the old truck rattled to life. He put it into gear, and they lunged back onto the road, both looking for the new Ford and any signs of the crazy man who would come to stay in this dying old town.

★★★

Emma heard the truck stop out in front of their house. She struggled not to run to the door. When she did get there, she had to fight back disappointed tears as the reverend and his wife stepped out of the truck. Henry hadn't returned.

Emma glanced down at her hopeless mess of a dress. She straightened it anyway, brushed some of the dirt away, and returned Mrs. Woodall's wave.

"We've got some things for you and the kids," Peter called from the back of the truck. He picked up a box, set it down, and retrieved another. A gust of wind blew swiftly by and just as quickly died off.

"I forget the wind as soon as it stops." Mrs. Woodall walked over to stand under the late-afternoon shadow of the house. "It's gone for a day or two, but when it starts back up, it's worse than I remember."

Emma nodded. "It was nice not to have the wind today, though." She watched Reverend Woodall at the back of his truck, then looked down to his wife. Her dress had long since wilted in the hot sun, and her hat sat limply on her golden hair. She had on stockings and shoes that at one time had been shiny. But she still looked fresh in a way. Of course she did. She'd not had any children. Each child sucked out a little more life as they grew and then ripped their way out into the world. And that little part, well, at least she'd never gotten it back.

"I hope we aren't interrupting your evening." The reverend's wife watched, and Emma knew the other woman could read things she didn't want her to see.

"No. Just cleaned up after dinner." Emma made it sound like more of a production than it could have ever been. Another day had come and gone without her husband.

"These are for you." The reverend walked up behind his wife and slid one box onto the porch.

"What is it?" Emma bent to look into the container.

"The government asked us to distribute some food to the families here." Mrs. Woodall's explanation sounded recited. Emma looked at the dirt encrusted in the faint lines around her blue eyes. She'd been doing this all day.

"Are you sure it's for us?"

"Absolutely." The reverend slid another box onto the porch.

One of the younger children sidled up behind her and peeked around her skirt.

"Have you heard anything from Henry yet?"

Emma shook her head and feigned interest in the boxed items. She didn't want them to know how worried she grew while hours stretched into days.

"Hello, Jessie." Mrs. Woodall aimed her greeting behind Emma.

Jessie inched forward. Emma felt a pang of guilt at the sight of her, all gangly arms and legs, too thin for a girl her age. At nearly sixteen, Jessie should be in school and more worried about boys and curling her hair than about whether or not her father would be coming home. After the last storm hit and brought with it a cloud of black that stretched to the sky, they'd all but given up on shiny hair. After that storm, they'd had to scoop the dust out of the corners of their front room with a shovel.

"Hi, ma'am." Jessie dipped her chin into her chest. "What brings you over this way?"

Mrs. Woodall smiled. Emma could see she tried to bring the girl out, tried to encourage her to come forward more, to think of things other than the fact her feet were bare. Emma twisted her apron and tried to wipe the dust from her fingers. She should be the one to worry about her children. Another failure. Like empty tummies and a missing husband.

She'd thought she was a good woman, a good mother, but here she stood, staring at a daughter who was frightened by her own growth, and more than anything, wishing to sink her teeth into one of the bright red apples that teetered at the edge of the box.

How many were there? Enough for each of them? Enough that she could have a bite without the prick of guilt? Mrs. Woodall's conversation with Jessie buzzed quietly behind the thoughts of the cans and bags of food. It would buy them time for Henry to get back. All they needed was time.

Peter brought a third box to the front of the house. "Well, we'd better be on our way."

They said polite goodbyes, and Emma waved as their truck chugged away. Once out of sight, Jessie, Jacob, and Emma each stooped to pick up one of the heavy boxes. If Henry had been home, he'd have never allowed it. But he wasn't.

They set them on the kitchen table and pulled out the shameful harvest. The apples gleamed, and the smallest of the children stood at the edge watching quietly.

Emma sucked in her lips and watched her entranced babies. She should slice the apples, dry them, preserve them for a later date. Instead, she picked up the first and handed it out for Jessie to take. Jessie smiled, turned the heavy, moisture-laden fruit in her dry hands, wiped off the thin coat of dust until the apple gleamed in the low rays of the sun, and handed it over to Little Henry.

Each child waited their turn, and Emma, at once ashamed that a piece of fruit had become such luxury and proud that her children would wait so patiently and then savor each bit so silently, couldn't keep the tears from flowing in trails down her dusty cheeks.

"Here, Mama." Jessie held out one more. "You too."

Emma took the fruit from her oldest child and sank her teeth into the delicate flesh.

***

Randall paced from the window in his tiny room above the store to the side of the bed and back. The town, if it could even qualify as a town, had nothing.

Not even people.

Except he had seen one girl. Perhaps a bit young but at least pretty.

It had taken him all of a few minutes to unpack his things and slide them into the drawers of the small flowered dresser. Where his brother, a man who'd never been married, had gotten such a thing, he'd no idea. Randall looked around the room at the faded pink patterned wallpaper. It probably came with the place.

There was bound to be some redecorating once he found a farm to purchase.

"You ready for dinner?" Justin called up from the store.

"Be down in a minute." Randall stacked a few of the papers he'd been reviewing on the side of his desk then thought twice about it. Instead, he pulled his trunk out of the closet that opened to the low space in the attic and unlocked it. A hidden compartment in the cover opened by way of push and a click, and the papers fit perfectly. He pushed the trunk back into the closet and closed the door again.

He glanced back at the room before heading down the stairs. He hoped he'd find a place in better repair, but if not, there were bound to be plenty of people looking to make a few bucks on the side. He could probably get the work done right cheap.

And if he married quick, a wife could help get the place in order.

Not someone like his last wife, though. He curled his lip thinking about her and her rather ugly death.

It was hard to feel sad for someone who could cause so much trouble with a single call to her father.

This time around, he'd find a wife who needed to rely on him. Like a wife should. This time, he'd be smarter about his choice.

Not that the money didn't have its uses. He'd been paid, and paid well, for his time.

CHAPTER SIX

L illian rolled over and pulled the sheet off of her face. The dirt-laden wind hissed against the side of the house like radio static, only louder, and it couldn't be adjusted.

"Wind picked up again." Peter sat up at the edge of the bed.

Morning had come but darkness still pervaded the room. Lillian kicked the sheet back, slipped her toes into her sandy house shoes, and made her way down the stairs to the kitchen, where she used a dusty towel to wipe out the inside of the tea pot, which she filled with water and set to boil on the stove.

At least the wind wasn't blowing as hard as it had the last time. So far. The haze in the weak kitchen light reminded her of the smoke from burned toast, enough to make her want to rub her eyes.

"It's a shame to wear nice clothes to church when we have to walk through this." Lillian glanced out the window and then to where Peter sat at the kitchen table paging through his sermon notes. "What are you going to speak about this morning?"

Peter remained engrossed in his papers and Lillian gave up. It wasn't as if she wouldn't hear it soon, anyway. "I'll go get ready."

"Okay. I'll be up in a minute," Peter said, still staring down.

Lillian walked past the front window and looked out at the clouds of dust whipping down the street between their house and the Owens' place. The children were not in the yard, and the front door remained closed, a sheet tacked up to cover the window again.

Lillian looked at the pile of folded rags sitting on the floor next to her chair. By this afternoon, when they returned from service, she'd probably be soaking them in oil and stuffing them into the little gaps and crevices they'd come to identify over the past couple of years, deficiencies in the home that under normal conditions would have remained a mystery.

But dust found its way into everything.

Lillian opened her jar of face cream. Brown grit swirled amongst the smooth white. She shrugged and dipped her fingertips into the cream. She could feel the grainy texture when she smoothed the lilac scent against her cheek. If she closed her eyes, the subtle perfume made the all but senseless ritual important in that it almost made her forget her lilacs hadn't bloomed this year.

She closed the jar before any more dust settled into the cream and walked into their room. Peter stood in a still, hot cloud, beating the dust from his suit. Sweat glistened on his brow. They knew better than to open a window, though. Everyone knew better than that.

They dressed in silence and made their way to the kitchen door. Lillian pulled two dishcloths from the drawer, shook them, dipped them in the water, and wrung them as dry as possible. She handed one to Peter and kept the second for herself. They held the cool, damp cloths over their faces and stepped outside.

It had grown darker.

Peter grabbed his hat and pointed to the truck. The church stood mere blocks away, but it grew harder to see by the second.

"I doubt too many will show up today," he shouted over the stinging wind.

Lillian nodded, climbed into the driver's side of the truck, and slid over, making room for Peter.

"I think it might be a bad one." Lillian looked out the back window toward the street. Waves of dust billowed between the houses. Mrs. Owen's door opened, and Jessie stepped out, holding a rag over the face of the baby on her hip.

Lillian pointed. Peter nodded and they backed up and pulled in front of the Owens' house.

Before the truck even stopped, Lillian jumped out and ran to the shelter of the porch. Had it been raining, had it been any other kind of storm, the overhang might have done what it had been designed to do: protect, shelter, comfort.

But it didn't. This was Oklahoma, and the storm was one of dust and dirt, and the roof hung as a loose reminder of their laughable attempts to tame the land.

Lillian wordlessly took the baby and held the rag tight. Jessie ducked back inside the house for the next youngest. Peter, right behind Lillian, opened his arms for that child.

In the end, Peter, Lillian, and four small children pulled up to the front of the church. They offered to come back for Mrs. Owen and Jessie, but the women waved them off and hollered through the wind that they would follow on foot.

With a limited ability to see much farther than the bumper of their truck, Peter drove slowly to the tiny chapel. He pulled in on the side of the church with the least wind. No grass grew anymore. He parked in the one big lot that made up their new world.

They tumbled out of the truck with the youngest children tucked into their arms and the older ones grasping Lillian's skirt and Peter's jacket so as not to be torn away by the wind.

Peter held the door open for them, handed the child in so Lillian could take her, and quickly followed. Only their breathing and the scratch of dirt on glass indicated their presence in the room. They stepped in, brushed off, and the children sat in their family pew, anxious for their mother.

★★★

Mr. Mitchell and his brother opened the door to the church as the scant congregation, maybe thirty in total, sang the final chorus of the last hymn.

Like everyone else, Emma turned to see who had let in the dust-disrupting wind.

The man with Mr. Mitchell looked nothing like him. They stood, close yet not. Emma made the easy assumption he was Mr. Mitchell's brother.

They took off their hats and shook off the dust with enough effort to make it obvious they were aware of the problem but not with so much gusto as to create another cloud for the rest of the congregation to breathe.

Jessie turned and stopped singing. Emma nudged her a bit when she noticed the other Mr. Mitchell sending a quick smile in her direction. She tried to make eye contact with her daughter, looking for a silent explanation as to how she knew the stranger, but Jessie looked forward and moved her mouth to the last words along with everyone else.

The men shuffled into the room, deciding on an empty pew in the front of the church. Emma couldn't remember the last time she'd seen Mr. Mitchell in service. He didn't seem to be the church-going type. Not to say he wasn't a decent sort, but single men tended to find other ways to spend their Sunday mornings.

They both wore nice enough clothes, although Mr. Mitchell's brother's ostentatious attire included a black derby-style hat with a green silk band. He'd topped his striped vest with a bright tie, and his recently ironed pants were cuffed at the perfect height above the edge of his shiny patent leather shoes. The song ended, and he sniffed in and coughed loudly in the stretch of space between the song and the sermon.

The pastor's wife sat in the front row on the opposite side. Emma hadn't asked her and the reverend to pick up her children, but she sure appreciated that they did. No one really knew what would happen to the kids who grew up breathing the black air, and Emma appreciated any bit of protection they could get.

But it didn't really matter whether they were inside or out. After a storm, they'd spend the day spitting and blowing streaks of mud out of their noses. Emma figured it best not to miss church seeing as how they got just as much dirt at home. A little church-going couldn't hurt.

She shifted on the hard pew and tucked her feet underneath. She wore her husband's old shoes, but wearing the ugly things was better than going with bare feet. Jessie would soon grow out of Emma's shoes, which she wore for now. If Henry didn't come home, her oldest daughter would have to wear his shoes. Emma closed her eyes. The pastor prayed. She felt it in her chest, but she was too busy praying that she could spare Jessie the humiliation of men's shoes this winter to concentrate much on the pastor's words. And then she prayed that Henry would come home.

The aisle seat where Henry sat each Sunday morning glared in his absence. Emma looked up once the prayer ended, and Reverend Woodall began the sermon.

Henry had to come home. She looked at her hands, still clasped in her lap as if they'd not yet finished praying, and swallowed. She could feel the grit of the dust in her teeth and in her throat, and Mr. Mitchell's brother looked around at the people in the congregation as if he could divine their level of desperation by a careful catalog of their possessions. Emma pushed her skirts as far down as she could. It was a useless gesture—hiding that she wore her husband's shoes was impossible. But she couldn't help it.

Emma reached for Jessie's hand. The girl nearly drooled over the fine fabric that made up the stranger's suit. Jessie was young, but not so young she couldn't have her head turned. A sick feeling stirred just below Emma's heart. The man had not turned to look back, had not paid them any attention since sitting at the front of the church, but Emma knew she had to watch Jessie.

She squeezed her daughter's hand, and Jessie turned her head the tiniest amount. Emma ignored the question in her eyes.

★★★

Peter looked out over the congregation. Their small group consisted of his wife, the Owens from across the street minus the father, a couple of widows who had hung on to their farms only because they hadn't been mortgaged, another couple of families who were at risk of losing theirs, and Mr. Mitchell and his brother.

The new man's clothes outshined, in the literal sense, any other wearable item in the room. Peter marshaled his thoughts back onto his sermon and moved to the next point.

He needed to get these people back to their homes. The wind hadn't slowed at all since service began, and the individuals seated in the pews took turns looking out the windows at the noisy black clouds obscuring any view of what used to be softly waving fields of new green wheat.

He remembered. They all remembered the crystal blue skies that shifted from a morning yellow to an afternoon turquoise and then celebrated with a lavender evening. Peter flipped over the sheet of paper next to his Bible and moved on to the conclusion.

And all those hues in the sky couldn't compare to the dazzling sea of wheat that had promised bounty and God's goodness. They'd all fallen prey to it. The farmers had flocked to the richest soil they'd ever seen and planted as much as they could. Then the next year they had purchased more tractors and combines, planted and harvested through the day, and kept the machines whirring and chugging through the night under the blazing headlights. For his part, he'd preached too many sermons about God's call to Adam to farm the land. He'd believed, like the rest of them, that the acres of rolling prairies and sky were there as a gift for those who were brave enough to reach for it.

They'd been wrong.

And now, as he preached about King David and his trials, as he preached about the parts of life no one understood, as he offered ambiguity as a source of comfort for the same congregation he'd earlier encouraged, he understood the consequence of it all.

The land didn't come with a blessing. They were not, after all, the Israelites, God's promised people.

They were people who saw opportunity, a chance for freedom from the factories and the festering cities of people who worked them. They'd found the land in a moment when the sun and the rain had agreed to grow prairies in a rainbow of wildflowers and interpreted it as a sign from the heavens. They'd landed, pulled up and tore down, dug in and staked out the black soil.

They'd felt huge, like masters on top of a flat world, but begged their own insignificance and looked the other way when they were reminded that the armies had pushed back the plains Indians, that the land they'd found had been found all along. They'd chosen to see God's providence in the easy times then wrestled with the flip side of the same coin.

Peter looked around at the tired faces. Disappointment had a way of aging folks. The wind and dust did the rest. If he believed as he'd preached in times of plenty, then the opposite would apply in times of want. He couldn't preach it, though. Couldn't bring himself to chastise people who had already suffered so much.

His preacher father would have said he was failing his flock, that it was his responsibility to make them repent, and then God would heal the land.

But repent of what? Peter scanned the faces. They were good folks. As far as people went, he'd seen more dastardly behavior in wealthy congregations. He'd stood at the bedsides of gamblers and drinkers who had had more money than he'd ever see and watched as they passed into peaceful eternity with the comfort of a priest at their side.

He couldn't bring himself to rail at starving children about God's wrath. His wife wore a concerned expression. He knew he plowed through the pages of his sermon without emotion, without conviction. He was as beaten down as his flock. She smiled up at him.

Peter paused and opened his Bible. They all waited. They watched him for direction and guidance. But in this time of want, he had no more to offer than any of them.

He cleared his throat. "Please stand and turn to Psalm one hundred twenty-one, verse one."

The congregation shuffled to a standing position, the sound of pages being flipped acting as the best song of penance Peter could scrounge up for them all.

"'I will lift up mine eyes unto the hills, from whence cometh my help.'" They read the verse in unison with quiet, scratchy voices. One of the children coughed in the silence that followed.

The new man, the brother of Mr. Mitchell, smiled. He had white teeth and slicked-back hair. He had money. That much was obvious.

It was a rare gift in these times—parishioners with means. Peter hoped he was a Bible-believing man and resolved to talk to him after church. Possibly the man wanted to help the community. In the absence of rain, maybe he was the blessing they were all waiting for.

★★★

Jessie watched the new man leave his seat and make his way over to their family.

"I'm Mr. Randall Mitchell." He greeted her mother, but she could feel his eyes shift in her direction.

Much to Jessie's dismay, her mother stood and nodded her greeting. "Nice to meet you. I'm Mrs. Owen." She stressed her married title with a well-timed pause.

Silence stretched. Her mother frowned and continued, "And this is my oldest daughter, Jessie."

"It's a pleasure to make your acquaintance, Miss Owen." Mr. Mitchell bowed slightly.

Jessie couldn't help but smile. No one had ever called her miss before, at least not that she could remember. And it had been obvious that he'd come over to speak with her.

"I hope to see you around sometime?" he asked, watching her mother.

"Sure." Jessie blushed. He smiled and turned away, and she couldn't help but think of the thousands of other things she could have said to the only man in town who drove a new car and had shoes shiny enough she could almost see her reflection in them.

"Let's get going." Her mother handed Little Henry into her arms. "You have the rags?"

Jessie pulled the two she'd kept out of her pocket and handed one to Little Henry. Even at two, he knew what to do with it. He placed it over his nose and watched the door.

It used to be at the end of church the reverend would stand just outside in the grass and greet everyone as they rushed home to their Sunday roasts. Not anymore. Reverend Woodall stood at the back of the church, a sentry for the door that let in the winds and the dirt. People used to mill about, they used to visit. The men used to chuckle and the women twitter about the goings-on that week. They invited each other to Sunday dinner or accepted invitations. But no one could afford a roast now. And even if they could, it would only taste like dirt, like everything else did.

Little Henry shifted uncomfortably. Jessie looked down at him, at his worn, gray clothes, at his blue eyes and hair of indiscernible color. He'd never even seen grass.

He didn't know the difference.

But she did. Jessie remembered their life before Oklahoma, in the green eastern mountains. She remembered hearing about her father's work on the railroad. And she remembered the decision to come out west.

She remembered the gently rolling hills of grass that went on as far as they could see. She remembered riding in their truck, and the game she played to entertain her younger siblings. One of them would watch out the back, and the other the front, and they would try to find a spot without a single tree in view. The first time it happened, her father had gotten out of the truck and pretended to swim in the waist-high grasses.

They'd laughed until they'd fallen down and then watched the clouds float by. Little Henry hadn't even been born. He didn't know how grass could be so soft it cut you or how they were sometimes allowed to splash in the water from the rain barrel. He wouldn't even know what a rain barrel was.

But the man the reverend spoke to, the younger Mr. Mitchell— Randall, he'd called himself—had traveled to this place on purpose. He'd found a reason to come.

Jessie couldn't help but hope that if he changed his mind and continued west he'd find a reason to take her with him.

CHAPTER SEVEN

Randall paced to the window at the front of the store. He expected the banker to stop by any time but felt compelled to watch carefully for him. The dust had kicked up again. Or rather, the dust had continued through the night and had not thought to desist just because the hour hand claimed the sun should be shining.

And the sun had certainly met its match.

Randall looked up through the windows at the dark sky.

Every once in a while a person would walk, or rather, run by. The reverend, for instance. He'd walked to the church early in the morning, clutching his coat collar over his face and smashing his hat down on his head. Randall could see now that he'd need a few extra hats if he didn't want to look like everyone else in town in a matter of days. Keeping them clean would be a job in itself.

"What you watching for?" Justin walked up behind him with a broom in his hand.

"I'm expecting the man from State Bank."

Justin snorted. "Most folks round here avoid that man if at all possible."

"He's going to pick me up to go look at a farm he thinks has been deserted."

"Whose farm?"

Randall crossed his arms over his chest and turned back to look over the store. Bare electric bulbs bolted into the ceiling blazed angrily against the cloud of dust that never seemed to settle. "I've no idea of their names. I just stopped at the bank on the way here, introduced myself, and told him I may be looking to buy if the price was right. He said he had some investigation work to do, that the judge down at the courthouse said some farmers had stopped by in the past month to report they would be leaving and said I could come along and take a look if I liked."

"Best watch out which farm you stop at. It's not unheard of for a shotgun to go off mighty close to the banker's car."

Randall grabbed the dustpan off the counter and held it for Justin to sweep in the pile of dirt. Once Justin did, Randall stood with the pan, wondering what to do with it. He pinched the dust between his fingers. "This stuff is so fine. It just floats, doesn't it?"

"That it does." Justin took the dustpan from Randall and opened a sack. He lowered it down, gently shook it out, then folded the sack over so just the handle of the dustpan stayed exposed. "Makes no sense to throw it outside, and it floats too bad to just dump it in a trash bin. So this is the best I can do."

Randall frowned and nodded. "Not many other choices."

A car rumbled to a stop outside the store. Randall rushed to open the door for the man wearing a suit that, before the wind kicked up, was probably black.

"Mighty blustery out there." The banker shook out the handkerchief he'd held over his mouth and coughed into it. "Picked a bad day to do this."

"There's been worse," Justin said from his place behind the counter. "At least the wind isn't so strong that it feels like it will tear your skin right from your bones. There's been a few days like that recently."

"I suppose so." The man brushed his shoulders off then shrugged at the hopelessness of it all. He glanced at Randall. "You ready to take a drive?"

"Whenever you are."

"Let's get going. If it's still blowing by nightfall, driving back might be near impossible, and I don't want to be stuck here overnight. You all even have a hotel or a place that lets rooms out?"

Randall looked to Justin.

His brother picked up a stray bolt off a counter and dropped it in the appropriate tiny drawer. "No. Used to have an old widow woman who would rent a room once in a while, but there's no one here anymore doing that. Most folks have a tough time just feeding their families."

The banker nodded and waved for Randall to follow him out into the brown cloud. Randall looked back for a minute then traced the other man's steps into the biting wind. He couldn't imagine it being worse than it was, but Justin said the blowing dust was nothing compared to what he'd seen earlier in the year.

No matter how bad it did get, he could count on property values sinking with each day of drought. And that was good for him.

★★★

Lillian didn't like the new man in town.

Of course she didn't mention it to Peter. He took the man's entrance into the sanctuary as an omen of hope. That possibly God wanted to bring someone to town with some resources, someone who could revitalize their dying farms, possibly someone to invest in getting the place back on track in the event the drought ever ended. It didn't hurt that the man had dropped ten dollars into the offering plate. That was more money than many of the people who shared the sanctuary that morning had seen in a long time.

Peter could be right, but she didn't buy it. She didn't voice her hesitation, and she'd agreed to have both of the Mr. Mitchells for dinner Tuesday evening.

Tuesday morning, she'd woken to the silence of no wind or birds. She left to celebrate a beautiful day by putting her bedsheets out to dry after she washed them. As long as she took care not to stir up the dirt on the path, and as long as she hung them high and walked carefully so as not to drag them, she'd have sunbathed sheets with minimal sand to smooth over their bed tonight.

She could see Mrs. Owen doing the same.

Lillian pinned a sheet to the line and waved. "Nice that the wind stopped." She set her empty basket on the porch and brushed the dust off her apron before rushing over to help Emma keep her sheets up and out of the dirt.

Lillian opened Emma's gate and walked over to where she held a wet, bunched up sheet. She pulled a clothespin from the bag that hung on the line and secured one corner of the faded fabric. Emma pinned her end, and after following up with a few fasteners down the middle, both women stood back and took stock of the yard.

"I miss sitting out under the tree and snapping beans." Emma nodded toward a dried-out old bench that sat crooked under the dead tree.

"I miss the beans." Lillian smiled and crossed her arms over her chest.

The sound of an engine roared to life, and the women looked for the source of the noise.

"That's the new Mr. Mitchell. Bet he's driving out again." Emma chewed her bottom lip.

"Do you know what he's looking for?"

"Not really." She paused. "You know, I've been growing some beans in a box next to my house. I've been careful to cover them when the winds start, and it looks like we might get at least enough for a meal or two in the next few weeks."

"I haven't even tried. I even lost the flowers in my window box." Lillian listened to the noise of the revving engine. "We're having both Mr. Mitchells over for dinner this evening."

Emma frowned.

"Why the expression?"

Emma pointed to the edge of her porch, and they both took a seat in the shade. "You ever meet someone who just sets your teeth on edge."

"Yeah."

"He does that for me. And I know it sounds crazy, but I think he's been watching Jessie."

Lillian glanced toward the house. "How old is she now?"

"Almost sixteen."

"She looks older."

"I know." Emma picked a rock out of the dirt with the toe of her shoe. "But that's not too young to have your head turned."

Lillian knew she was right. She'd been in love young too, or at least she thought she had been. "How old do you think he is?"

"I've no idea. I'm a terrible judge of age, but I'd have to say nearing thirty, at least."

"I think I'd have to agree."

Mr. Mitchell's car rumbled slowly down the road. They watched for him to become visible through the frame of his lowered window. They could see he scanned the house and yard, and when he noticed how the women watched him, he tipped his hat and smiled a brilliant white smile.

"How do you suppose his teeth look like that?" Emma furrowed her brow. "Even my baby's new teeth don't look like that."

"I was thinking the same thing. I know out east my mother made me visit the dentist, but my teeth never looked like that."

"Do you miss it?" Emma met Lillian's gaze.

"Miss what?"

"Living back east?"

Lillian leaned back on her hands and let her eyes follow the new car until the dust hid it from view. "No. I really don't." She looked up at the blue sky. "I mean, I miss some things. I miss grass." She snorted slightly and then shrugged an apology for the unladylike noise.

Emma covered her mouth and smiled.

"I miss being in a church where more people were involved in the functions. But I suspect that lack here has more to do with the drought than any lack of desire to spend time as a community."

"We used to have potluck dinners on some Sundays, after service. Not since everything dried up, though. Not enough food. And not enough money for gas to get into town for a lot of the folks. And not enough grass so the kids can sit and play." She leaned back, matching Lillian's posture. "And too much dirt to get in the little food we have."

"I've almost forgotten what it's like to eat without feeling that grit in my teeth."

"Maybe it will be like sand, and it will clean them, and we'll end up with teeth that look like the new Mr. Mitchell's."

Lillian smiled and stood up. "I doubt it." She brushed off the back of her dress. "You know, I was looking through some old boxes, and I found a couple of pairs of shoes the ladies' auxiliary at our sponsoring church in Virginia sent last year. They don't fit me right. I was wondering if you or Jessie could use them."

Emma looked down at her worn shoes, and Lillian forced her eyes not to follow. She didn't want her to know that she'd noticed there could be a need.

"We sure could."

"Good. Is it okay if I bring them over this afternoon?"

"That would be great."

Lillian could tell Emma didn't want to meet her gaze. They'd just had a nice conversation, the kind that made you forget how bad things were, and Lillian had pulled them back down to reality. She wished she could do more. She wished she could do something to make Emma forget the threat of hunger and her missing husband.

Lillian took a step toward her house. "I need to go and make some lunch for Peter when he gets home. I'll stop by after he leaves again."

"Thank you."

Lillian offered half a smile. The kind someone gave when the pain in the other person's eyes didn't need to be addressed but did need to be acknowledged. *Dear Lord,* she thought. *Just send her husband home. Please.*

★★★

Jessie watched for Mr. Mitchell to return. He'd left while her mother and Mrs. Woodall leaned back on the front porch talking, so she hadn't been able to wave as he'd passed.

His car had a thick coat of dust but still bragged its shiny newness by the smooth rust-free paint underneath. It lumbered by, and Jessie imagined how the smooth seats might feel on a cool day, imagined silky cool relief of a new dress—the kind that flowed and smoothed against her legs, the kind in the magazines. And a hat—a white hat with a lavender flower and a checked ribbon. If she had that, and if he pulled up to their gate to pick her up, and if he held the door open for her, and then closed it with the heavy thump that said he would buy her dinner at a nice restaurant; Jessie imagined having it all.

Ten dollars in the offering plate. She'd watched him put it in. If she had that money, she could make sure her brothers and sisters had every fruit they wanted. And she'd buy her mother new shoes.

Jessie buried her toes in the dust and rested them there, feeling the heat seep into her skin. If Mr. Mitchell picked her up, maybe he could drive her to a place where she could sink her toes into sweet-smelling, dew-covered grass and lie by a stream, listening to the clear water gurgle over rounded stones. Oh, they could find someplace new together. Someplace where things stayed clean. Someplace where the heat couldn't reach.

"Jessie? Where'd you get off to?"

Jessie took a deep breath of the hot, dry air and slipped her toes from the dirt.

She stood. "I'm coming."

"Can you pull the sheets off the line?" Her mother's face appeared in the kitchen window. "Be careful not to drag them through the dirt."

Jessie frowned and plucked one of the pins from the line. Of course she knew not to get the clean sheets dirty.

Working her way down, she pulled the second and third pins while she bunched the fabric up to keep it off the ground. Nearly sixteen was old enough to gather sheets from the line. It was old enough to watch her brothers and sisters while her mother was out. It was even old enough to get married and have her own if she wanted to. That's what her cousin had done. Everyone tittered about it, and the women in the family shook their heads, but her cousin married and went off, and she was fine.

Jessie looked as far as she could across the barren brown landscape behind their house, where the fields once waved with the slightest breeze and where her father would press on with his tractor, waving and smiling. The limitless landscape, the rolling hills and the sky that stretched forever, had once seemed all the more beautiful because it was uninterrupted by trees or buildings or even streams. Now the desolate reach made it seem as if the whole world had withered, and she stood on the summit, looking out over the open prison of devastation.

She bunched the second sheet tightly to the first and looked to the house with its gray, unpainted wood wishing she could brush the dust away and something shiny, something new, anything not coated in dirt would appear. But she couldn't. Jessie wiped a trickle of sweat from her forehead, knowing it would leave a black smudge. Even the things she cleaned were only dirtier for the effort. No amount of rubbing or scrubbing or dusting accomplished anything but to make things worse. Like everyone else in what was left of the little town, she had no choice but to watch as each day dawned a little worse than the last.

Jessie tossed the last of the faded sheets into the basket and held her breath, hoping she hadn't kicked up any dust with her little flare of temper. When the dust didn't react, she picked up the basket and glanced down the road one more time before she opened the door to their house and stepped into the still, heavy weight of a home existing under the threat of her missing father.

He'd had a choice, though, or at least he'd made a choice. Jessie dropped the laundry on the kitchen table and picked up the dishrag. She, on the other hand, had work to do.

CHAPTER EIGHT

"Have you had much luck in finding places you'd think about purchasing?" Peter speared a chunk of potato and lifted it to his mouth. The stew that had simmered on the stove for most of the afternoon filled the house with the delicious kind of fragrance he remembered from better times.

"There are a number of potential farms available, but I want to confirm the depth of the wells and find out who owns the neighboring acreage." Randall wiped the corners of his mouth then settled his napkin back into his lap. His collar was the whitest thing in the room.

"Has the banker driven you by the Drapers' old place? They had a lot of land, and they just recently left town." Justin lifted one brow.

Randall nodded and moved a carrot around in the thick broth. "There's the Drapers' place, and the Smiths'. They moved on and didn't tell the banker."

Peter glanced at Lillian and set down his fork. "We drove by there, too. Looks like they lost their young twins. Didn't tell anyone. Just left."

After a pause, Randall cleared his throat. "Both those places are possibilities, but the people across the road own the neighboring acreage."

Peter could feel Lillian's eyes aimed in his direction. "Yes. Well, I haven't heard they've any plans to sell just yet."

Lillian's swift intake of breath reminded Peter to tread lightly.

"What do you mean by 'just yet'?" Randall carefully spread a generous smear of butter across the roll he'd torn apart.

Peter used his knife to open his, and Lillian slid the butter over so he could reach it. The man was sharp. "What I mean is that, like the rest of these folks, they're hanging on so far." Hopefully, Randall would accept the vague explanation.

The new Mr. Mitchell nodded and, with a quick gesture, shoved the piece of bread into his mouth. The man's teeth were white, almost as white as his shirt. Peter looked at the stew resting in his bowl. Part of him hoped the new Mr. Mitchell would find the farm he searched for quickly so the town could settle once again, but if he wanted to be honest, a small part of him wanted the man to go away. Peter lifted his fork and drew lines through the gravy that had drifted to one side of the plate.

"You think they may want to sell?" Randall continued the discussion.

Justin folded his napkin and set it on the table before sitting back in a conversational pose. "You know her husband is gone. Been gone a while. She may need to sell soon." He sucked on his front teeth before reaching in with his fingernail to pick out the remains of dinner. "I've extended her credit quite a few times."

Lillian stood quickly. "Who's ready for dessert?"

"Dessert? Mrs. Woodall, you make the thought of becoming a married man a downright tempting one." Randall smiled and placed his fork on the edge of his plate.

Dessert sounded like a fine prospect, but Peter knew his wife only offered as a way to move the evening forward. She thought she hid her distrust of the new Mr. Mitchell, but he knew better. His wife, although quiet, had an openness about her eyes that she gifted to nearly everyone she met.

Except Randall. Her eyes shuttered when he'd walked into the room.

Peter only hoped Randall stayed unaware of her feelings. It would not do the town any favors to alienate the only chance to breathe life into the place that they'd seen in years.

★★★

"Where'd they come from?" Jessie turned her foot back and forth, wishing for a mirror that reached the floor.

"Mrs. Woodall brought them over." Her mother kicked out her foot so that Jessie could see she also sported a new pair. Well, they were new to them. "She said the ladies' auxiliary from her home back east sent a box with a few pairs of shoes. These she couldn't use."

Jessie examined the soft brown leather. They were women's shoes, not children's, with the stubby kind of heel that spoke of work, but not so much work that the wearer couldn't look good doing it. The slight scuffs on the right toe were buffed until they had almost disappeared. Diagonal lines darted from the bright buckle to the toes and added a dimension of whimsy.

Jessie looked down the side of her leg and tried to get a view of what she might look like with the added two inches. If she worked as a secretary in a big building in a city, the shoes would be perfect. Jessie let her mind wander to stacks of papers, the buzz of adding machines, and the office-like noises she'd heard on the radio programs they waited for every week.

She blinked and looked up, listening to the silence. No noise meant no work. In the country, the noise that spoke of success— the whirring of the tractors late in the night, the chirping and buzzing of the bugs in the light—had made them all want to keep going. Noise meant hope. Not like now.

"Do you like them?" Hope hung on her mother's words. She rubbed her hands on her apron and watched for Jessie's reaction.

Jessie nodded and smiled as best she could. "How about yours?"

Her mother slipped them off and stuffed her feet into her old shoes. "They're nice. But I think I'll wear these ones around the house. No sense in wearing out two pairs."

"But you'll wear the new ones to church and the store, right?"

"Of course I will."

"And if we get visitors? You'll wear the new ones for company?"

Her mother lowered her brows in a question. "Who are you expecting?"

"No one," Jessie lied. Not really lied—rather, she didn't voice her hopes. They were silly, anyway. "Do you want me to get the rest of the laundry off the line?"

"Go ahead." Her mother bent to pick up the new shoes then lifted them to the top shelf of the closet that separated the kitchen from the rest of the rooms. "I'll finish up the rest of the dishes."

Jessie escaped outside. The setting sun burned deep orange on the horizon. But instead of the brightest color clinging to the edge of the earth, the light speared up into the darkening sky. The line between earth and sky roiled angrily against the remnants of sun, and the static in the dry air buzzed around her. The small hairs on her arms stood on end, and Jessie whipped around, searching the deep colors of the setting sun for any warning.

Her brother and sister piled rocks in the dirt, playing some game that had been invented only because of the lack of grass. Jessie rested the full basket on her hip and watched them and the crackling air.

"I think you need to come in." A gust of wind ripped the words from Jessie's lips, but they'd heard, abandoned their game, and ran to the door. They'd felt it too.

Jessie glanced around the yard, checking to make sure the chickens were all in and that nothing that could blow away was left loose. But they were used to this now. They were prepared. The only thing left unknown was how long it would last.

The cloud in the distance swelled and rose to block the fire-colored sky. Jessie turned her head. As far as she could see, the dirt wall rose against what was left of the day. She grabbed the bag with the clothespins, a chair with a missing back, and ducked against the growing wind. The wall boiled, and agitated fists rose against the backdrop of their tiny house as if they would smash down at any second.

Jessie ran with the basket on her hip and hit the front door just in time for the cloud to envelop the house in a loud hail of soot.

Her mother rushed past, locked the door behind her, then hurried to the few windows to make sure they were closed as tightly as possible.

"Get the oiled rags. Quickly!" she yelled over the hissing needles of sand that battered the panes of glass.

Jessie nodded her answer in the room that had grown too dark even to see mere gestures. Her little brother struggled to light a match and set the kerosene lamp to burn against the dark cloud that invaded the room.

The three smallest already held damp rags over their noses and mouths. Her mother must have seen the cloud approach and attended to them right before running to the door for her.

Her brother shook out the match, and the flame throbbed to life against the growing thickness of talcum-fine soot. Jessie covered her mouth with her apron and helped stuff oiled rags in the corner of every window sill and across the threshold of both doors.

She turned to look at her siblings seated together on the threadbare sofa. This was it. This was what they would do until the wind stopped punishing their tiny house and until the sun found a way to beat down against the barren fields. It was funny—she didn't even think to wish for the one thing that would stop it all anymore. Rain. A heavy rain could bring new life. It could beat the dust down and give the dormant seeds the life they needed to sprout green.

But it had been so, so long. Jessie looked at the dark room, at the pounding of the flame against the glass, at her mother's furrowed brow. She tried to smell something besides the dirt and oil, something that reminded her of life. And she imagined breaking out of that little gray house. Any way she could.

★★★

Randall pushed the gas pedal as far down to the boards as he dared. A black cloud billowed behind him. A behemoth of a creature that pulsed and roared in silent threat.

Birds raced ahead of the dark wall. He glanced up at the sky through the dusty windshield and pressed the pedal farther down, urging his car to go faster, goading the machine to fly ahead of the flock.

What existed of a town loomed ahead. Houses spread apart only because there was so much land to be had that seeing neighbors' barns seemed almost to be an intrusion. The farmland reached behind the houses. Fenced near the road, but then not ... the farmers knew where their lines rested. Randall jerked the wheel to the left and then to the right, dodging holes as big as his tires and trying to keep his car in one piece.

If he ended up buying land here, he'd have to buy a truck. The car, although comfortable, was impractical.

The sky in his rearview mirror swelled black and menacing. He didn't know anything could be so high. Even the cities back east with their buildings that stretched into the clouds couldn't compare in height to the monster behind him that grew by the second.

He thundered past the few homes that shared the street with his brother's store, skidded to a stop, pulled the parking brake, and leapt out before the engine had even finished sputtering. He slammed the door closed just in time for the cloud to rush in and swallow his parked car.

He glanced out the store windows. The tiny building was enveloped in black. He couldn't even see where he parked. Heck, he couldn't see to the edge of the planks that ran the width of the porch.

"Pushed that to the very limit, didn't you?" Justin carried a bucket of foul-smelling oiled rags and motioned for Randall to move over. "Gotta shove these against the threshold. Here..." He handed one to Randall.

Randall sneered at the dingy, drooping scrap of fabric, took it between his fingers, dropped it to the plank floor, and shoved it into the corner with the toe of his shoe. "Are all the homes here built so ... well so that the dust can get in everywhere?"

"This is good." Justin shook out a sheet and covered the bolts of fabric. "You should see some of the homes. By the end of this storm, people will be tossing full buckets out their front doors." He smoothed the cloth and tucked it under the corners. "Most folks have given up on brooms—tomorrow, if it stops by then, they'll be using shovels to clean their homes."

"How long has this been going on?"

"Years."

"And they still live here?"

Justin stopped and looked at Randall. "What else are they supposed to do? Most folks gave up everything to move out here. Everything they have is in these farms, and after a few years of drought, most of the farms are mortgaged to the hilt. They've no place to go and no money to get there."

Randall nodded and looked to the floor to conceal the bit of smile he couldn't hide. That was precisely why he was here.

CHAPTER NINE

The storm hit fast and hard. Lillian looked up from her cup of coffee and watched Peter's unwavering expression. His furrowed brows appeared to be stuck where they were, with his eyes darting to the windows every time a particularly fierce gust hit their small house.

Dust floated in swirls on top of her black coffee, and every time she took a sip, she avoided clamping her teeth closed so she didn't have to feel the ever-present grit.

"Hope everyone made it in. This one came on pretty quick." Peter stood, walked over to the sink and slowly dumped his now cold coffee down the drain. He watched it swirl in the white porcelain sink, swallowed into oblivion. Instead of turning on the water, he grabbed the dish rag and wrung it out over where the coffee had left a trail. Even though their well was good, even though running water wasn't in short supply for them, living where the air sparked with dry energy, where everything seemed too old or too worn, meant they conserved everything.

Lillian stood and shooed him away from the sink. "I'll wash it with the other dishes later. Maybe after lunch when there's more to do."

Peter took in a deep breath then coughed. "No sense going to the church office today."

"I would think not." Lillian frowned. "You'd likely get lost and die trying to get there."

She'd meant to say it as if it were a ridiculous notion, to say it to lighten the mood, but the silence that stretched after her sentence revealed the harsh truth of her words.

"I wonder what happened to Henry Owen." Peter glanced toward the front of the house. Even though it was late morning, the black cloud that refused to dissipate shrouded any room without burning lamps.

Lillian walked ahead of him and set the lamp on the coffee table. They both sat, gingerly, careful not to stir up any more dust than necessary. She crossed her legs and leaned forward. "How long has it been?"

"At least a few weeks."

"She can't have much money, and they have an account at the store."

Peter nodded.

"And he took their truck, which means she has no way to get out of here if she decides they need to go."

"I know."

"How much longer do you think they can hold out?"

Peter leaned back, locked his fingers behind his head, and looked up to the ceiling. "I've visited, but she's always careful to have her cupboards closed and everything cleaned up best as anyone nowadays."

"Same here. I took them over a couple pairs of extra shoes. It's hard to tell what they need."

Peter stood and crossed to the window. The drapes were drawn tight against the barrage of dirt and wind. Not that the fabric held any power to stop the onslaught, but because it felt better not to look out and see nothing but thick black. "We could be the only ones on the planet right now." He stared at the fabric as if he could see through it.

"Has the new Mr. Mitchell found any property?"

"Not sure." Peter turned around and crossed his arms over his chest. "Why do you ask?"

"No reason, really." Lillian leaned forward and adjusted the lamp so it burned brighter. "What do you think brought him? I mean, it seems strange that a man would want to buy land right now."

Peter shrugged and sat back down next to her. "I don't know. I suppose it may seem strange, but this area was once coveted farmland. No reason to think it may not be again someday."

"And you think it's okay for someone to come in and buy it out from underneath struggling farmers?"

"Either someone like him or the banks. I suppose once the owners can't pay, someone has to do it."

"What about the Owens? What if he wants to buy their land?"

Peter closed his eyes and rubbed his face. "I'm not sure what kind of mortgage he has, but I did see the banker stop there last month, so I assume he's doing business with the bank."

Lillian slumped against the back of the sofa. "I wonder if Emma even knows. Is Henry the kind of man to talk to her about such things?"

"I've no idea."

Lillian could taste bile at the back of her throat. "I wish this would end." She crossed her arms over her chest and held tight as if the gesture, the closeness, the reality of touch itself might produce some impossible solution that she'd yet to consider.

Peter stood again. "I'm going upstairs to try to get something written for Sunday's sermon."

The house groaned and shuddered, and the wind picked up speed. She could hear it. "I hope some of the other farmhouses can stand up to this."

"There's no telling until the storm's over." Peter grabbed the newel post and took the first heavy step up to his study. "All we can do is pray."

Lillian nodded. She should pray. She should pray for Emma and her children. She should pray for anyone who hunkered down in shacks waiting for the wind to stop. She should pray that the drought would end. But all she could do was wonder why a stranger might drop ten dollars in an offering plate.

★★★

Justin carried the pot of stew to the kitchen table, tossed his mother's hand-knitted potholder down, and rested the simple dinner on it.

It felt late in the day for dinner, but as the clock on the wall of the store chimed only four times, Justin realized he'd been ahead of schedule all along. The constant black had a way of doing that. A way of making a man forget about time. Not his brother, though. Randall checked his pocket watch what seemed to be every five minutes and kept glancing at the door.

"Dust storms don't run on a schedule, you know."

Randall frowned and walked over to the sideboard where earlier he'd placed a stack of papers. "Maybe you can help me with trying to figure out who owns what around here." He pulled one large, folded piece out from the pile. Blue lines ran to and fro, and tiny scribbled numbers covered the page. Names and landmarks—the post office, the gas station, and the hardware store that had closed—anchored the rest of the map with tiny symbols and familiar drawings. Randall flattened the creases and pointed to a large plot of land that ran from one place in town and down back behind most of the other farms. "Whose is this?"

Justin set the bowls he'd been holding down on the corner of the table and leaned in to get a better look. "That looks like the Owens' place."

"They're still in town." Randall tapped his finger in the middle of the plot.

"That was one of the families in church. Don't think they'll be wanting to sell, especially with the husband out of town." Justin grabbed a towel to protect his hand from the hot cast iron pan and lifted the lid. Steam rose through the hazy air. "That's a pretty big place, though. You got that kind of money?"

Justin knew his brother had come to town with money—it was obvious by his new car and his clothes.

Randall shrugged in a gesture that at once told Justin to mind his own business but also bragged. Justin fought the urge to scowl.

But the kind of money that it takes to buy out a full farm—Justin took in a deep breath, trying to enjoy the aroma of the stew—that kind of money didn't come along very often. Randall had contacted him after his wife had died, and he'd talked about life insurance. Justin glanced back to his brother's inscrutable face. At the time, the whole conversation had made Justin a little queasy. Only now did he know why: Randall hadn't even mentioned his wife's suffering or her family or even what he did for a living. He'd simply made the call to scope out opportunities. What kind of a man never looked back?

His brother studied the plat maps like a surgeon might draw a line across a leg in need of severing. But Randall was his younger brother—half-brother, to be more precise—by more than fifteen years. And he'd had it tough growing up. Justin felt a kind of responsibility for him. Felt like maybe he should be the dad that Randall hadn't had. At least he should help him out here and there where he could.

"The Owens." Randall looked up at the ceiling and then back to the papers. "There was a woman and a bunch of kids—and older daughter. They sat near the back, right?"

"That would be them." Justin waved to the chairs.

Randall folded up the papers and set them back on the sideboard before joining him at the table. "How long has the husband been gone?"

"At least three weeks now." Justin uncovered the loaf of bread, sliced off a piece, and handed it to his brother.

Randall took it, lifted the lid off the butter, and slathered some on before replacing the cover. "That's a long time." He paused to bite into the bread, chewed, and swallowed loudly. "Think he's coming back?"

Justin blinked and tried to hide his level of discomfort with the harsh question. Of course, he wanted to say. But he didn't know. No one knew what kind of trouble was brought in by the winds.

"No matter. I can talk to his woman about it. That's a nice farm. And if I remember right, it looks like they can use the money."

"I don't think it's that easy." Justin lifted his brows, willing his brother to get into the habit of thinking of other folks and what their needs might be before whatever his plans were.

"Maybe not." Randall used the flat side of his fork to crush a potato and mix it into the gravy. The resulting blob dripped all the way to his mouth, but somehow he avoided any sort of mess. "Doesn't hurt to ask, though."

Justin frowned into his glass of milk. Sometimes it did hurt to ask.

★★★

Emma ripped the now dry sheet off of the doorframe. They'd nailed it up during the worst of the dust. It had been of dubious help. She didn't care about the nails left sticking out, or the frayed, torn ends of what had once been lovingly smoothed across her and Henry's bed. It was white, sprinkled with tiny yellow roses. Sunday had come again. He still wasn't home.

She took a deep breath of the dusty air and coughed it back out. The little ones lined up behind her with their rags pressed to their faces, ready to dodge into what was left of the storm and walk to church.

The wind had died down considerably, but even the slight remaining breeze kicked up enough to make her worry about the long-term consequences of breathing black air. Worry. That's all she had left.

More than one child had died of the curious pneumonia that struck without conscience.

"I'll take Little Henry?" Jessie scooped the littlest of her brothers up and balanced him on her hip.

Emma nodded. With big Henry still gone, the division of labor had changed. Drastically.

She glanced out the window at the dust devils that stirred and disappeared, only to reappear down the road in front of someone else's house.

He wasn't coming back. Emma looked at her children. Five of them lined up in the front room of their tattered farmhouse, ready to go to church and pretend that they still had a father.

Jessie knew. Emma could see it in the way she watched Emma carefully measure out the oatmeal, stretching every staple to its furthest extent, praying like the woman with the oil, that somehow, if she didn't look at the levels of supplies, there would always be enough.

"Let's get going. Service will be started by the time we get there." Emma picked up the second youngest, adjusted the rag she held to cover her face, and ducked into the blowing dust.

She hadn't even been sure that they would go to church, but Jessie surprised her by insisting they do. And her daughter was right. They'd all been cooped up for days while the wind ripped apart the town. At the very least, they would have a chance to look at four different walls.

Pastor Woodall held the door open as they approached.

"I thought we would be late," Emma rushed her children in and then let him close the door. She took off her hat and tried to shake some of the dust out of the folds of her skirts. Not too hard, though. Better on the skirt than in the lungs.

"You are. Didn't think you were coming; otherwise, we'd have stopped to pick up the little ones. The house looked quiet this morning."

Emma shrugged. "We ran behind." She offered the weak excuse.

"Well, we're glad to see you." The pastor leaned closer to whisper. "We can talk after service, but Lillian and I were hoping you might join us for dinner this afternoon."

Jessie had heard the invitation and smiled. It was too late to decline. "That would be lovely."

Emma ushered the children into the pew ahead of her and followed them to sit. She picked up the hymnal from the slot in the back of the pew in front of her and flipped to page one hundred thirty-one. Jessie and Jacob followed suit while the little ones stared at the ceiling.

Emma looked at the page. "In the Sweet By and By" was printed boldly at the top. She took a deep breath and began singing when the pastor's wife led out the first few notes.

She wished it was over. Emma looked down at her children as the words of longing washed over her. He wasn't coming home. She had no way to feed her children. But she sang of the eternal hope. *"We shall sing on that beautiful shore, the melodious songs of the blessed."*

But what were they to do now? She looked around the room to the other equally ragged families all wishing for the same thing ... that it would just be over.

"And our spirits shall sorrow no more, not a sigh for the blessing of rest." The song mocked them. She knew Pastor Woodall had chosen it, hoping it would be a source of strength, a hope for what was to come. But Emma couldn't help but doubt as she looked at her children who, without a father, would be hungry. They had nothing. Nothing. The song teased of the pleasure they might find if they just gave up.

She could stop eating. That way there would be more for the children ... but then who could take them in? No one had that kind of money. The tasks would fall to Jessie. Emma wiped away a betraying tear. She had to keep going.

Keep going, and sing of the hope that could fill her mind, but not her children's bellies.

★★★

Randall fought the urge to look back when the Owens stepped into the church at the last second before service began. He wanted to assess them a little more closely.

The maps had their farm in the center of it all. They had a narrow strip of acreage that ran all the way to town—where the old farmhouse stood—and then an expansive network of fields that connected more than a few of the other farms he'd talked to the banker about.

One farm stood out. A small one, but one with a good well and a strong windmill. After service finished and he'd had some lunch, he hoped to take a ride and talk to the widow. He had money to offer, and although she didn't have a mortgage and wasn't at risk for the bank stepping in, an old lady could only stay out here in these conditions for so long.

Besides, her house was one of the nicest in the area. Sure, it had been blasted nearly clean of its paint like every other building in the panhandle, but it stood strong with a front porch that refused to lean.

Randall glanced to the next hymn on the list and turned to page forty-seven.

He needed a place of his own. Living with his brother was fine, but a man needed space, especially if he wanted to find a wife. Even if that old widow's house had been roughed up a bit by the wind and dirt, it was still the nicest place in town he'd seen. And that meant he'd have a better time of finding a willing woman.

Randall stole a glance at the back of the room and caught the oldest Owen girl's eyes. She'd been looking at him. He nodded slightly enough for only her to notice and concentrated on finding where they were in the song. She was young. But not too young.

He smiled in spite of trying to keep his expressions in check.

After service, he'd talk to her. And her mother, of course.

CHAPTER TEN

Sidney leaned back on his chair and watched the new car struggle to navigate the deep ruts.

The wind had completely died after noon, and for the first time in days, he took in a deep breath of clean air.

Clean for now. Not the old kind of clean that smelled of growing things and rich, damp soil. This kind of clean was hot, with the air scrubbed and scraped by stinging sand.

He'd spent the morning shoveling out his house, and now the sheets he'd nailed up were set to soak in the wash tub. The water had grown muddy twice already. He needed to check it again.

He stood up, stretched, and scratched his chest under the front flap of his overalls. Long ago he'd lost the button on the right, but like most other folks in town, he'd lost a bit of weight since the drought started, and so he'd had some extra fabric. He'd slit a hole in the edge, strung the strap through, and tied a knot. He looked down at his fix and smiled. It had held up perfectly fine.

A man didn't need so much as he thought he did.

A car turned down the drive across the street to Old Widow Ruby's place. Sidney rubbed the dust from his face and walked over to his wash tub. Strange kind of day to be paying a visit. The only folks out on a Sunday were the ones either cleaning up after the storm or those going to the church. And Old Widow Ruby didn't need to do either.

Her house was up off the ground, so she didn't need to shovel dirt out from her front door. Besides, the strong construction and good lumber didn't let in much in the way of the kind of dirt that had to be shoveled.

And she never went to church. She said she was too old for that and that if God wanted her, He'd take her. She didn't need to get up and put on a hat and crank her old Ford to life just so she could convince God that she was worth it.

Old Widow Ruby made Sidney smile.

Sidney plunged his hands in the warm, murky water and swirled them around before pulling up one of the sheets. Every week they seemed to come out darker.

He wrung them out, tossed them over the thick branch of the dead tree, and reached for the bottom of the barrel. Testing the weight first, he heaved it up and dumped the water in the direction of his miserable garden. No matter how much water he poured, he couldn't make the dirt change back to when it smelled fresh and new, and when just touching told him it would be a good harvest. All that dirt had disappeared. Sidney scowled at the few bean vines that still fought to sprout something of value. A thick stem had finally pushed a flower from its nearly leafless branch. Overall, he didn't hold a lot of hope for any plant that spent half of the summer covered in the dark and the other half burning in the sun.

Sidney kicked the tub back into place and dumped in the full bucket he had heating over a fire. The steam dissipated before the water even pooled into the bottom of the tub. He filled the bucket again and set it to heat over the fire before walking back to his chair under the shade of the porch.

A dust cloud from that new car still hung in the air over the road that led to Old Widow Ruby's place. Sidney sat down and leaned back again, watching to see how long until the old woman chased the fancy man off with her ever-ready shotgun.

★★★

Lillian told Emma to relax in the front room while she set the table for them all, but Emma refused and instead followed her into the kitchen.

"You know, you didn't have to invite us all over. This is very generous." Emma ran her fingers along the blue flower pattern on the china. "This is all too nice."

"To tell you the truth," Lillian opened the stove and reached in to tap the biscuits to check if they were done, "if I had to eat another dinner with just us, I think I may go mad."

"It was a long one." Emma smiled. "I have to admit, by last night I was beginning to wonder if we were the only ones left on the earth, and maybe it was the end of times."

Lillian nodded. "I think I might have been almost wishing it were." She grabbed the towel off her shoulder and used it to pull the pan from the hot oven. "I used to like the times where Peter and I could be home alone and relax together in the evenings. Right now, I think I've had enough home-alone time to last the rest of my life." Lillian sent Emma a smile after using Peter's given name. Because of his position, everyone referred to him as "Pastor" or "Reverend," and Lillian knew many of the other ministers' wives did the same when speaking with the parishioners, but whenever she did, it felt like a lie. Calling him "Pastor" placed the importance of his position above their relationship, and she just couldn't do that. Emma didn't even seem to notice.

Lillian folded the towel she'd been holding and set it on the counter, adjusting it while she tried to think of a way to broach the topic of Emma's husband. "Have you ... I wish I could ask this in a way that didn't feel like I'm prying, but have you heard from your husband?"

Emma shook her head and sank onto a nearby chair, staring at the window with its closed curtains. Taking a deep breath, she rubbed her arms and shook her head again, as if she'd forgotten that she'd already answered the question.

Jumping up again, Emma let the breath go with a hiss and started distributing the stack of plates Lillian had set on the table.

"I can do that," Lillian said. She rested her hand on Emma's arm, and Emma jumped, holding tight to the plate.

"Let go, sweetie." Lillian slid her hand down to cover Emma's.

"He's not coming back." Emma handed the plate to Lillian.

Lillian quickly set it down and pulled Emma back to sit.

"I know that now. But I don't know what happened." She avoided Lillian's gaze. "How could I not know?"

Lillian shook her head and sneaked a glance at the doorway, wishing her pastor husband would come in. He knew how to talk to people, how to help them. Lillian knew how to make a good potato salad.

"I'm sorry. It's really none of your trouble." Emma sniffed and wiped her nose on her handkerchief. "All we can do is keep going." She looked around the room. "Where do you keep the flatware?"

With nothing to say, Lillian pointed to the drawer next to the sink. She looked at the woman she now considered a friend. Sometimes work, the business of living, was the only clear path forward.

★★★

Justin leaned on the counter, counting out his inventory of nails. The full boxes he didn't mind so much.

The door handle rattled and outside Randall lifted his hand to shade his eyes and see through the glass and into the store. Justin waved at him and walked around to open the door. He rarely opened the store on Sundays—only in the case of an emergency—so he typically kept the door locked. Justin frowned. Right now it was probably the only locked door in town. All the other businesses had moved on long ago.

"Wasn't sure you were here." Randall stepped in, took his handkerchief from his pocket, and wiped the sweat from his face.

As the breeze had died down, the heat had swelled. Justin pulled the window shades down in anticipation of the late afternoon sun.

"Did you get a chance to speak with Old Widow Ruby?"

"No." Randall tossed his hat onto the counter, heedless of the dust. The rounded top, turned-up brim, and royal-blue ribbon looked out of place against the worn wood. He slid a bench closer and sat down. "She's dead."

Justin stopped with the last window shade halfway closed. "Dead?" He looked at his brother settling more comfortably onto the bench. Justin slowly pulled the shade the rest of the way shut, trying to process what his brother had just said. "You mean dead, as in dead?"

Randall rolled his eyes. "I'm not sure how many kinds of dead there can be, but she's the dead kind." He stretched his legs out. One of his knees made a popping noise. "It's blistering hot out there."

Justin concentrated on staying upright. Old Widow Ruby. Dead. He didn't think that old battle-ax could even die. There wasn't a kid in town—his younger self included—who wouldn't have crossed the street for the sole purpose of concealing dirty fingernails. "How'd she die?"

"I found her outside. Maybe the dust got to her?"

Justin took a deep breath of the hot, dry air. A body in this heat ... he didn't really want to think about the condition they might find her in. He swallowed. "How long do you think she's been there?"

"Not long. She's just lying there in the sun."

"What did you do?"

"Left her." Randall shrugged and looked up, confused. "What should I have done?" He brought the edge of his thumb to his mouth and chewed at a hangnail.

"Did you at least cover her?"

Randall stopped chewing and dropped his hand onto the counter. "Didn't think of that. Does she have family nearby?"

"No. Some distant nieces in Ohio or someplace like that."

"What'll they do with the farm?"

Justin slid the nails he'd been counting into his hand then dropped the fistful into the container. He'd lost count anyway.

"We need to go talk to Reverend Woodall. I'm not sure what we're supposed to do without a doctor in town anymore."

Randall nodded. "You want me to come with?"

Justin closed his eyes for a minute and held his breath and his tongue. "Yes. You found her. You should come."

Randall heaved back up off the bench and made a show of the unwelcome trouble.

"You were the one who found her," Justin explained. "It's only right you be the one who goes to the minister."

"I suppose." Randall shoved his head back into his hat. "Besides, I'd like to find out who owns that parcel now. The house there seems mighty fine, and, well, it's empty now."

Justin felt nauseated. "Let's just get over there and see what needs to be done."

He unlocked the door and stepped out. Heat rose from the dirt road in nervous waves. Justin pulled his hat farther down and stepped into the sun. "Taking our time sure ain't going to make things better out at her place. Come on."

Randall closed the door behind him, and the two men crossed the deserted street together. "This dirt isn't like anything I've ever seen before." Randall glanced back to the cloud of dust that had risen behind them both. "It's like talcum powder, only black."

Old Widow Ruby was dead. Justin shook his head. Everyone had to die sometime. He just wished it hadn't been Randall who'd found her. He looked at the unruffled man who walked next to him. She had deserved better. At least someone who pretended to care.

CHAPTER ELEVEN

Jessie tucked her knees up under her work skirt, rocked back on her heels, and watched the Mr. Mitchells go up to the reverend's door. They took their hats off when Mrs. Woodall opened it, and she invited them in.

No one went for a stroll in the midday sun.

Jessie took a deep breath and turned back to the front room where her brother sat reading the same book he'd read a dozen times. The younger ones fought over the wooden tractor their father had made.

He wasn't coming back. That much she knew.

Her mother hadn't said anything. But there weren't a lot of other conclusions.

He might have died at the side of the road, and they might never know. Or he might have run off, jumped on a train, and headed someplace not plagued by the clinging dust. Jessie picked at the cracked wood of the windowsill. Anyplace would be better than here. She couldn't really blame him, except that he went without them.

He could have at least left the truck. Jessie frowned. When she got married, she'd make sure to squirrel away money any chance she got. Just in case she ended up left behind with children to tend.

★★★

Peter picked up the phone, stuck his fingers in the worn holes, and circled the face. His wife had gone into the kitchen to make some tea, and he stood there, receiver to his ear, hoping someone at the hospital would answer.

The simple truth was that no one in the town knew what to do if someone died. Especially on a Sunday. With the doctor long gone, and no one filling the position in the interim, there was no one to pinch hit in case an undertaker became necessary.

And delaying a burial in this heat simply wasn't an option.

Peter glanced up to Justin and Randall. The news of Old Widow Ruby's death still hung in the air like an unwelcome fog. Justin fiddled with the rim of his hat.

The phone rang three times before someone picked up. "County Hospital. How can I help you?"

Peter took a deep breath and explained the situation. The other men stared at him while he talked, agreed, and finally hung up.

"What'd they say?" Justin stood and walked over to stand by Peter.

"That we should try to notify next of kin if we know anyone, but the coroner will come out tomorrow to interview all of us. If her plan was to be buried in the churchyard, and if the situation calls for an expedient interment, then we can go ahead as planned. The paperwork can be filed on Monday."

"Good." Justin nodded and then shrugged an apology they all understood.

Nothing about the situation was good.

"I suppose we need to go out and bring her back." Peter couldn't move. He didn't want to.

"Have some tea first." Lillian carried the tray into the living room and poured cool glasses of tea for the men.

Peter thanked her. He remembered when ice deliveries were regular, when condensation from iced drinks would dampen his hands on hot summer days. It seemed unlikely that would ever happen again. But the underground water at least stayed cool enough. Better than hot tea on a day like this.

"You got any coffins in stock?" Peter asked Justin.

Justin frowned. "In back. A couple of them. We'll need to take your truck, pick up the coffin, then drive out to her place."

"That's what I was thinking." Peter drained his glass and set it back on the tray that Lillian had left. The other men followed suit.

Peter picked up the tray and backed through the door into the kitchen. "We're going to go get her. Probably bring her to the church. You want to call some of the neighbors and spread the word? I think we'll have a small service for her tonight."

Lillian nodded and dropped the glasses into the dishwater one at a time.

The men were waiting for him on the front stoop. They walked together to the truck, rolled down the windows, gave it a second to cool off, and then sat three across. It would be a hot trip, but the longer they waited, the worse the drive back would be.

★★★

Lillian rang a couple of the families who lived out of town then pulled on her floppy sun hat and stepped outside to cross the street to Emma's house.

Jessie opened the door before she knocked.

"Is your mother home?"

Jessie opened the door wider and waved her in.

The front room consisted of a sagging sofa, a ladder-back chair, an old rocker, and a bookcase with a large Bible and a few other school-type books. A picture of mountains hung over an unused fireplace mantle, and a huge rag rug marked the center of the worn linoleum floor. It had an indecipherable pattern. A hairless baby doll rested listlessly, slumped against the leg of the sofa.

"Oh." Emma brushed her hands on her apron and stood with one foot atop of the other in an attempt to hide the bareness of her feet. "I'm sorry. It's such a mess." She stooped to pick up a few things and fluff the sofa pillows. "I keep telling the children to put their things away." She bent to retrieve the baby doll and handed it to Jessie.

Jessie bit her lower lip and backed out of the room.

"I'm sorry to surprise you like this." Lillian pulled off her hat and let her arm drop to her side. "We just got a visit from Mr. Mitchell. Seems his brother went out to visit Old Widow Ruby this afternoon and found her dead."

"Dead?" Emma sank into the rocker and motioned for Lillian to take a seat.

"Said he found her outside."

Emma looked to make sure none of the children eavesdropped at the doorway. She lowered her voice. "How long was she out there?"

Lillian shook her head. "Not long, from what he says."

"Poor Old Widow Ruby." Emma looked down at her apron and smoothed her skirt against her knees. "Wish she hadn't been alone. Any guess how she went?"

"Peter and the Mr. Mitchells are on their way out. They picked up a coffin and plan to have a short service for her this evening. That's why I'm here. To invite you, and to spread the word."

"Of course we'll come." Emma half smiled then covered her mouth with her hand. "That woman scared me when I was younger, and if I were completely honest, she still scared me now."

Lillian smiled and stood. "Good, I thought I was the only one." She put her hat on and walked to the door. Emma followed to let her back out into the sun. "You know, the first time she came to church, I made sure I was sitting straight. And she only came the once. Said that she wanted to make sure we were okay for the town and that she probably wouldn't be back again."

"I'm surprised she even came the once."

"At the end of service, she told Peter that he 'would do.'"

Emma laughed again, this time not bothering to cover her smile.

"We'll see you tonight then? I think it will be around seven."

"We'll be there."

Lillian waved and then turned to walk to the next neighbors. Only a few in town needed to hear the news, and then she would have to go back to the house and come up with something to bake for after the service.

It would be modest but then so was everything else.

***

Peter walked around to the back of the house, followed by Justin, Randall, and Sidney. They'd stopped on the way by to inform him, and Sidney had hopped in the back of the truck for the ride down Old Widow Ruby's drive.

"She seemed fine last week. Was out tendin' to her chickens. I walked over to make sure she didn't need anything. She told me to mind my own business." Sidney laughed. "Gotta love a woman like that."

Peter didn't have to ask where they would find her body. The humming flies led the way.

"They sure make quick work of things." Sidney crossed his arms and ducked into the house.

In a few seconds, he returned with a sheet and handed it over to Peter. Peter took a deep breath and walked over to where she had collapsed face first into the dirt. Her legs shot out at a strange angle, and her arms rested, flailing at her sides. Peter looked at the other men in the group and knelt next to her. The smell of death had just begun to gather around her.

He swatted at the swarming flies, tucked one stiffening arm close to her body, and flipped her over. They gasped at the purple pooling of blood on one side of her face. Her mouth gaped. Flies crawled in and out, and her cloudy eyes stared up at the men still standing.

Peter covered his mouth and stood back up. "Get the coffin."

Justin and Sidney jogged back around the house. Peter looked up. Randall stood a few feet back. His eyes roved the old woman's body, and Peter felt a wave of nausea rise. "Maybe you should go in and see if you can find a few more sheets."

Randall nodded and backed away with his gaze locked on her face. Finally, he turned and climbed the steps to the house.

The dirt hadn't drifted around her body, so she'd died after the storm ended. Peter lifted his arm and wiped the sweat out of his eyes with his sleeve. With the heat, figuring when the Old Widow died would be impossible.

Peter tried to remember anything he could about death and rigor and decay, but thoughts of Old Widow Ruby walking into that one Sunday service swam in and crowded out anything useful. She'd worn a blue dress with a leather belt and carried no purse. Instead, she'd had her dead husband's wallet tucked under her hat. She'd taken it out when the offering plate passed, dropped a couple of bills in, then shoved the wallet back into its home on top of her head.

She had been so wholly unconventional that at the time it seemed the most natural thing to do. Only on later reflection did the habit of carrying her husband's wallet under her hat make him wonder.

Justin backed the truck up, and it rumbled to a stop only a few feet away from Old Widow Ruby's body. The men jumped out, lifted the empty coffin out of the back, and set it down next to her.

"How you want to handle this?" Justin chewed his bottom lip and tilted his head, as if a better view could make the task any easier. "Where'd Randall go off to?"

"I sent him to find more sheets." Peter walked over and lifted the lid of the coffin. "It's hard to believe her years on this earth ended like this."

Sidney snorted. "Wasn't her time to die, I don't figure. But we'll never know." He squatted down and lowered her eyelids. One refused to budge. He took a deep breath, swatted at the gathering swarm of flies and stood back up. "Need to get her covered proper."

Justin shook out the sheet that they'd already brought out and nodded to Peter. Peter took the other end, and they laid it out flat on the ground.

Then they stood back, knowing what came next, and not one of them wanting to do it.

"Here's a few more sheets," Randall called from the back of the house. His loud voice boomed through the circle of men, and Justin turned and frowned. "What?"

Justin waved him over with one impatient swipe of his arm.

Peter looked back to the body. "We'll lift her together, lay her on the sheet, and then try to get her limbs tucked closer to her body so that we can get her in the box." He glanced up at the other men in the circle. The sun punished them. Their shirts, soaked with sweat, already clung to their chests, and they hadn't even done any work.

Old Widow Ruby looked at the sky with her one open eye and her open mouth and jaw that lolled to one side. Peter gestured for Justin and Randall to take each of her feet and for Sidney to help lift her by her shoulders.

She weighed nothing. They set her on the sheet, straightened back up, and looked at each other.

Peter gave one nod, and the men went to work straightening her limbs enough to get her into the coffin. Sidney tore the last sheet into strips that they tied around her to keep her still. Finally, they lifted her into the box and nailed down the lid.

They took a step back from the truck.

"I'll ride in back, keep her from bouncing too much." Sidney followed the box into the back of the truck. He sat with his back against the hot metal of the cab and one arm over Old Widow Ruby.

The other men piled into the bench seat, too exhausted and hot to worry about anything but driving so that they could feel the hot air at least pass against their skin.

CHAPTER TWELVE

The funeral would start late. The sun had already burned its way down to the horizon. It sat there, pausing, resting up for the final burn into the flat Oklahoma desert.

Lillian stood outside the church. The men had just finished digging the hole in the small graveyard. They'd stood, wiped their faces with sweat-soaked handkerchiefs, and leaned their shovels against the side of the old shed where the idle lawn tools had long ago surrendered their meaning to rust.

The sanctuary windows were open, and the hum of conversation escaped the small hot building. Lillian leaned against the siding under one window and picked at a string that hung from the button on her cuff. She knew she shouldn't, that if she gave one tug too many the thread would unravel and the button would fall to the dirt and her cuff would hang useless. She lowered her hand a couple of times and watched the sun teeter on the edge of the earth, but her fingers always seemed to find their way back to that thread.

She lifted it to her lips, bit it off, and dropped the thread into the dirt, where its insignificance magnified.

All that struggle, and for what?

In a few years Old Widow Ruby would be equally as unimportant, resting in the dirt.

A group of children dashed around the back of the church and skidded to a stop when they saw Lillian. She smiled and waved them on. They continued their path with a more dignified run.

"I think we're ready to begin." Peter walked around the back of the building, his business-like pastor voice—the one he relied on when he needed to disconnect from the emotion so he could do his job—announcing his need for Lillian at his side.

In a flash of orange and purple, the sun lost its grip on the Oklahoma plain and sank. Lillian nodded, shivering with the approaching darkness despite the heat that radiated from the baked ground.

"Are we still planning to invite everyone to our house after the funeral?"

"Yes." Lillian kicked up from her leaning position and took her husband's arm. "I've put some refreshments together. We should have enough for everyone."

"Good." Peter paused before opening the doors to the church. "Are you okay?"

Lillian looked up at him. "Why?"

"I don't know. You seem quiet."

Lillian shrugged, knowing the hesitation he sensed was his own, not hers.

"It's the funeral. It's sad." Lillian didn't want to give him anything more to think about right before he had to perform his duties as their minister.

He patted her arm and they walked in together. Most of the people had already found seats. Peter led Lillian to her typical pew then stepped up to the podium.

The casket rested on a table, closed. Weedy wildflowers did the best they could to comfort.

Lillian looked across the aisle. Randall sat motionless, his hands folded in his lap, staring at the casket. Nothing in his clothes or his mannerisms appeared out of place. She let her eyes roam over his perfect form. He'd dressed to impress. That much shined obvious. She looked back to his face in time to find him staring back.

He smiled.

★★★

Jessie didn't know whether to stand with her mother and pretend to be interested in the ladies' discussion or if she should join the children and end up trying to keep them out of trouble. Instead, she found herself wandering out back behind the pastor's house while the people inside spoke in hushed tones and remembered the dead.

"Too confined in there for you?" The new Mr. Mitchell walked around the house and stopped a few feet away.

She looked down. "I guess so."

Mr. Mitchell leaned against the side of the house next to the kitchen stairs and crossed one elegant leg over the other. His shoes shone in the light that spilled from the open windows as brilliantly as they did the first day he'd stepped into church. "The stars should be nice tonight. No wind and no clouds."

"I guess so." Jessie chastised herself for her lack of conversational skills. The richest man in town was talking to her, and all she could think of to say was *I guess so?*

"You plan on staying in this area for long?"

Jessie forced something besides *I guess so* from her tongue. "My mom needs the help now. Besides, I don't have anywhere else to go."

Mr. Mitchell cleared his throat. "You have to have suitors here ... you're too pretty to not have the men in town scratching at your door."

Jessie stole a look at the man, and their gazes locked. She had no one and couldn't keep the truth from him.

"No one?" he guessed. "What are the men in town thinking?"

"Well, there's not too many single men in these parts. Most who don't have mouths to feed have moved on to better places."

"I suppose. Still, it seems a crime." Mr. Mitchell pulled his pocket watch out and flipped it open. He held it up to the truant window light. "It's getting late." He tucked the watch back into a perfect little pocket hidden under a flap in his vest. "I'm sorry, I'm not sure I remember your name."

"Jessie Owen."

"Well, Miss Owen, it was lovely to have a chance to steal away for a bit and chat." He held out his hand. "In case you don't know my name, it's Randall Mitchell."

Jessie rested her fingers in his, but instead of shaking her hand as she expected, he closed her fingers in his and trailed his thumb across the back of her hand. He smiled, waited for her to meet his gaze, and watched her eyes as he lifted her hand to his lips.

Jessie couldn't move. She knew her flushed face betrayed her reaction, but she couldn't stop watching the man tend to the sensitive skin on the back of her hand. Her fingers trembled with jolts of electricity like the static that came with the storms. "Nice ..."—she tried to swallow the lump in her throat that changed her voice to a soft pitch she didn't recognize—"... It's nice to meet you, Mr. Mitchell."

He lowered her hand and let go. Jessie felt the air rush across her empty fingers. A hollow feeling spread all the way to her stomach.

He leaned in closer. "Please, call me Randall."

She nodded. "You can ... I wish you would call me Jessie."

He smiled and tipped his hat. "Well then, Jessie, I'll look forward to calling on you soon?"

Jessie nodded and couldn't keep the smile from her face.

Randall ducked back behind the house, and Jessie concentrated on breathing steadily. Would he be interested in her? Could he be? She was young, but nearly sixteen. Old enough to be married if she wanted. She pressed her hands against her hot cheeks and tried to remember the feeling of his lips on the back of her hand. She trailed her lips over where his had caressed.

He had a car and money. A marriage to him could save their family. He was a little old, but still handsome in a city kind of way. Jessie dropped her hands into the pockets of her skirt and took a step deeper into the darkness, chastising herself for the foolish thoughts. A man kissed the back of her hand and already her imagination jumped to marriage.

The guests still mulled around in the house. She could see them as they stood near the windows with their cups of coffee in one hand and tiny tea cakes in the other. Her mother helped by carrying the tray around to let the other guests pick out the cake of their choice.

The pastor and his wife seemed like nice folk, but Jessie knew if she married a man with money, her mother wouldn't have to serve others. She could be the one holding the parties. Better yet, Jessie could be.

Jessie looked down at her new shoes and calf-length skirt. If she turned up the waistband, she could shorten it a bit, and her mother probably wouldn't even notice. The heel on the shoes made her legs look nice—she'd caught her reflection in the store window—and if she wanted to catch Randall's eye, she needed to do the best with what she had.

★★★

Lillian had given up on falling asleep as soon as her head sank into her pillow. It would be one of those nights. She rolled to her side and waited for the stars.

A metal fan oscillated, clicking twice every time it reached its limit to the right. No noise announced the left restriction.

"I guess it went as well as we could expect." Peter rolled over in bed and faced Lillian. "I won't feel easy about it until the coroner stops by."

"When is that?"

"Tomorrow, hopefully."

"I think it went fine. Did something happen I didn't see?"

Peter shook his head. Lillian could hear the stubble on his beard scrape against the sheets.

She reached out and pressed her hand against his face. "Was seeing her that way difficult?"

Peter took a deep breath in and covered Lillian's hand with his. He turned his face into her palm and kissed the soft skin there.

"How long do you think she'd been gone?" Lillian tried to think of a delicate way to ask the question she knew her husband needed to answer, but there simply were not too many ways to ask about the stages of decomposition.

"I don't think she'd been gone long at all. She must have died right before Randall visited her..." Peter left the thought unfinished.

"Something is bothering you." Lillian pulled her hand back and shuffled around in the bed until she sat cross-legged, facing him. "What is it?"

Peter sat up and kicked his legs off the side of the bed. She could hear him slip his feet into his slippers. "I'm going to get a glass of water. Do you want one?"

"Peter?"

He paused. "Yes?"

"You do think her death was natural, right?"

His shoulders slumped and he rubbed his hands over his face. "I have no reason to think otherwise."

"But you do."

Peter stood and crossed to their open bedroom door. "Let's just say I wish the coroner had been able to visit before we had to bury her. It would have been nice to hear someone else say that she died of natural causes, that she'd not been in pain, that she didn't suffer."

Lillian nodded, knowing he couldn't see her agreement in the darkness. But she had nothing else to offer. Putting her concerns to voice only made the doubts swell, and with the heat of the day and the still-hot night, with every dust-laden breath and each grit-filled swallow of water, ideas let out to roam in the open had a way of revisiting, of pressing down, of becoming real even in the face of no substance.

Everyone knew it and held their thoughts in check. Peter left and Lillian crossed to the window. The moon rose over barren fields and the drifts of waste from years of cash-crop profits. She crossed her arms and closed her eyes, trying to remember the sweet tang of sprouting wheat fields. She used to look out the window at night and see combines with their blazing electric lights humming and crashing through the rows and rows of promise.

Now nothing disturbed the black landscape save the line of horizon stretching as far as she could see in every direction.

Things went on forever here. Land. Drought. Disease. Rumors. Lillian walked back to her side of the bed to lie down before Peter returned. The best she could do for them both was to roll over and pretend to sleep.

That way, their concerns didn't risk springing to life with the potent, fertile, spoken word.

CHAPTER THIRTEEN

Randall locked the door to his bedroom in the upstairs of his brother's store and shrugged out of his suit jacket.

The day had been long, and if he'd planned things himself, they couldn't have gone much better.

He tossed his jacket over an empty chair and fished around in the interior pocket for the papers he'd been able to find at the old widow's house. He hadn't been sure how he would get an opportunity to find out about her personal matters, but when that minister had sent him in to gather more sheets, he'd made good use of the gift of time.

He spread the papers out on the small desk and shuffled through until he found what he was looking for. A letter, dated for earlier that spring, from a niece out east. Old Widow Ruby did have family, but from what the people in town claimed, no children of her own.

The letter read of trifles. Nothing important, save the address and names. Randall ran his hand through his slicked-back hair and sneered at the feel of the oiled soot. For as much as he needed to keep his appearance presentable, he conceded that until the drought ended he might have to discontinue the use of the hair oil.

A moth battered itself against the shade of the electric lamp. As far as he could tell, only about half the homes were wired for electricity, and most still had outhouses leaning out behind the main house.

But Old Widow Ruby's house sported all the conveniences. Electricity, running water, indoor plumbing, and even small touches like ceiling fans that one typically only found in the city. Her sofas had somehow maintained their brilliance during the drought and the dust. The wood furniture didn't lack for polish, and even the china in her cupboard gleamed.

Doors and windows had tight rubber seals installed, and even though the sun beat down hard when he'd arrived, the house felt at least ten degrees cooler inside.

He knew it would be his as soon as he'd stopped the car and looked out at the wind-beaten, white-painted gingerbread that adorned the corners of the front porch.

Randall flipped to the next sheet of paper, a bank statement of her accounts.

She had almost nothing there.

He bit the inside of his bottom lip. The coroner planned to investigate tomorrow. He'd be out at the house, and he'd be interviewing the three men. Old ladies never put all their money in the bank. They hid it in mason jars stuffed in stored pots and shoe boxes, and in cans buried in tool sheds. They sewed stock certificates into sofa cushions and hid silver certificates in the attic. The woman had money ... she had to—just not in the bank.

Unless her niece were dull, she'd never give up the property until she'd inspected it closely. The coroner would contact Ruby's next of kin, and then there would be a reading of her will, and then, most likely, the property would go up for sale.

He had to wait. Randall stood and paced to his door then back to the small desk in front of the window. Lacy, feminine curtains hung still in the open space. He sat down and drummed his fingers against the worn wood of the desk.

He wouldn't have to wait long, though. If he gave the authorities at least a few days to contact her niece and then dropped a letter of condolence in the post, with the time it took to deliver it, her niece should receive his note just as she considered the problem of what to do with her old aunt's worn-down property in the drought-weary Oklahoma panhandle. And if his expression of solace also contained an offer for her aunt's property, then, if she were a practical person, she couldn't help but consider it.

Randall smiled, but it quickly faded. That didn't solve the problem of finding her hidden money before anyone else did.

He stood again and grabbed his jacket off the back of the chair. He folded the papers he'd borrowed and stuffed them back into the compartment of his travel trunk. After securing it, he opened his bedroom door and listened for his brother's movements.

Nothing. He closed the door and toed off his shoes before easing his way down the hall to listen outside his brother's bedroom. Soft snoring floated out from behind the door. Randall slipped down the stairs and outside.

Walking was the only option. The rumble as the car sputtered to life would likely wake everyone in town. Randall tied his shoes, grabbed the lantern that hung on a nail next to the back door, and stepped out into the dirt.

He would have to take the road. Only a mile, maybe two including her driveway. He didn't know the area well enough to cross the fields, nor did he want to leave a path from the back door of the store to Old Widow Ruby's stoop.

He kept the lantern shuttered and followed the ruts of the moonlit street. He had imagined, before now, that at night the sky would sink into the land, that the blackness would be immense, that without hills or trees or any sort of topographical definition it would seem as if he could walk forever into the abyss, or reach the end of the earth, only to fall into the dark.

The opposite was true. The moon added depth. Ruts existed in the road that during the day had disappeared under the punishing white blaze of the sun. Dead trees lived again, quivering against the impossible spin of the stars. The more his eyes adjusted, the more he realized the lack of need for any kind of lamp. The land, when it bloomed again, would be astounding. No wonder families had flocked to the open expanse of sky. The town existed under a sparkling glass dome, like a cake under glass at a rooftop party in the city. The protective curve in the corners where the sky and land met lent a sense of security. They lived like fireflies under an overturned glass big enough to allow them freedom to fly and do as they pleased, but small enough to protect them from the rest of the world.

The only problem was whoever set the glass above forgot to feed and water the creatures within.

Randall stumbled over a rut. He should be watching the ground. It wouldn't do for him to get lost in the promise of the place while forgetting the danger.

★★★

Jessie couldn't sleep. The bed she shared with her sisters was suffocating, even on a rare night when they could enjoy an open window.

She eased off her stomach and up onto her knees, and then crawled over their small bodies. The metal springs creaked under her weight. She grimaced at the squealing sound. She couldn't wake her mother.

A curtain hung over their doorway. She moved by the moonlight past the rough fabric and to the stairs that were little more than a ladder. The second and seventh stairs squeaked with the littlest of encouragement. She skipped them.

The kitchen still radiated warmth from the stove, and the welcome aroma of carefully collected pork fat hung in the air. Jessie pulled at her clinging nightgown. The collar tightened in the syrupy heat, strangling her with dingy lace and mismatched buttons. She had to get out of the stifling house and cool off.

She eased the kitchen door open and stepped barefoot down onto the cool dirt. But as soon as she stayed still for more than a second or two, the residual underground heat seeped up to meet her toes. She couldn't get cool.

She hiked her nightgown up over her knees and sat on the old broken bench near the water pump. Her nightgown rode as high as she dared, and she worked the pump until cool water ran over her knees and into the basin below. She dangled her feet there, in the water, and looked up to the sky.

A magazine she'd read said some stores and theaters in the big cities had cooled air, cold enough for some women to bring sweaters. Jessie tried to imagine what it might feel like to walk in from the sticky summer heat and feel a blast of cold so intense she'd shiver. Every day the list of things she'd never experience seemed to grow. She wiggled her toes in the cool water and wished for a breeze to skim over her bare legs.

The Sears catalog sold women razors for their underarms and legs. Jessie couldn't help but wonder if men like Randall were used to women who had smooth skin everywhere, and then she blushed at her own thoughts.

Jessie glanced at the dark windows across the street then both ways as far into the black as she could see. She worried her bottom lip with her teeth and reached up to unbutton the top few buttons of her nightgown. Night air rushed in, and she took a rare deep, dustless breath. She could smell the water in the basin where she soaked her feet. She reached out again to pump more water over her knees.

And then she heard something.

She stopped, hand still on the lever, and listened for the sound to repeat.

Nothing.

And then she saw him.

He strolled along down the edge of their fence. Jessie held her breath and held as still as she ever had. If he saw her now, like this, half dressed, her feet in a bucket, her shirt gaping open, he'd never speak to her again.

All her mother's warnings about modesty and propriety even when they didn't have money flooded back. Three heartbeats roared into her ears and then stopped. For a moment, she worried her heart had stopped beating altogether and that she would die right there in the dirt in her nightgown.

She refused to die that way.

Jessie forced her eyes down. She didn't want him to feel her gaze. She concentrated on his passing footsteps, willed him to keep walking on his way out of town.

But why he'd be walking when he had the nicest car around, she couldn't figure. She stole a glance at his back as he slowly moved away. Maybe, like her, he couldn't sleep. Or maybe he tended to walk in his sleep. A dangerous habit when every direction offered only fields of desert. But by the time she put clothes on and chased after him, he'd be long gone.

She'd never forgive herself if something happened, though.

She stood and tiptoed out of the water. She dropped her nightgown and buttoned it up to her neck. Then she followed him down the road a bit.

Her feet were bare, but that wasn't anything she wasn't used to. And she kept to the shadows of buildings, darting between the open, moonlit spaces and ducking into empty corners.

He stopped. She crouched against the building, wishing for everything she was worth that her nightgowns had not all been white. He didn't see her, though. He stooped, lit a match against the heel of his boot, and made the lantern come to life.

It illuminated his face with the only bit of color for as far as she could see. In a landscape of black and white, the planes of his face glowed yellow. He checked behind him, and Jessie held her breath. Then, he turned for the last time and continued down the road out of town.

Jessie stood, relieved at not having been caught. She shivered once and wished for the warmth of her bed.

He hadn't been sleepwalking, or if it was sleepwalking, it wasn't any kind she'd ever seen. She didn't worry for his safety.

But what could he have been doing leaving town on foot in the middle of the night?

***

Randall doused the lamp as he neared the turn at Sidney's place. He didn't need trouble, and he especially didn't need the kind of trouble that came with arms as big as tree trunks.

Old Widow Ruby had a long straight drive, and Randall watched for the silhouette of her house to rise up into the sky and block out a house's worth of stars.

The moon had risen early when the sun had still lent its late afternoon red to the desert around them. Randall wished he could check the time, but he'd have to wait until he got inside. He didn't want to light the lamp again. Whatever he did, he figured he would be in the house for a while. By the time he started back, the moon might have fallen below the horizon, and then it would be a challenge to get back in the pre-morning blackness.

The front porch yawned its black welcome. Randall paused and scanned the acres behind him before taking the first creaky wooden step. The moon failed to pierce the shadows under the roof, so Randall felt his way to the front door, running his fingers against the grain of the wind-battered wood and finally finding a cool shiver in the metal of the knob. He twisted it and stepped into the black parlor.

He could see nothing. In the absence of light, decades of polish, diligently rubbed into tables and banisters, surrounded him. Old perfume, cloying and long worn free of any particular brand or flower, threatened to choke him. He stood still for a moment, hoping to name another element that he couldn't quite place. He blinked in the dark. It was cooking oil, and with it, childhood memories of his mother standing over their own small stove. He quickly opened the lamp, struck another match against the trim on the door, and lit it, being careful to shutter it to a narrow line.

The stripe of light darted from one object to the next: an armchair with a crocheted doily hanging over the back, a pair of shoes at the base of the stairs, a glass china case with a gleaming silver service.

He turned, using the lamp to scan for the roll-top desk he'd found that afternoon. Earlier that day, he'd driven out here just to talk to the old bat. Providence had smiled on him. Securing the place without her in the way should be a simple task.

He set the lamp on a table and aimed the beam at the desk. An old wedding picture stared at him from an oval metal frame. He looked closer. The woman in the picture vaguely resembled Old Widow Ruby, and the man, well, he looked like any man on his wedding day: trussed up, hair combed straight back, and uncomfortable. Randall chuckled out loud. Soon, there might be a picture like this of him again. Possibly setting on the same desk. He'd left the pictures of his last marriage with his wife's things in her parents' attic. No sense reliving that nightmare.

He slid the top up and fanned through the papers. Mostly bills and statements. A few torn-out pages of a catalog. A receipt for the new stove in the kitchen. He held it up to the light. Thank you, ma'am. It had been quite expensive. He smiled and tucked it back into its rightful place under some other meaningless slips of paper.

Randall only found more of the same in the drawers, with the bottom one holding old glass candle holders. He kicked it closed, enjoying the responding jolt of glass on glass. Not hard enough to break, but satisfying nonetheless.

Grabbing the lamp, he made his way to the kitchen. He rifled through cabinet after cabinet, looked in cookie jars and every pot he could find, slammed open the pantry and shuffled the preserves to the right and to the left, pushed aside sacks of flour and rice, and then paused. His fingers had brushed against something that didn't belong. Twisting open the bag of rice, he dug through it until he could grab the metal box buried inside.

Carefully, he pulled it from the rice and shook the loose grains back into the bag. This old woman wouldn't be the kind to stand for a mess, and leaving one now would only raise questions. He carried the box and the lamp to the kitchen table and sat down.

Cash. A lot of it.

Randall tipped the box over into his palm and felt the weight of the stack. Andrew Jackson stared up from his palm. Twenty dollars. If there were a whole stack of twenties ... Randall let himself dream for a few moments before sliding the top bill to the table top.

Rapidly, he flipped from one bill to the next, and then stared at the stack of bills that represented more than a year's salary to the folks in these parts. Randall looked out the kitchen window at the still-black sky. He had more time.

He thumped the stack on the table a few times to straighten it then tucked it into his jacket pocket. Another quick search of the pantry revealed only a jar of coins—he didn't need to mess with that—and a few dollars, maybe household money, hidden in an empty sugar bowl. That he left as well. He set the empty metal tin up on the shelf above the sink.

Upstairs probably held a few surprises. Randall glanced at the ceiling and picked up his lamp before making his way back to the front room.

The stairs didn't squeak in the least bit. A well-built home would make a wife happy. He passed a bathing room and couldn't resist looking in. The older model tub still appeared to be almost new, and the sink basin shone as if the old lady had just polished it. There was nothing in the place not to like.

He slipped into the main bedroom and aimed the lamp at the nightstand. A cursory search of the drawers there, and then the obvious hunt through her dead husband's sock drawer offered a host of valuables he would have to take to the city to pawn. That really wasn't much trouble. He left enough jewelry—the cheap stuff—and stepped back into the hall, hearing the trinkets jingle with each step.

It had been a fruitful visit, but the larger things of value he'd been unable to locate. Wherever she'd hidden the deed to the farm, certificates of ownership for the equipment waiting in the barns, he had yet to uncover. This time, he took his watch out and held it to the light. The hands already read close to three.

Randall glanced at the hall window that looked out over the front of the house. A cushioned seat built into the place welcomed him to sit and relax. He yawned and shook the impulse away, turned into the next room, and stopped. Slowly walking to the bench, he bent and ran his fingers along the front edge. Diminutive hinges lined one side. Dropping to his knees, Randall aimed his light again and found the opening.

He reached into the dark space and found a large envelope. Randall sat back on the floor, leaned into the light, and opened the flap.

At least a dozen stock certificates in a multitude of colors cascaded out. Some of them he thought might hold value, while some came from companies he'd never before heard of. He folded a few of the promising ones—utilities, railroads, heavy farm equipment—and stuffed them in his pocket with the rest of the things he'd found. The rest, he would leave for anyone who might know where to look. When he bought the place, he could always check again.

Randall stood, snuffed out the lamp, and made his way to the front door and back outside. The moon hung low but hadn't yet disappeared. Randall didn't waste time. He half walked, half jogged back to town, his pockets thick with all he'd found. More than his brother had. At last. He had more. And unlike Justin, he'd started with nothing.

Randall smiled. Tomorrow he'd answer the coroner's questions; tomorrow he'd make the rounds with the banker.

Which rang much more promising now that the one piece of land with the best house sat vacant and waiting.

CHAPTER FOURTEEN

Emma shook out Little Henry's trousers and hung them over the line. They were the same ones he'd worn in the autumn, and they stretched a bit tighter around his waist, but not as much as a mother hoped to see. Food had been scarce for too long.

Over a month and still no word from her husband.

A cough erupted from the backyard. Emma didn't have to call out who'd coughed or ask if they were okay. Everyone coughed and somehow survived until the next day. But that was the second time Anna had coughed in less than an hour, and she was only six.

The supplies in the kitchen dwindled more each day, and the scraggly beans wouldn't be ready for a while. The challenge of letting them grow, of not plucking the tender, soft shoots, of hoping that the sacrifice today wouldn't become worthless because of a freak dust storm tomorrow, the challenge to leave them be while listening to the music of the children's stomachs, it all made the sun hotter.

Emma pinned a child's shirt to the line, and then a nightdress, and then some underthings. She used to take pride in bleaching everything to white, find satisfaction in the bright laundry swaying against a backdrop of newly green waving fields of wheat. The cool sweet breeze that blew through her kitchen window—the kind that smelled like apples and forced her to stop sloshing in the dishwater and say a prayer of thanks—the sound of her children laughing and splashing after the miracle of a summer storm ... it was all gone. Everything gone.

Emma dropped to the broken stool under the line, covered her face, and let her head fall onto her lap.

"Are you okay, Mama?" Jessie walked around the house and over to the water pump.

Emma dried her eyes quickly and smiled. "Everything is fine. It's just so hot. The sun is relentless."

Jessie's wise eyes searched her face. Blue, like her father's, like the sky. "What are we going to do?"

"I'm not sure." The words came out before she'd even thought about them.

"I've been thinking. Maybe I could go to the city and get a job. Find a family to work for? I may earn enough to send back some money and help out here."

Emma shook her head and secured a shirt with one more pin.

In the distance, an engine sputtered to life. Emma listened. "The new Mr. Mitchell?"

"No. I don't recognize that one."

Together they stepped around to the front of the house. "Oh," Emma said. "It's the banker. Probably here to take another farm."

"What do you mean?"

Emma sucked in her lips. "Sorry. It's not something you have to worry about."

"Will he take our farm?"

"No, baby. He won't. We don't have a mortgage, so as long as we can scrape enough together for the taxes, we'll be fine."

"But how will we do that."

Emma smiled at her oldest and reached for a strand of Jessie's hair that had fallen to stick onto her sweaty face. She tucked it behind her daughter's ear, and they turned back to the laundry. "Worry accomplishes nothing." She glanced to the water pump. "How about we gather the little ones. I'll fill the tub, and we'll scrub their hair." Emma tightened her apron. "As long as the wind isn't making a nuisance of itself, maybe we can keep them clean for a few minutes."

Emma watched Jessie glance over her shoulder and down the street one more time before nodding and taking a step back toward the house. She had grown so much, and she deserved more than Emma had to give her. Jessie deserved to learn in a school so that she could go to the city and get a job as more than a servant for some other family. Emma pictured her smart daughter working behind a desk, her hair shiny and set in a fresh style. She would be lost in thought and clicking her pencil against her teeth. Emma sucked in a breath. Visions for her children could be so real, so intense, like a part of her died to make it happen. But Jessie, here, now, was too young to go. She hadn't enough education to make it.

And Emma had no way to change that.

★★★

The post office opened only on Mondays. And no one actually delivered the mail anymore. There weren't enough people left in the town to warrant the luxury.

Lillian shaded her eyes and peered through the dusty glass. Mrs. Porter rocked in the corner chair, head back, eyes closed, hands folded across her ample bosom.

Lillian knocked softly and opened the door. "Mrs. Porter?"

Without a notion of weariness, her eyes shot open. "Hello, dearie. I believe you received some mail today." She waddled over to the counter, pulled a few envelopes from the small, dusty mail slots, and slid them across to Lillian.

"Shame about Old Widow Ruby." The woman leaned forward, elbows on the chipped Formica top. "I never considered that she could even die. I suppose that sounds simple, but, well, some people seem like they've been in a place forever, and like they'll be in that place forever, and it's hard to imagine the place without them."

Lillian nodded. She fanned the letters out and glanced at the return addresses. The letter from her mother had arrived. Hopefully, the church back home was able to respond to their needs. She nodded to the lady behind the counter and tried to edge her way back into the conversation, but she was afraid she'd missed at least a couple of sentences.

She smiled and took the conversationally safe route. "Even though we didn't see her around town much, I'm afraid we're all going to miss her." Lillian tapped the envelopes on the counter and silently promised to pay better attention to casual conversations.

"I couldn't agree more." Mrs. Porter pursed out her lips and cleared her throat.

"Well, thank you. Will we see you in church on Sunday?" Lillian began the process of extracting herself from the room. Sometimes with Mrs. Porter, it took a while.

Mrs. Porter's hiccupping gait got her back to the rocker where she eased back down. "Sure thing. Unless, of course, the wind picks back up too bad."

"Of course." Lillian reached for the door handle and pulled it open. "Nice visiting with you."

The older lady waved one plump hand high enough to say that Lillian had accomplished what she'd intended with the niceties. By the time Lillian offered one final wave back through the window, Mrs. Porter had already resumed her previous position.

Lillian looked up to their church across the street. Half an hour until lunch. Peter would still be in his office.

Justin's brother's car sat in front of his store, but she'd seen Randall leave with the banker and hadn't noticed their return. The coroner had already left. Lillian brushed the dust from her favorite skirt, a straight-cut that flared at her calves, and stepped into the hush of the sanctuary.

Dust motes floated in and out of the spears of sun that stretched from the tall windows to the floor. "Are you here?" she called to the empty room.

"In here." Peter sat behind his desk in a small room behind the cross at the front of the church. "Is it lunch already?"

"No. I stopped for the mail. Thought we could walk home together."

Peter hummed.

Lillian sat, dropped her floppy hat onto the floor, and brushed the hair from her eyes. "How did it go with the coroner this morning?"

"He found nothing out of the ordinary." Peter inhaled loudly and then let the breath out slow. "He wants me to handle the notification of her next of kin. I've called a minister in her town, and he will pay Ruby's niece a visit."

"That's better than a letter."

Peter looked up, his eyes revealing nothing. "Randall will follow up with a letter."

Lillian paused, allowing for the comfort in the quiet sounds of an old building. "What does he have to do with it?"

"He wants to buy her place."

Lillian didn't try to hide her surprise. "What for? There's nothing left in the land."

"That's why he's here. He wants to buy the farms while they're cheap as an investment in the possibility this desert will once again become tillable."

"He didn't wait long, did he?"

Peter stood and crossed to the small, open window. "At least someone has hope. There's nothing out there."

Lillian clasped her hands in her lap.

"There's nothing out there, and there's nothing in here." The sheen on Peter's forehead glimmered in the shape of a sunlit rectangle that overflowed onto the desk and to a stack of books and finally the chair Lillian occupied.

She crossed her legs to block the shape.

"I have nothing left to give, nothing that they need."

Lillian looked up. "Do you remember fireflies?"

Peter turned to her. "Of course." His perfectly arched eyebrows betrayed his dour mood. Even when things were at their worst, he had a difficult time appearing stern. Someday, she hoped, he would make a wonderful father. So far, they'd been denied that blessing.

"No." Lillian stood and slowly walked over to stand by her husband. "Do you remember *that* night? The one where we drove out into the prairie, the part that hadn't been farmed, and strolled down to the stream that only existed because it had been a rainy spring."

The corner of his mouth twitched into a tired smile, and his eyebrows lifted playfully. "Of course, I remember."

Lillian shook her head. "Shame on you," she chastised him. That night they'd made love in the field, then lain naked under the stars on a quilt she kept tucked behind the seat of their truck.

His smile made it all the way to his eyes.

Lillian took a step nearer. "Do you remember the fireflies? How many there were? And how when the sun had finally sunk far enough for the stars to flicker through, we felt like we were floating in space because there were stars above and stars below and telling where the sky ended and the earth began had become impossible?"

"I remember." Peter whispered his answer.

Lillian pressed the tips of her fingers against the front of his shirt. "And how we said we wished we could stay there, between the real world and the one we could see?" Lillian ran her fingers along the sewn seam of his shirt pocket. "I knew in that moment the real world was not the one my senses recognized."

Peter lifted her hand to the side of his face and kissed her palm. "I know."

"The real world is about who we are together. The things we see and taste and hear when we are alone, they fade ... we don't even remember them after a while. But the things we do, the people we are to the others who walk our same road..." —Lillian pointed to the doors leading out of the chapel— "...how we help them, that is our reality. That is the thing that doesn't diminish.

The lack of rain may have faded the land, it may have made life hard, but the souls who step into this church are as vibrant as ever. Hardship has no hold on reality. Because you are what is real, and I am what is real, and Emma and her children are real, and Sidney and everyone else."

Peter nodded. "I'm sorry."

"Don't be sorry. Be who you need to be for them." Lillian smiled up at him.

Peter took a deep breath in and held it. "What's for lunch?"

Lillian rolled her eyes and took his hand. "Corned beef hash and applesauce."

Peter laughed and grabbed his hat. "I don't know. Sometimes reality feels awful real."

★★★

The day kept getting better.

Randall stretched his arms over his head and twisted the stiffness out of his neck. The farm next to Old Widow Ruby's had recently been abandoned, and the banker didn't waste much time hinting they might let it go cheap.

On top of that, the coroner stuck to simple, matter-of-fact questions and actually encouraged Randall to contact the next of kin by letter in order to inform her of his interest in the property. Of course, the official did so with surprise registering on his face. No one understood Randall's interest in the area. He didn't care. They didn't have to.

Randall glanced out the window over the desk in his room above the store. No one milled about. Too hot. Too dry. The fan, sitting atop the other chair in the room, whirred and clinked like some kind of excited clock. Randall glanced at his watch: 4:30. Fifteen more minutes and he'd be on his way to visit the Owens. Particularly the daughter. He chased back through to the conversation they'd had after the funeral. Jessie. Jessie was her name.

A bit too young but old enough. And pretty enough.

Heck, if he wanted to take some time, he could step in and maybe sway the mother. But who knew where the husband had taken off to, and filing a divorce, that simply took too long. The daughter, though, she'd work out fine.

He folded the letter he'd written to the Old Widow Ruby's niece, slid it into an envelope, and sealed it. The letter would go out with next week's mail. A delay he didn't appreciate but a necessary one.

Unless he found a person going to the city. Then he could send it with them.

Randall stood, fastened the top button of his shirt, and straightened his tie. He checked his reflection in the small pockmarked mirror that hung over the dresser. He'd used less oil in his hair today. The look suited him.

Downstairs, Justin still sat at his bench behind the counter, waiting for the hands of the clock to tick over to the five. Randall cleared his throat as he took the last step.

"Going somewhere?" Justin glanced up from his ledgers.

"I thought I'd pay a call on the Owens and possibly bring them over something."

Justin tilted his head up with a measuring glance Randall was sure he thought he controlled. He didn't. His questioning always betrayed the suspicion Randall knew hid beneath the surface. "What takes you there?"

"I heard that the man of the house has been gone a while. I thought they may appreciate a few things."

"That's true. What kinds of things?"

"I may do a little shopping here in your store." Randall walked down one aisle and turned on his heel. "You don't happen to know what the children may like, do you?"

"Maybe a tin of biscuits?" The question in Justin's tone revealed his confusion.

"You think it's strange for me to do a bit of visiting? I am, after all, hoping to someday be a neighbor."

Justin rolled his pencil back and forth between his fingers. "I think that's nice."

Randall gave one curt nod and picked up a few boxes of what he knew would be a rare treat. He set them on the counter and returned to the shelves for a couple dusty cans of peaches and a pound of coffee.

"How about this?" He stood back and looked over the collection.

"You don't think it's a bit much coming from a stranger?" Justin's hesitant tone mocked Randall's efforts.

"You don't think they need the items?" Randall challenged his older brother.

Justin stood and unrolled a long line of brown wrapping paper. "I think what you are doing is nice." He made quick work of securing the packages with twine.

It was just like his brother to doubt Randall's ability to do something as simple as give someone a gift. To his right, beaded bracelets hung on a spinning display rack. They sparkled despite the fine sheen that had covered them for who knew how long. Randall picked one up and rubbed the glass beads until they shone. "Add this, too."

Justin nodded and avoided eye contact. He tallied the items. "You want to pay for these now or do you want to open a tab?"

"I'll pay now. Wouldn't want to request credit from a family member."

Justin's expression deadened, and Randall enjoyed a rush of adrenaline.

CHAPTER FIFTEEN

The new Mr. Mitchell walked down the street, his arms loaded with parcels. Jessie ran around the back of the house before he could see her and then through the kitchen to the stairs. She rushed up, sifting her fingers through her hair, trying to gauge the state of matters.

Glancing down out the window, she watched him pause at the gate and shuffle the brown-wrapped packages to one arm. Jessie looked down at her dress and then to her little sister, who had crawled in bed early because of a fever. She knew her mother stood in the kitchen, stirring something or other for dinner. That left her to answer the knock when it came.

She dragged a brush through her hair and splashed some water on her face, scrubbing her cheeks dry with a towel.

"What ya doin'?" Anna rolled over and stared at Jessie.

"Nothing. Mind your own business."

"Is someone here?"

"You just go to sleep now. You've got a fever. No sense in worrying about what's goin' on downstairs."

Anna frowned and crossed her arms over the worn patchwork blanket.

Jessie sighed. "If you're good and stay in bed, I'll tell you all about it if you miss anything interesting."

Her little sister considered the offer like a seasoned gambler. "I guess," she paused, "but you best not leave out any good parts."

"Of course not." Jessie brushed her hands down her waist and peered at her reflection one more time before ducking out of the room. Her sister could be a pain, but that was only because she was smart. Really smart. Jessie chewed on her bottom lip. There wasn't a schoolteacher left in town, and Anna needed one. There had to be something she could do.

The anticipated knock at the door had her mother poking her head out of the kitchen. "You going to see to that, Jessie?" she called up the stairs.

"Yes." Jessie nearly tripped in her rush to slip on her shoes and get to the door before one of the other siblings opened it and said something embarrassing. "Go on," she said to her hovering brother. "I'll get it."

He shuffled out of the front room, but not so far away that he couldn't hear. Oh, what it must be like to live in a large house.

Jessie opened the door and tried to look surprised. "Mr. Mitchell, so nice to see you."

He stepped into the living room and held out the packages. "I thought I would stop by to be neighborly and maybe bring a few things over. And please, call me Randall. We are, after all, practically neighbors. I only live down the block above the store."

"Who is it, Jessie?" Emma stepped into the room, wiping her hands on a dishtowel she'd slung over her shoulder. She stopped when she noticed Randall. "Oh, we weren't expecting company." She lifted her hand to her hair to check for loose strands. "What brings you around?"

Randall shifted the packages to one arm. "I wanted to get to know a few of the families in town, so I thought I would bring over a few things."

Emma glanced at the pile. "We really can't accept anything. It is very nice of you but not necessary."

"I know it isn't necessary." He handed the pile off to Jessie. "I just wanted an excuse to visit."

Jessie watched confusion dance across her mother's features. "Thank you, Mr. Mitchell. We appreciate it. Won't you have a seat?"

"Again, please, both of you, call me Randall."

Emma shot Jessie a warning look that Jessie ignored. "I'll take this into the kitchen and put some coffee on." Jessie juggled the packages into the kitchen and dropped them on the table while her mother gestured for Randall to sit on the sofa. She took the chair across from him.

"What's that?" Jacob crowded her and pulled at the twine on the package.

Jessie slapped his hand away then glanced out the kitchen window to make sure the younger ones were still in sight of the house. "Mr. Mitchell brought these for us," she said with a harsh whisper. "He's sitting in the front room with Ma."

"What for?" He matched her tone but didn't drop the string.

"Don't know."

"What you doin'?"

"Making coffee."

Jacob picked up a package and shook it. "I'm opening it."

"You better not."

"You can't stop me."

Jessie frowned but short of a brawl in the kitchen, she knew he was right. "Just be quiet." She set the water on the stove to boil and watched Jacob work at the knots.

The flaps of paper opened to reveal boxes of biscuit cookies.

Jacob's eyes grew wide. "You think we can have one?"

Jessie glanced to the front room. She couldn't see them from where she stood. And she couldn't hear their conversation. Just the drone of overly polite tones. The yellow box with red lettering bragged of the shortbread inside.

"Please, Jessie? Just one?"

"Fine. If you take it outside and stay there."

Jacob held up his right hand and put his left over his heart. "Scout's honor."

Slipping a nail under the cardboard flap, Jessie tore it open. The sweet aroma of cookies drifted up. She almost closed her eyes. Floating dust and acres of dirt where the grass used to be masked every scent with hordes of sameness. When something different came along, something sugary or new, their minds somehow magnified the effect. Suddenly, a single sugary cookie stood in place for a holiday kitchen and a grandmother's plump hug. A piece of fruit meant visions of cool brooks lined by bushes of berry-laden branches hanging over the water, slumping under the weight of abundance.

"That smells so good." Jacob held out his hands.

Jessie counted out three cookies. "One for you, one for Betsy, and one for Henry. And you better make sure to keep track of them out there. I'll take one to Anna later. She's not feeling so great."

As soon as the cookies dropped into his hands, Jacob was out the door.

Jessie stared down at the open package. Her mother didn't want to accept the gifts. Too late. She shook a few more out of the box and onto the small plate from her mother's incomplete collection of wedding china—at least the porcelain wasn't chipped—and then set the offering on the edge of the tray with the coffee cups. A couple more minutes and she could join them in the front room.

Jessie checked her reflection in the back of a spoon and wondered at Randall's age. He might be nearly thirty or he might be younger. Some people were married with twenty years between them, so if he might be interested their difference in age shouldn't be a problem. Jessie turned down the burner on the stove. He might be as old as her mother. But he'd talked to her like an equal, and he'd brushed her hand. Jessie ran her thumb over the place he'd touched, searching for that warmth again.

The coffee finished percolating. Jessie poured the hot liquid into the cups and carried the tray out to the front room. The cookies, although small, felt huge, and Jessie ignored her mother's questioning look.

"I was just telling your mother how I hope to purchase some land in this area."

Emma picked up a cup and sipped gently, locking gazes with Jessie over the rim. She set the cup on the saucer in her other hand and held it in her lap. "And I was asking why he may want a dried-up old farm in these parts."

Randall smiled and shifted his gaze from mother to daughter, giving Jessie the bulk of the time with his stare. "I explained"—he paused to take a sip—"that not so long ago this was rich country, and it stands to reason it will become so again."

"I suppose that makes sense." Jessie took a sip herself, ignoring how her mother's brows shot up into her forehead. Just because she'd not liked coffee before didn't mean she couldn't like it now.

Jessie swallowed. Or at least learn to like it.

"I think I need to be going. I've a few things I'd still like to get done this evening." Randall looked from Jessie to her mother. "Would you mind if Jessie walked me out? I'd like the opportunity to speak with her."

Her mother paused, cup in midair. Then her spine stiffened and she took a deep breath in. "I suppose that would be acceptable." She eyed him with enough suspicion to make Jessie uncomfortable.

But Jessie couldn't tamp down the fluttering just below her heart. He wanted to speak with her. Just her. Alone.

Despite her efforts, her smile wouldn't stop spreading across her face.

"I'll take the tray." Her mother stood and picked up the few dishes. "Thank you for your visit, and thank you for the gifts." She carried the tray into the kitchen and disappeared around the corner.

Jessie looked up at the man who'd taken a step closer. Before she had time to adjust to his nearness, he held his arm out for her to take. It was all very old-fashioned and debonair, and Jessie couldn't help but step onto the front porch of her home hoping someone was there to see them walking, her hand tucked securely in the crook of his arm.

★★★

Emma dropped the tray on the table and scurried out the kitchen door. Without a doubt, that man had intentions on her daughter.

The other children sat under the shade of the house, digging in the dirt and burying the ends of dead twigs: makeshift roads and minuscule telephone poles. Jacob pushed a rusted toy car through the town, earning scowls from Betsy when he ran over her imaginary building and knocked down fences. They all looked up as she passed, six eyes blinking questions at her. She pressed the tip of her finger to her lips, signaling they should be quiet, and made her way around to keep Jessie in view, and with any luck, to catch a bit of their conversation.

He had to be in his late twenties, at least. Emma shook her head. That put him nearly fifteen years older than Jessie. She'd heard of more, but fifteen years would raise a few brows. Jessie would turn sixteen soon. People did get married at that age. If Henry hadn't gone off and left, he'd not be happy, but he wasn't exactly here anymore.

Emma closed her eyes for a minute and leaned against the side of the house. Nearly sixteen. Old enough, with the right man, to have her own place, maybe a job, and maybe children soon.

And young enough to be dazzled by the thought of freedom.

Emma rubbed her hands together and glanced back at the pair by the fence. Jessie had the stance of a woman waiting, and Randall the assurance he could get what he wanted. But what he wanted made no sense.

A wife? A home on drought-burdened land? Emma watched him pull his hand from his pocket. Something hung from his fingers, shimmering in the sun. Jessie reached for the bait, toyed with the glimmering beads, and took the bracelet.

Emma watched her oldest daughter hold her breath as Randall fastened the sparkling costume jewels around Jessie's wrist then held her young fingers a fraction of a second too long.

★★★

Lillian watched the pair from the front-room window. Randall had found a potential wife.

Out of habit, she eased down into her favorite upholstered chair. Any quick movements released a cloud of dust that never seemed to land.

He'd given Jessie a bracelet. A brilliant move, she had to concede. It wouldn't take much to turn the head of any young woman in town. With the promise of a good meal and another shiny gift, he might just convince her to marry him.

Lillian looked up at the clock, and pieces of her thoughts fell into place. The promise of a home—arguably the nicest home in town—would be too much for Jessie to resist. Too much for her mother to resist on her behalf.

She stood, pulled on her sun hat, and listened as the phone rang.

Lillian looked back to the kitchen. Some days, she almost forgot they even had a phone. It never rang anymore. There were so few left in town. And of those who remained, no one wanted to talk. There were too many needs—those who had resources worried they would have to offer help they really couldn't afford, and those who didn't have anything to spare, well, they were too proud to admit it.

She crossed over the bare wood floor and picked up the receiver. "Hello?"

"It's me," Peter said. The reception, so strangely clear up against her ear, without wind or dust, made her pull the phone away for a second and glance at the holes that pushed out her husband's voice.

"What do you need?" She hesitated to ask too much. After all, what couldn't wait a half hour? What couldn't wait until they shared dinner?

"I need you to go across the street and speak with Emma."

Lillian looked down at her shoes. "I was just on my way to visit her."

"Good. She needs to come and see me."

The silence stretched the distance between the house and the church where she could imagine her husband sat, phone to his ear. "But why don't you visit her?"

"Because we will need to make some phone calls and some arrangements, and I think it best if we do not try to accomplish that at her house."

Lillian swallowed. "Did you hear of her husband?"

A crackle came over the line; an auditory agitation insinuated itself into the conversation. "I've some news for her."

"He's alive, right?"

"Yes."

"Is he, well, is he in jail?"

"No."

"Then what happened?"

"He's been hospitalized. He had no identification, so they only now discovered he had family."

"Oh, dear." Lillian glanced out the window at Emma's home. Her children were back out, at least a couple of them. "I'll go get her, and we'll walk down."

Peter agreed, and Lillian dropped the receiver back into the cradle. Every comforting word flashed through her mind, and at once, Lillian dismissed them all.

She opened the door and stepped into the dirt. A small cloud of dust rose against her haste. The children across the street waved. Lillian did her best to smile at them, but it felt more as if she bared her teeth. She carried bad news, the kind that would change their lives forever. Smiling as she made her way across the street felt like the worst kind of betrayal.

CHAPTER SIXTEEN

Emma's hands shook with relief or fear or simply with too much emotion.

Her husband hadn't left them. She'd not been abandoned. He'd not found another woman, a younger woman. He'd not given up on her because after five children her body had lost its resilience. He'd not been overcome with the work of life. He'd not been overwhelmed because the last two children had been her fault. They'd not wanted any more, and she hadn't been smart with her dates, but that hadn't chased him away. She hadn't chased him away.

Her children had a father. Nothing important had changed. There was no reason to think he'd stopped caring for them, for her.

No tears fell. Why wasn't she crying?

"Are you going to be okay?" Peter's voice sounded like it came from far away. Emma heard him from across his office desk. She felt Lillian's fingers flutter down to rest on her arm. In her mind, she stood, thanked the couple whose job it was to take care of the meatier chunks of life, and then walked out with the pride of a wife who still held her husband's fancy.

But her legs wouldn't move. She willed herself to look up.

"He's in the hospital. Do you understand what that means?" Lillian's words landed all around like feathers from a ruptured pillow. Like Emma should do something with them, clean them up, use them in some way, preserve their softness.

"How ... what ..." Emma glanced to Lillian, willing the other woman to make the decisions for her.

Lillian let her hand slide down and grasped Emma's fingers with a grounding squeeze. "We'll get the truck ready. We'll drive you to town."

"What about the children?" Emma abandoned any pretense of control. *Just make the decisions. Just tell me what to do. I don't want to be in charge anymore.*

Lillian stood and pulled Emma to her feet. "We're going to go back to your house. We'll pack you a bag. Jessie is old enough to keep things together for a couple of days, yes?"

Emma's mind twirled with visions of her husband in a hospital bed, so sick he'd been unable to communicate even his name. "Yes. Yes. I think so. She's nearly sixteen."

"And we'll let some of the ladies in town know to look in on them. I'm sure they would be glad to help. Peter, you'll make the arrangements? Get us all a place to stay in town?"

"Yes. Yes. Of course." Peter retrieved the faded directory from a desk drawer and flipped through the pages. "I'll call the hospital first." He glanced at the lines of numbers. "Maybe I'll call the operator. She'll likely know the best person to speak with."

"We'll leave then. You'll pick us up at our house in a while?"

Peter stretched his arm to reveal his watch. "About a half hour?"

"That should be fine."

Emma followed Lillian back into the sun. The Mr. Mitchells watched them walk down the street from the filmy store windows, their faces almost pressed to the glass. She still had a husband, she wanted to scream. She had someone who could settle the bill at the store, maybe, or at least deal with it. Someone who would take any man who was too old for Jessie to task with the barrel of his shotgun. She still had someone. They had someone.

But she said nothing. She watched as her small house loomed closer, as her children congregated at the gate, curious to hear the news that had called their mother away in the middle of the day.

★★★

Lillian slid across the torn leather seat and tried to keep her knees free of the gear stick. It would be a hot, undignified ride. She looked into the cracked side mirror and watched her husband take Emma's bag.

"Go ahead. I have this," Peter said. He nodded her toward the passenger side door and lifted her small suitcase into the back of the truck.

Emma slid into the empty space to Lillian's right, tucked her skirt in under her thigh, and nodded for Peter to close the door.

"Thank you. I'm really not sure what we would have done." Emma clasped her hands tightly in her lap and stared out the front window.

Lillian nodded. She wanted to tell her not to thank them. That for all any of them knew, they were taking her to more heartbreak than if she'd never known what had happened to Henry. She wanted to say so many things that couldn't be put into words. Instead, she gave half a smile and waved to Emma's children, lined up across the street, with Jessie standing behind them like a sentry.

"They'll be okay." Emma sounded more like she needed convincing than that she was assured in the truth of the statement.

"Of course they will be," Lillian agreed. "Jessie's a good girl. She knows what to do."

"She's getting older." Emma continued to watch the five at the gate. "She'll want her own things soon. She'll want a life this town can't give her."

"We're looking for a teacher still. We're hoping to find one before autumn. That would help, don't you think?"

Emma frowned. "If fall isn't too late." She met Lillian's gaze and shrugged. "Don't you remember sixteen? Two months were a lifetime."

★★★

"So they found him?" Randall dropped back to all four legs of the chair on the front porch of the store and called through the open door to his brother. The truck with the minister, his wife, and Mrs. Owen lumbered down the road, slow and respectful, careful not to stir up an unnecessary dirt cloud.

"From what I heard. He's in the hospital."

"What's wrong with him?"

"I think he got caught in a storm. Something happened to the truck, ended up in the middle of nowhere. I would guess he got that dust pneumonia the old folks get."

"But he's been gone a long time."

Justin walked out and leaned against the porch post. He crossed his arms over his chest and looked out over the buildings. "I think he was just real sick. Didn't wake up for a long time. Took a lot of doctoring to get him back."

"How long you suppose they'll be gone?"

"Don't know. Why?"

"Just leaving a whole family of kids like that. Suppose it's safe?"

"Women in town will look after them."

Randall nodded, slapped some of the dust off his pant legs, stood, and stretched. "I've got a bit of work to do upstairs. When do we want to have dinner?"

"Not a bit hungry yet. How about you?"

"No. Maybe I'll take a drive for a while. I'll heat up a can of beans tonight when I get back."

Justin nodded and took the chair Randall had vacated. "Where you going to go?"

"I'm still trying to make sense of who owns what land out here. When I ride around with the banker, sometimes I'm not even sure he understands where one farm ends and another begins. Seems to me like when the grass starts to grow again, maybe everything will have shifted, scrambled somehow."

Justin nodded and leaned back, balancing on two legs like Randall had done earlier.

He didn't last that long, though. Randall heard the chair drop as soon as he stepped into the deeper shade of the store. Some people couldn't relax unless everything balanced. Some people needed things to be perfect before they could find peace.

Randall climbed the steps to his room, remembering which boards creaked, and cataloging where the wallpaper had peeled from the corners. Justin, like everyone else in town, had decided to stay and survive.

But Randall planned to do more than survive. His previous father-in-law had accused him of a lack of patience and said that he'd never amount to anything. On more than one occasion, Randall had been informed by his in-laws that he was so much less than their daughter deserved. She'd been a simpering whiny woman who'd done her best to make his life miserable. She'd sneered at everything he said, and her family had tolerated him at best. Like his own family. Justin the golden child, and Randall, the fatherless.

Was it his fault Justin's father had died? Was it his fault his father had abandoned Justin's mother? Randall opened the bedroom door and turned the knob to close it quietly, without the finality of a click. He'd never understood what had happened. But Justin had known. He'd always known. And he never bothered to tell Randall why their mother would cook their meals but could hardly look at Randall when she set his plate down in front of him.

CHAPTER SEVENTEEN

Jessie stirred the oatmeal and replaced the cover on the pot. They were tired of oatmeal, all of them, but little else remained. The only thing left in the cupboards were the dishes, but with no food to put on the plates or in the bowls, the space they occupied was little more than a cruel joke.

Her dad was alive. Her mother had gone to fetch him, maybe. It had been a hard lesson, but they'd all learned not to believe something until it sat there at their table. At least her mother had gone to see what had happened.

"When we gonna eat?" Anna backed down the steep stairs and stumbled into the kitchen.

Jessie frowned at her sister's flushed face and glassy eyes. "Come here. Let me feel your head."

Anna lifted her own hand to her face. "Think I'm fine now."

Jessie crossed her arms and waited for her little sister to sigh and march over like a court-martialed soldier. Her forehead was warm again.

Jessie crossed to the sink, dipped a cup in the pail of water and handed it to her sister. "Drink it, and then back upstairs," Jessie ordered. "I'll bring you some dinner in a bit."

"I'm going to eat down here. I'm tired of upstairs."

"I don't think so. Ma wouldn't be happy if she knew I let you out of bed with a fever."

"Ma's not here and you can't boss me."

Jessie took a deep breath. "Ma's not here, and that's exactly why I can boss you."

Anna widened her stance and crossed her arms.

"You want me to tell Ma you didn't listen? And when she comes home with Dad, you want the first thing I tell him to be that you misbehaved?"

Anna's shoulders dropped a fraction. Jessie knew it had been a tad mean, bringing their dad into the contest, but she didn't have time for nonsense.

"Fine." Anna turned on her heel and stomped back to the stairs. "But when Ma gets back, I'm telling her you're mean."

Jessie turned to the table and set out five bowls and five spoons. She mixed the powdered milk with the water out of the bucket and poured it into glasses. The oatmeal still needed to bubble for a while longer so she could give each glass another stir after they'd set awhile. The milk always tasted better after it had had some time.

The last can of peaches caught the sun from where it sat on the counter. She'd given it a lot of thought. The sweet, thick syrup would make the oatmeal taste like summer. She licked her bottom lip, grabbed the opener before she reconsidered, and snapped it onto the lid.

The scent released by the first trembling twist was at first dewy, and then sugary, and then the peachy aroma came through. Jessie lifted the sharp edge of the top to her mouth and licked the syrup off the lid. She measured out five equal portions, even cutting the last two slices into equal bites. Then she set the small bowls of shimmering fruit next to the bowls for their oatmeal and stood back to enjoy the look of a table with more than one dish per person.

With the oatmeal ready to dish out, she called in the others. They all paused to brush the dust off their knees and clothes before piling into the kitchen. Jessie inspected each one with a damp cloth at the ready, then ushered them into the chairs.

In awe of the fruit next to their bowls, they sat, hands folded, ready for the memorized prayer they always recited. Jessie glanced up the stairs to where Anna had retreated minutes earlier.

"Anna, you still awake?" Jessie called up through the hole in the ceiling.

"Yes."

Jessie smiled at the peevish tone. "If you feel good enough, you can come down to eat, but you have to go back up as soon as you're done."

Anna's feet appeared on the steps before Jessie finished her sentence.

"Go ahead. Sit down. I'll dish out the oatmeal."

Jessie acted as the mother, scooping and wiping and shushing through the meal. And when everyone finished, she cleaned and scrubbed and made sure the dirty rags were hung so they would dry instead of mold.

And when the children were finally tucked into bed, and her hair straightened back out, and her face washed of the day's dust, she sat down on the front stoop, looked up to the clear sky then down to her bracelet, and listened for his footsteps, in case he decided to walk by.

He could be their ticket out. She had to do something.

★★★

Randall paced back and forth in the shadows of the store.

The young girl, Jessie, was pretty. Young, but pretty, and not at all hard to imagine as someone whom he could come home to every night.

But going near her place when her mother had left for town, it wouldn't be looked upon kindly by the watching neighbors.

That's why he'd waited until dark.

He didn't know her well enough yet. Didn't have any idea of her plans. But if she had the same dreams as any other sixteen-year-old, she had dreams of freedom. And right now, in this town, there were few paths to freedom for anyone, let alone a sixteen-year-old young lady.

He couldn't walk down the road. That would draw attention. He'd slip behind the houses and come up on hers from the back. If she sat out, then they could visit, almost as if he'd been out for a stroll and happened upon her. If he didn't see her, then he'd return to the store.

He looked up to the sky and the countless stars and the half-moon hanging there. A few houses still flickered with electric life and human sounds. He'd never get used to it, the unsettling lack of noise.

Not only were there no city noises, but the lack of grass, water, and live trees meant that the chirping of summer crickets, the deafening cicadas, and the enormous buzz of tiny mosquitoes and gnats were sporadic, if not missing entirely. This left the houses with only the silent hum of stars and the occasional responding crackle of a radio when the quiet became too much.

Randall crept up next to Jessie's house. No light shone and no whispered conversations floated down out of the open upstairs windows. He continued, keeping the water pump in view, hoping to see a glimpse of her pale skin.

She sat on the front stoop, her legs and bare feet dangling over the side of the porch. Randall sucked in a deep breath, surprised by the level of attraction he felt for the teenager. He slowed and watched her dip her big toe down to the earth to draw a lazy circle in the fine dust. He didn't want to frighten her, so he shuffled his feet and let her hear his approach.

"Who's there?" Jessie whispered loudly.

Randall smiled. She'd realized the discretion he wanted even without his direction. "It's Randall. I wanted to check on you to make sure you were all faring well with your mother gone."

Jessie peered into the dark and lifted a hand to pull back the hair that had slid down over one cheek. He couldn't make out her eyes in the dark, but he knew they were an ice blue. What surprised him, though, was the long curve of her neck, the hollow where it met her shoulder, and the smooth line of her long bare arms. She reminded him of one of the paintings that hung in the museum his wife required they tour almost weekly. The one with the ballerinas.

"We're fine," she whispered again, still watching for him.

He stepped into the light and watched the smile spread across her face. "While I do want to make sure you don't need anything, I don't want to risk being seen calling while your mother isn't around." He watched her expression grow serious as he let the truth that he desired to call on her sink in.

She slid from the stoop and walked a woman's walk to the shadows. "We're doing well. I'm not sure how long they will be gone."

"I heard your father is alive, though."

"Yes. But I don't think he is well. I should know more tomorrow."

"Good." Randall let the silence stretch. He waited for her to meet his eyes before he reached for her hand.

Jessie didn't resist his touch.

"I see you are wearing the bracelet I gave you. Do you like it?"

"I adore it." She smiled and didn't drop her gaze.

"Good." He lifted her hand to his lips and dropped a light kiss on her knuckles. "You do realize that I would like to call on you when your father comes back, right?"

Jessie nodded and swallowed. His heart beat faster at her blatantly trembling response. Not only did her parents own the farm on the right location, but it occurred to him he might actually enjoy wooing her. He reached for her other hand and lifted it so their palms met. He waited for her untutored fingers to realize the feel of his, and he smiled when they slowly curled down the back of his hand.

"It feels wrong to visit with you like this, without your parents around."

"I don't think so," Jessie whispered.

She watched his face when he spoke. He could feel her gaze; he could feel the draw.

"Do I have your permission to call on you when they return?"

Jessie nodded, not taking her eyes from his lips.

Randall had to fight the urge to pull her closer into the kiss he discovered he wanted as much as she. "I think I should go now." His feet didn't move.

Jessie took a step closer. She was bolder than he'd expected. He looked out at the front street. No windows faced them. No one was there to see.

She reached up on her toes, uninvited, and unwound her fingers from his. He felt the loss keenly, but when her fingers trailed up to the side of his face, he forgot everything he'd planned and dipped low to take her mouth in a gentle kiss.

It was the most innocent kiss he could remember. He pulled back. Any more and he'd scare her. There was no doubt she'd no idea what a simple kiss could do.

There was more at stake, though. He smiled and took a step backward. She watched him until he knew she couldn't see him anymore, and then she continued to stare into the dark.

Randall smiled. Things couldn't fall into place more providentially. He'd have his wife and house and land before long.

And then when the drought ended, even though he'd had to do it on his own, he'd be the successful brother.

★★★

Jessie crawled up the wall side of the bed she shared with her sisters and turned over to stare at the boards that made up the ceiling in their tiny room. She tried to keep her mind from racing, but she could still feel his lips against hers, and her pulse wouldn't stop pounding through her veins.

Her mother would be furious. But it wasn't his fault. He'd said he wanted to leave, that he only visited to check on her, and she'd been the one to stop him. She tried to feel bad about how boldly she'd acted but couldn't muster the necessary guilt.

Did that make her bad?

Jessie skipped over the thought. Even if it did, she still didn't feel bad about kissing him. She bit her bottom lip, trying to erase the feeling of him. She had to think straight.

His age might be a problem for her parents, but for her needs, the fact he had a few extra years couldn't be more perfect. After all, she didn't care to date him. She didn't need endless nights of sitting in the front room entertaining him like the proper old folks tried to require. She needed a husband. Someone who had some money. Someone who could help out the family.

And if he happened to be handsome, and he happened to want her back, all the better. Love could come, she knew that much, especially when his kiss felt like that.

She'd done the math. Any man who hadn't been tied down by family and farm had left long ago. No opportunities for work existed within the town. They'd not yet replaced the schoolteacher, so the chances of graduating with a diploma had diminished.

If she didn't make this happen, she'd be sitting in the same place, sleeping in the same bed with her sisters, and they'd all still be wondering where their next meal came from.

Especially if her father returned still sick.

Jessie took a deep breath and closed her eyes. A lot of girls went to try to find work in the cities so they could send money home. Marriage to a man with money who gave her gifts and who made her want nothing more than to feel him kiss her again—well, that wouldn't be so much sacrifice as opportunity.

She didn't know when her mother would be back. Jessie rolled to her side and felt Anna's cool forehead. The fever had lifted. She let a relieved breath escape, and little Betsy, between them, shifted to drape one loose arm over Anna's ribs.

They all needed help. And, if Jessie planned right, she might be able to make all their lives better.

CHAPTER EIGHTEEN

Emma shifted in the hospital room chair, searching for a spot of comfort that had, for the past week, remained elusive. Her husband slept, except for the short bouts of wakefulness, offering a strange mix of reality and hallucination.

In the hallway, doctors whispered, nurses pushed carts, patients rolled wheelchairs, and families cried quietly into handkerchiefs. In her husband's room, nothing happened. She sat, wondering about her … their … children, and watched him wither away.

It had been an accident. That much was evident. Maybe the dust had whipped up and obscured his view as he barreled down the road, maybe he caught a rut, maybe another truck drove him off his path then didn't have the humanity to stop. Whatever had caused it, he'd broken both legs and his pelvis.

That wasn't the problem, though. It had been the time it took for someone to find him, lying twenty feet from the truck, half covered in a dirt drift. He'd breathed too much of the black dust, and his lungs hadn't recovered.

Emma stood up and looked out the window. His portion of the shared hospital room had half a window. She looked down over a view that at one time probably boasted green lawn and bright blooms of flowers. Now cars rattled down the road, and kids kicked balls and used cans or faded pieces of cardboard signs substituted for bases.

Three weeks had gone by before he'd been able to even tell the doctors his name. It took another week for the hospital staff to put together where he came from. Where his wallet had disappeared to, Emma had no idea. It didn't matter. Whoever took his wallet experienced more disappointment than Emma did. There hadn't been money in it for a long time. Or, it might still be buried in dirt at the side of the road.

Emma looked at the bed again. At the white sheet stretched over her husband's body, and then at the table, with the pile of correspondence the hospital hadn't known where to send. Bills, mostly.

Emma hadn't the fortitude to open them. This latest hit would cost the farm. No doubt of that. And if he survived the pneumonia, the financial ruin might take him out anyway.

She couldn't be sad, though. He breathed. Her children had a father. He cared for them. In some ways, even if he didn't make it, it would be easier to deal with than if he'd abandoned them all. She stifled the one loud laugh that had threatened for days. Sometimes, no matter how hard she tried at life, the worst happened. And somehow, the sun still rose, and kids still needed to be fed, and cars still drove by.

Life was like waiting for a bomb to fall from the sky. She braced herself, covered her ears, and squeezed her eyes closed. But then, nothing. And when she opened her eyes, she could see the destruction, but she hadn't been knocked to her knees, hadn't been deafened by the crash, hadn't been bruised or hurt. So she picked up a broom and kept doing the same thing she did every day, marveling at how big the clean-up could be and wondering why she was still there.

"How is he doing?" One of the nurses floated on silent white shoes into the room. Red curls sprang from underneath her geometric hat, and Emma found she spent more time thinking about how long the nurse's hair might be if she let her bun out than anything else in the past day. Focusing on meaningless details kept her mind off the things she couldn't control.

"Nothing has changed."

"The aides will be in after the dinner hour to change his bedding. Is there anything else you need?"

Emma tried not to notice the look of pity on the young woman's face, then felt a pang of guilt for all the acts of pity she'd accepted at the expense of others.

The list was long. Pastor and Lillian said they'd bring groceries to the children and check in on Jessie. The hospital administration veiled the mounting bills in terms of payment plans and the always nebulous words like assistance and help. The women in town promised to look after the kids and then, under their breath, mentioned bringing over dinner. They needed it. She needed it. All the help they could get. But every gift felt at once a cool river that brought relief and certain drowning.

"Ma'am?" The nurse took a step nearer, leading with her shoulders.

"I'm sorry. We'll be fine. I don't need anything else right now." Emma sank back into the hard chair, and when the nurse backed out of the room, she brought her eyes back to her husband's shuttered face.

The doctor didn't know how long it would go on, said they had to wait for his body to expel the dirt and heal itself.

Emma didn't know how long they could go on. A few more days, and she would have to call the banker herself, put a mortgage on the land that for years they'd owned outright.

Henry would be furious.

★★★

Randall dropped the open letter onto his desk. The response had come quicker than he'd anticipated. And the niece would take the steps he'd expected her to make.

Any day now, according to her letter, she'd be in Oklahoma to facilitate the sale of her aunt's farm. She had no desire to take it over herself, and after only a little digging, Randall had discovered, like nearly everyone else, her small family could use the money from the sale. He should have no problem negotiating a good price for the deserted place.

Randall checked the postmark on the letter. It had been over a week in the process of traveling to the panhandle. The drought slowed everything down except for trains. Ruby's niece would be traveling by train to the city, and then she'd need to find a vehicle to bring her out to her aunt's house. If he'd have had time to follow up with another letter, he'd have instructed her to call so he could meet the train.

But he didn't have time. Instead, he had to wait.

Randall folded the letter and slid it back into the envelope. He added it to the small pile of correspondence he'd received since living with his brother. Randall smiled. In less than a week or so, he could be taking residence in the old widow's place.

And then he could properly court Jessie. Surely her parents wouldn't find any objection to the man with the largest farm. Especially if Jessie wanted the marriage.

Of that, he had little doubt.

Despite his best intentions, he found the past week's evening walks agreed with him. And if she happened to be waiting in the shadows, that was darn convenient. Randall raked his hand through his hair, remembering the feel of her soft skin. A quick wedding would be welcomed by all.

He glanced out the window, wondering if the woman would have the sense to check in at the store first before heading out of town to the old place. He'd have to keep watch.

Randall plucked his hat off the hook, flipped it in the air, and snatched it back before it could fall to the floor. A playful gesture he'd spent weeks perfecting. Now he just had to add the flick of his wrist to pop it up onto his head.

He closed his bedroom door and made his way down to the store. For now, he'd sit on the front porch and wait. He hated waiting. But he'd learned one important lesson during his wife's long death: waiting always paid off.

★★★

Lillian piled the church's mail with her own and tucked it under her arm for the walk back home. She'd stopped by a few places in town on the way to the post office and waved as she walked by the new Mr. Mitchell. For the rest of the morning, she and Peter would make deliveries—the government had come through with more provisions. Peter would have to read the mail at home instead of at his office.

One thing about getting mail once a week: it sure made for impressive stacks. The letter from her parents sat on top. She'd already opened it and scanned the words scrawled in her mother's perfect penmanship. The church sent best wishes for weathering the continued drought. The depression seemed to be easing around their neighborhood: empty homes were filling again with families. Also written was the news that the funding from their sponsoring church would continue for the next year, and the ladies' group wanted a list of anything they might need.

Lillian paused and lifted her face to the burning sun, giving thanks for the people back home. As far as the list went, what didn't they need?

She skipped up the stairs and dropped the pile on the table by the door.

"You ready to go?" Peter called from the kitchen.

"Is the truck loaded?"

"Did it this morning with old Mr. Mitchell's help."

"We should look in on the Owen children first. Any news from Emma?" Lillian leaned against the kitchen doorframe and stuffed her hands into the pockets of her skirt.

Peter rinsed his coffee cup and set it in the strainer. "Yes, actually, I just hung up the phone with her."

Lillian straightened and walked over to where Peter had left a dishcloth crumpled on the table. She shook it out, folded it over the handle on the cabinet, and waited for Peter to elaborate.

"Seems Henry's doing better. He's sitting up and talking, his fever is gone, and he's gunning to get home."

"Sounds like Henry." Lillian smiled. "Can we tell the kids, or does Emma want to speak with them over the phone?"

"No. Emma wants us to let them know what's happening. If all goes well, I'll travel back in the next week to get them both." Peter paused for a few seconds and turned to face Lillian. "He's not the same, though. They'll need a fair bit of help. They may have to sell the farm and go back to family."

Lillian frowned. "From the tidbits I've garnered, their family will not be much help."

"I guessed as much. Anyone with even the most modest of prospects back home has already left."

"We can help them." Lillian closed a cupboard door that refused to stay shut and watched it to see if it would stay in place. "Nothing has to be decided right now. If we can help them get through the winter, well then, spring may bring rain." She wanted to sound assured but couldn't keep the questioning lilt off the end of her sentence. "Never mind. It will be what it will be."

Peter nodded and rolled up his sleeves. "Ready for another hot, dusty, sweaty afternoon?"

"It sounds like a delightful change..." Lillian let the dry tone in her voice do the work her words didn't do.

"Yes, well, we'd better get moving anyway."

"I'm going to run over to check on the children. We should drop off some things there first. I'm sure they're running low on supplies." Lillian opened the door. "I'll meet you across the street."

"Okay."

Lillian closed the door and stepped into the yard. The house across the street looked as if it had hemorrhaged its live contents into the dirt outside. Jessie sat near the pump, tending the youngest while she played in a washtub full of cool water. Two of the children chased around to the front of the house, one with a stick, the other with mock fright pasted on her face. And the oldest boy busied himself with creating a city grid in the pile of dust under a small dead tree.

"How are things today?" Lillian waved and flipped the latch on the gate. "We heard from your mother."

Jessie looked up and shielded her eyes from the glare of the sun.

"It sounds like things are going well at the hospital."

Jessie smiled. Across the street, Peter's truck chugged to life. It backed up in one long shudder from their yard to the Owens'.

"You got plans for the day?" Jessie asked.

"We have more deliveries to make. You all are first."

Jessie looked over to the truck and stood up. "I can carry them in." She motioned for her brother to come over and sit by the baby. "No need to trouble yourselves with that."

"No problem." Peter heaved a box up to his shoulder and made his way to the front door.

Lillian walked with Jessie to the back of the truck. "If you want, you can take these." She handed her a bag of apples and then picked out a bag of other groceries. "I'll grab this, and then that should be it."

Jessie rushed to the door and followed Peter in. "You can set them right here. That box looks heavy."

"That's alright. I'll just set them in the kitchen."

Lillian followed Peter and Jessie and stopped as soon as she saw the table, already stacked with groceries. It wasn't that an unreasonable amount sat on the table but more the kinds of foods that seemed off.

Peter slid his box onto the table, edging the cans of fruit and cookies off to the side. "The ladies in town have been quite generous, I take it?"

Jessie set her bag down and looked at the floor. "They've been nice. Bringing us dinner every night."

"Is that where these things came from?" Lillian took a step nearer.

Jessie twisted her fingers into the hem of her untucked shirt. "No."

"Then where did you get them?" Peter picked up a can and shook it before setting it down. "Did you make a trip to the store? You didn't have to do that. We told your mother we'd look after you."

"I didn't. Randall ... I mean Mr. Mitchell ... the new Mr. Mitchell brought them over last night."

"Last night?" Lillian furrowed her brows.

"He only stopped by quick. Didn't even come in." Jessie clarified.

The need for clarification grabbed Lillian's attention. "Why would he do that?"

Jessie lifted her chin. "I suppose because he wanted to be helpful."

Unless Lillian interpreted it wrong, Jessie's stance held the tiniest bit of a challenge. She nudged Peter. "We need to be going. That was very nice of Mr. Mitchell ..."—she stressed the word mister—"... to bring these over."

Jessie nodded and followed them back to the door. "Thank you for the groceries." She put her hand on Lillian's arm then withdrew it quickly.

Lillian smiled and reached for her fingers before she could start twisting her shirt again. She watched her face until Jessie looked up and met her gaze. "If you need anything ... anything ... no matter what time of day or night, you come to us, okay?"

Jessie bit her bottom lip and nodded her understanding. "Yes, ma'am," she said before closing the door.

"That's interesting." Peter grasped Lillian's elbow, helping her down the steps.

"I should say so."

Any number of things needed to be said. The house stood in good order. The children played contentedly. Nothing needed to be tended.

Lillian looked down the street at the parked new car young Mr. Mitchell owned. There was nothing more they could do for the children. But she couldn't shake the feeling that Emma needed to come home, and soon.

CHAPTER NINETEEN

R andall kicked the crooked bottom stair. It didn't move. Like everything else in the place. Nothing moved.

Nothing changed.

He'd waited all week to see the niece chug down the road, or, at the very least, to hear from her, but the only thing his waiting had accomplished was a thorough understanding of the uninteresting habits of the townsfolk.

He walked back up to the door and leaned in. "Think I'm going to go for a drive."

Justin looked up from his ledgers. "Sounds good."

Randall rolled his eyes and felt his pockets to make sure he had his wallet. Not that he'd need it in this place.

He let the door slam behind him and walked over to his car, ignoring the dust on his shoes. Honestly, the thought that the people living here had endured the dirt for nearly three years made him want to cough. And he'd be lying to himself if he didn't admit to some worry that the drought would persist for another three.

"No risk. No reward." He said it aloud, not even bothering to see if anyone had overheard. The town was beginning to look like the pictures he'd seen of old abandoned mining settlements: unpainted shutters hanging from one hinge, leaning houses, stores with empty shelves. No souls here.

With the car parked, he kept the windows rolled up to try to keep out some of the dust. But overall, his pointless efforts accomplished little. The coating in the interior looked about as thick as the coating on his shoes. Still, if the winds picked up like he'd seen earlier, at least he wouldn't be shoveling the dirt out by the bucketful.

The engine roared. He pushed the gas a few extra times to clear the exhaust and because he liked the sound of it. The purring of the well-oiled engine and the smooth leather seats of his Oldsmobile felt more alive than anything else in the town. He cranked down his window and started down the road.

Mrs. Owen had yet to return. From the sound of things, her husband would recover, which, Randall suspected, worked in his favor. Mr. Owen would come home with medical bills, and people tended to do what he wanted when they owed a lot of money. Financial desperation had a way of making every opportunity attractive.

He slowed, passing the Owen house, and bristled that he couldn't control a pang of disappointment when Jessie didn't step out to wave. She had to have heard him start the engine.

He pushed the pedal down enough to kick up a respectable cloud of dust and continued out of town. The old widow's place needed to be looked in on. It wasn't good for a house to sit empty with no one tending to it.

To his left sat a broken-down shack with the only colored man in town, like always, sitting outside, watching the road. Randall frowned. The only problem with the old widow's place he could see so far was Sidney's shanty across the street. Once he got things arranged with the niece, he'd spend some time thinking how to solve the problem of an undesirable, nosy neighbor. With a quick flip of his wrist, Randall waved and then turned down the drive onto land he hoped would soon be his.

An unfamiliar car sat in front of the house, and every window in the place gaped open. Parlor curtains, flattened against the screens from the suck of the breeze, blazed white against the dull, sand-eroded exterior of the house.

Randall cursed and jammed the brake. The car skidded to a halt, and the dust cloud that had followed him from town crashed into the house.

When it dissipated, Randall stepped out of the vehicle, plastered a smile on his face, and took the steps two at a time. Standing in front of the closed door, he took a second to straighten his vest and smooth his hair. If the niece had come to town and not had the sense to check in at the only place in town first, then he needed to make a good impression to someone who might not be that bright.

The door opened before he had a chance to knock on it.

"Who are you?" The woman who stood on the other side of the threshold reached up and adjusted the curls of her bobbed hair. Her dress had likely fit her matronly figure better before the last child or two. Pink with exertion, her cheeks rose in two bunched-up hills with her smile.

"You must be that man who wants to buy the house. I figured you'd come out, or I was going to come looking for you. Have you taken a look at the place?"

Randall paused to wait for her to continue without the benefit of his answer. She didn't disappoint.

"I'm Mrs. Cooper. Ruby's niece." She held out her hand.

Randall took hers and shook it gently. "I'm Randall Mitchell. I sent you the letter."

"Ah, yes. I thought so." She turned and waved him out of the sun. "Come in."

Randall closed the door behind him.

"I've been here for a couple of days, so I was getting ready to come and find you. Have you decided if you really want the place? I mean, there's not a lot left here." She glanced out the window at what used to be fields.

"Oh yes. I recently moved to town. I've been waiting to find the right place."

"And this is it?" Her eyebrows lifted almost to her hairline. She had one of those flexible type of faces, the kind that changed expression as easily as the sky changed color. She looked like a completely different person with each new thought.

"Yes. I'm counting on the drought ending sometime. I can hold out. A lot of folks have."

"I suppose." She did little to mask her doubt. "Have you looked through the place?"

"Not in detail," he lied.

"Well, let me give you the tour, and then we can discuss the price." She looked around as if missing something important. "Maybe we should start upstairs?"

"Wherever you prefer. No matter to me."

"Good then." She took the first step and then turned to face him again.

He pasted on a patient smile. It would be a long visit.

"Do you think you might want the furniture or the other things in the house?"

"I moved here with only what could fit in my car, so I'd be more than glad to have anything you see fit to leave."

She nodded and took the next step before turning again. "Maybe we could work out a price for the house as it stands now?"

"Maybe."

"That would be great because I'm not even sure what to do with most of this stuff. I mean, she had nice things, but I've no room for them, and I'd pay a fortune to ship them back home."

The woman was not a skilled negotiator; that much Randall could plainly see.

"To be completely honest, my husband told me not to come home with anything unless I found jewelry or something like that. And I've only found a little, and nothing with much value."

Randall nodded. Speaking was not required for a conversation with this woman.

She turned and took another step, this time talking while she climbed the stairs. "You have a wife? Someone who might like to make this place their home? It is a lovely house to raise a family. Do you have children? We have two. My husband's sister is helping out while I'm gone."

Randall kept smiling. He could endure anything for a time.

★★★

Jessie tucked Little Henry in last. He missed their mother the most and sometimes had to cry a bit before he fell asleep. Jessie ruffled his hair and yawned. Tonight, he was quiet.

Taking care of the five of them took a lot of effort.

She'd done it in bits before, when her mother had other things to do. She didn't mind—in a way she liked it, but when they'd gone through laundry and when she finally finished dishes only to find the dinner hour approaching, those times made her miss her mother.

She tiptoed out of the room and down the stairs into the kitchen. The sun had set completely, and she shuddered at the dark room. She'd never liked the dark. She didn't like to be alone either.

"Jessie?" Randall's voice floated through the kitchen window. He'd seen her standing in front of the sink.

"I'm coming out."

Jessie hurried behind the door so he couldn't see her straighten her dress and tuck the loose strands of hair behind her ears. Then she slipped on her shoes and stepped into the cooling night.

"Where are you?" she whispered.

"Back here."

They'd chosen to meet at the back of the house for the past few days. The pastor and his wife were too curious about her comings and goings to count on the shadows in the side yard to hide them.

It wasn't as if she didn't appreciate their attention. But she sometimes wondered if anyone realized she would turn sixteen tomorrow. And it wasn't as if they were doing anything wrong. Randall had always been respectful, and although he did kiss her sometimes, he never forgot he was a gentleman. Jessie couldn't keep the smile off her face at the thought of him waiting for her.

"Over here."

She followed his voice through the yard to the space behind the broken down old shed where her mother kept the gardening tools. No one bothered to go in there much anymore. There was no need to.

"I didn't expect you tonight," Jessie said as she rounded the corner.

"I couldn't stay away." Randall took her hand in his. "I've good news."

Jessie looked up into his eyes. The dark made it impossible for her to see any details or color, but she could feel the intensity of his stare.

"Today I bought a house."

"Old Widow Ruby's?" How she knew, Jessie wasn't sure.

Randall cocked his head. "I don't remember telling you I was interested in it."

She shrugged. "I think it was a lucky guess. It makes sense. No one is living there, and I don't think anyone else would want to buy it. And it is lovely." She let the dreaminess infect her tone.

Randall took a deep breath and let it out slowly. He turned to take in the land behind the house. "I bet you remember when acres and acres of wheat grew in these fields."

"I'd never seen anything like it. When I was little, I used to walk away from the house and down that bit of a hill." She pointed to the desolate stretch that appeared to go on forever. "When I couldn't see the house anymore, I would concentrate only at the wheat and how it waved until I got dizzy and had to sit. Almost like being seasick." She looked at Randall, suddenly aware how childish she sounded. "I'm sorry. This is silly to talk about."

"No. I love to hear about how this place used to be."

"So, is it Old Widow Ruby's place?"

"It is."

"I'm glad for you."

Randall turned and stared at Jessie. "I was hoping you may be glad for us."

Did he mean what it sounded like he meant? Jessie tried to imagine another way to understand.

"Did you hear me?" Randall took a step nearer. "I know we only met a short while ago, but when your parents come home, I'd like to talk to them both about courting you."

"They'll say I'm too young." Jessie tried not to smile. His insistence on an old-fashioned courting made him seem even older than he was. But her parents would like the term; that much she knew. Besides, a man who looked forward to courting her at home made more sense than one who wanted to date. There was no place left to go. Even a picnic lacked appeal.

"I know. It may be hard at first, but I have the means to support you, and after next week, I'll have a house."

"It's a big house. Do you have furniture?"

"I'm buying it as it is. Her niece was happy to accept my price. We'll finish the paperwork in town tomorrow."

"Tomorrow my parents come home."

"How is your father doing?"

Jessie shrugged. "It will be hard. He'll be in bed for a long time." She kicked at the dirt. "It's a good thing nothing can grow, because he wouldn't be able to be out in the fields anyway."

Randall slid his arm around her shoulders and pulled her closer. Resting her head on his chest felt good. It relaxed her to feel his breath go in and out and to be this close to another person. She spread her fingers against his hand and invited him to weave his between hers. An excited trembling began in her stomach and worked its way up her spine.

"Will your parents have to sell the farm? The medical expenses must be significant."

So much had happened. She had no idea if the farm would have to be sold. If her parents did have to sell, her family would have no place to go.

But she might. She looked up at Randall's silhouette and rubbed her hand against his, warming her fingers against his palm.

Her marrying Randall might be the only thing that could get her family by. She looked out over the dark landscape and concentrated on not lifting her hand to bite her nails. One old-fashioned idea atop another—negotiation. After Jessie and Randall married, he could help her parents keep their farm. It wasn't unheard of. And so far he'd been generous. He just had to want her enough to make her worth the expense.

Jessie ran her hand along his sleeve and lightly squeezed his bicep. He didn't have a farmer's muscles. She tried to like his softer build.

She could get used to anything if it meant her family had a place to go.

CHAPTER TWENTY

Emma sat in the back of the truck next to her husband. They'd filled the small bed with blankets and anything else they could find to cushion him for the journey. Once he'd woken enough to comprehend the impossible numbers on the bills, he simply refused to stay.

The pastor took the road slowly, but the jostling still made her sick. She swallowed convulsively and pasted a smile on her face before shaking Henry until he opened his eyes.

"Do you need a drink of water?"

He closed his eyes against the movement and held up his fingers to signal he couldn't talk. The doctors warned of excruciating pain if he rode home now. But Henry, stubborn as always, wouldn't listen. Emma tried to be angry with him but pity won.

She craned her neck to peer over the cab of the truck. The town's few buildings rose in the distance. "We're almost there," she leaned in and shouted to Henry.

Almost two weeks ago she'd left home, and although she received regular reports from Lillian, the thought of Little Henry's arms squeezing her neck forced tears to the surface. She wiped them away and watched for signs of pain from her husband.

What they would do once they returned home, she'd no idea.

Waving and jostling, the children lined up along the leaning fence. As soon as the pastor parked the truck and came around, Emma jumped down and hurried over. Little Henry nearly dove out of Jessie's arms in an effort to reach her. She squeezed him too hard.

"Now, your father is still very ill. He won't be able to do much of anything. You will all need to help out around here."

Jacob nodded, his face serious.

They walked together over to Henry, who did his best to sit up. He masked the pain with a cringing smile. Jessie's calm expression faltered but she recovered quickly.

Henry reached for her hand. "Happy birthday," he said quietly.

Jessie nodded and lifted Betsy to see over the edge of the truck.

Emma glanced to Lillian and Peter, standing by, waiting for directions. No one looked forward to moving Henry. Least of all, Henry.

"It will be nice to be home again." Henry twisted to better see the house then winced from the effort.

"I'm going to run over to the store and see if I can find some help. I think it will be easiest to lift and move him with the blankets he's on now."

"I moved your bed to the front room," Jessie said. She held out her arms and took Little Henry from Emma so she could climb back up next to Henry and try to get him situated to move.

"You think you're ready?" Peter was back already, with both Mr. Mitchells and a farmer that had the unfortunate timing to be shopping at the minute Peter walked in. Emma nodded thanks to the men, and each one took a corner of the blanket.

"This is going to hurt, you know that, right?" Emma spoke quietly to Henry. He clutched the edge of the quilt and squeezed until his knuckles turned white. The new Mr. Mitchell took a corner at his feet and smiled at Jessie. Jessie's returning smile had Emma trying to make eye contact with Lillian. Something had changed between her daughter and the newcomer. Lillian was too busy herding the children out of the path to pay much attention.

"Wait." Peter took a step back. I think it might be better if we rolled him to his side and slid a board underneath him. That way he's not bending so much. Might be better for his bones."

"I'll be right back." The old Mr. Mitchell ran back the way he came and returned with a wide flat piece of lumber. "This should do the trick, I think."

"Perfect." Peter climbed up next to Henry. "Everyone reach in so we roll him at the same time. Try to keep everything as still as possible."

A smothered moan escaped Henry's lips, but they managed to get the board under him. Each man took an edge of the blanket, and they maneuvered him into the house and into bed.

"We're very grateful for all your help." Emma walked the men to the door and waved to Lillian. She had stayed in the yard, helping Jessie keep the children from underfoot.

"No problem, ma'am." The new Mr. Mitchell tipped his hat and smiled. "You folks need anything, you know where we are."

Emma tried to swamp her caution with appreciation but failed. His smile was too wide, his hands hung lank at his sides, and his eyes kept drifting to where Jessie stood. He'd done nothing wrong, but the whole picture made her grit her teeth in preparation for what she did not know.

★★★

"Anything interesting happen here today?" Randall lifted the lid to examine the contents of the pot on the stove. Beans with pork for dinner again. In town, lunch had been better—much better. Thin slices of roast atop toasted bread with a scoop of mashed potatoes and gravy smothering the whole plate. And the banker had paid for it. Nothing like that out here.

One could argue the beans were free too. But they still didn't taste as good as the roast.

"Nothing out of the ordinary. It's pretty hot out there. Not many folks moving around. What'd you do?"

Randall slipped a stack of folded papers out of the inside of his vest, dropped them on the table, and slid them over for his brother to examine. "Finalized the sale on Old Widow Ruby's place."

Justin's eyebrows shot up, and he reached for his spectacles. Unfolding them with meticulous care, he took more time to balance them on his nose then slowly smoothed the papers out to read. He stopped at the first line.

"Shameful good price." Justin looked up and met Randall's gaze.

Randall didn't even try to hide the half-grin that had taken over his face.

He read in more detail. "You bought the place, equipment, furniture, and all?"

"Everything out there."

Justin folded the papers back up and slid them across the table. Both men sat, facing each other. "When you planning to move out there?"

"Probably tomorrow." His brother's store had been nice and all, but Randall couldn't wait to be in his own place again.

"Big place to take care of on your own."

"That's what a wife is for."

Justin snorted. "Easier said than done in these parts." He frowned at his bowl of beans. "You meet someone in town with the banker? Because I don't think you're going to have a very easy time convincing some city woman to hie out to this desert."

"Not a city girl." Randall picked up his fork and speared a chunk of pork. "The oldest Owen daughter down the road. I've reason to think she may consider me."

"Reason to think?"

"She's pretty enough. And..."

Justin held up a finger, interrupting him. "Don't you think her parents may have something to say about it?"

"If she fancies me, what problem would they have?"

"Maybe that you have to be nearly twice her age. Is she even sixteen?"

"Turned sixteen on the day her father came back."

Randall watched Justin wrestle his reactionary look of disgust into something more like mild discomfort.

"Don't think they're gonna like it," Justin said.

Randall imagined punching the smug look off his brother's face. How old would he have to be before his brother would see him as an adult? He'd already been married once. He knew what it was all about. The beans grew cold. Randall didn't care. "She may be a bit young, but it's not like there are other options for her out here. Not to mention, if she married me, there could be benefits for her family."

Justin buried his interest into the beans.

Good. Randall took a sip of coffee. Soon enough he'd see he didn't have the last say in everything.

★★★

Jessie chewed the cuticle on her thumb. She'd only seen Randall once in the days since her father had come home. She looked out over the black, moonless landscape. It had been a bit of trouble getting out of the house without anyone knowing. She hoped Randall would walk by tonight.

Her father couldn't do much of anything. He spent the days in bed, in the front room, frowning out the window or scowling at the pile of bills her mother finally pulled from his grasp. A pencil and a piece of paper, he'd demanded of Jessie, but at the shake of her mother's head, Jessie didn't comply. He only wanted to add up the sums. And everyone knew what the outcome would be.

Devil in the Dust

So she'd eased out the kitchen door into the darkness, waiting for Randall, hoping he might happen by.

She didn't have to wait long.

"What are you doing out here?"

Jessie took a deep breath. She'd decided days ago to do what she could to help her parents. And the only way forward she could see stood right in front of her. They didn't have a lot of time. "Waiting for you."

Randall's eyebrows shot up. He slowed as he approached. "Everyone's asleep."

He glanced to the open windows and nodded in the direction of the old shed where they'd spent so much time while her mother had been gone.

Jessie stood and followed him, twining her fingers between his as they rounded the back of the shed. When he turned to look at her, she lifted up on her toes and kissed him fully on the lips.

Randall took a step back. "What's this all about?"

Jessie shrugged. "I've been thinking about you asking to court me."

"And?"

"And I like the idea." She glanced back at the house. "I wish we didn't have to tell my parents. They won't be happy."

"Are you sure?"

Jessie leaned back against the shed wall. "They want me to finish school. I don't know how that will happen." She picked at a splinter hanging from the wood siding. It broke loose and she let it drop. "We don't even have a teacher this year."

"I need to be honest with you." Randall turned her so she faced him. "I'm looking for a wife. The old widow's farm is mine now. I'll need help. I don't have time to pretend I'm not shopping for a wife."

Jessie trembled at his words. It started deep in her chest and moved out to her fingers. She clenched her hands together. She hadn't dared hope it would be this easy.

"If you want to finish school, I understand. I know your parents want the best for you." He paused and let the silence drag out. "But with jobs like they are, I'm not sure how much good it will do. You can read and write and do math, right?"

Jessie nodded.

"Anything more than that, well..." he ducked closer so his lips nearly brushed her ear. "Well, do you need anything else to be a good wife? A farmer's wife?"

The trembling spread to her knees. He made her feel things, delicious things, and for a while she fought the guilt that came along with hoping that the choice she'd made to help her parents might also be a choice she wanted to make.

No one got what they wanted anymore. Why should she?

"Would you consider marrying me? We don't know each other well, yet, but sometimes even strangers marry and things go well."

Jessie didn't trust her voice to answer.

"Do you want me to speak with your parents?"

They wouldn't be happy. That she knew. But they could make mistakes just like everyone else. "I don't think I can do that to them yet. They have so many things to worry about right now."

Randall nodded and took a step back. Cool air slipped between them, and Jessie quelled a shiver. She didn't want him to know how keenly she felt the loss of his nearness even with only a step between them.

"You want to think about it?" Randall reached up and twirled a lock of her hair around his finger. He pulled her closer.

He smelled warm, of mint and cologne and paper, like she imagined people who worked in offices might smell. She closed her eyes because she wasn't sure what to do. In the magazine chapters her friends used to talk about every week, the women always knew what they wanted, and then they found a way to make their dreams come true. They fell in love, conspired to ensnare their beau, and lived happily ever after.

Things were finally coming together, there was some hope for her future, but the bold girl who knew what she wanted failed her now, just as things were going exactly as she'd wished. Really, she didn't know what she wanted. She didn't want to think about it. The only thing she wanted to do, other than to feel his warmth, was not to have to make any decisions.

Jessie looked out behind him and in the direction of the house he now owned. Her parents worried about money. Randall was wealthy. That made the decision a simpler one. She needed to be brave, to stop the worrying little girl who had taken over.

"I'll think about it," she agreed.

Randall reached up and adjusted his hat. "Would you like to see the house? Have you ever been to her place?"

"Only when I was young, and then never inside."

"I think you'll like it. I could pick you up tomorrow, and we could take a look around together."

Jessie's stomach sank. She didn't want to disappoint him. "I ... I don't think my parents would let me go out there alone with you."

"What if we take your brother with us? He could go as a chaperone of sorts." He cupped her cheek. "You don't have to feel bad because your parents are going to want some protection for you. You're young. I know that. If I were your father, I'd demand the same thing."

CHAPTER TWENTY-ONE

New Mr. Mitchell's car stopped in front of the Owens' house. Lillian pulled the curtain to the side just enough to watch him get out of the vehicle and walk up to the door. Emma answered, and by the looks of things, she'd been expecting him.

"What do you suppose he's up to?" Lillian called back to Peter.

"What's that?"

"Why is Randall over there?"

Peter dropped the newspaper he'd held onto his lap. "How should I know?"

Lillian backed away so her shadow didn't show in through the curtains. Snooping on one's neighbors was one thing. Getting caught was another. "He makes me uneasy."

"I know, but he's generous and always helpful." Peter lifted the outdated paper back up and turned the page. "He always gives to the offering. In fact, I've been able to pay a number of grocery bills down for folks because of his generosity."

Lillian bit her top lip and held it there for a while. "Why do you suppose he does that?"

Peter dropped the paper again, and this time folded it and set it on the table. He stood and crossed to stand next to her to better watch the neighbors. "Maybe he does it because he is generous, like I said."

"Or maybe he wants something else."

Peter placed his hand at the small of Lillian's back. "If he wants something, he's sure in the wrong place."

Lillian nodded, signaling for Peter to look out the window. "Not if he wants a young girl."

Together, they watched Randall walk Jessie out to the car, Jacob in tow. "He must be acting as a chaperone," Peter said, the dark tones of his voice matching Lillian's suspicions. "Jacob's ten, right?"

Lillian nodded.

"He's not old enough to watch Randall."

Lillian dropped her hands in exasperation. "See? You have the same concerns I have."

Peter frowned and turned to head into the kitchen. "The difference is I want to give him a chance." He checked his watch for no reason then sighed. "Do you think I should speak with Henry?"

"No. What is he going to do?"

He shook the water kettle to check if it needed refilling, then turned on the stove and set it to boil. "I suppose there's not a lot he can do."

The engine across the street turned over. Lillian listened to the sound of the car until it disappeared in the distance. "Part of me wants to follow them."

Peter stared at the pot that refused to boil. "I'm sure we're overreacting. A big age difference isn't unheard of, and it's not like she has a lot of opportunities around here."

"That's no way to start your life." Lillian pulled out a kitchen chair from the table and slouched down onto it.

Peter crossed his arms over his chest and continued to stare at the silent pot. "Nothing here is any way to start a life. There's no teacher in town." He glanced up to Lillian. "Is it even fair to expect people to make the same decisions in times of need as they would make in times of plenty? That's not even possible."

Lillian examined her house slippers, chosen specifically because the color would hide dirt. All of their decisions changed with the drought and the dirt and the grit that invaded every part of their lives.

That didn't mean there wouldn't be a price to pay. That part of life never changed.

Peter tipped his head back and closed his eyes, and Lillian knew he prayed for Jessie out of his, their, and the town's hopelessness. Sometimes nothing else could be done.

★★★

The countryside sped by, and Jacob, on his knees in the back seat, could hardly contain himself.

"For the last time, sit down." Jessie wanted to throttle her brother. She regretted making the suggestion of bringing him along, but if she hadn't, she'd still be at home.

Little mystery surrounded Randall's interest in her and hers in him. There had been no doubt in her parents' wary glances and lack of conversation. Jessie breathed in the freedom that came with the fantasy of her own house and her own life.

She'd spent most of the night deciding if she wanted to be married or if she only considered it because it could help her parents. Jessie glanced at Randall's determined profile. She still didn't have an answer, but either way, the most obvious path forward included marriage to the man she now sat next to.

"How long of a drive will we take? Can I try it? I mean driving. Can I try driving?"

Jessie sent the most hateful stare she could muster to the backseat, but Jacob remained resolute in his mission to embarrass her.

"On the way back I'm sure you could take the wheel for a bit." Randall turned slightly and laid his arm across Jessie's shoulders. He smiled at Jacob, who responded by sitting properly.

Randall didn't drop his arm. Instead, he let his fingers fall to brush her neck. Every jostle of the car brought his hand in further contact with her skin.

The house rose in the distance. A two-story with an attic. There were five windows on the front of the house: two on the bottom floor with the front door nestled in between, and three on the top floor. Jessie guessed the house had three rooms downstairs and three bedrooms upstairs. Had Old Widow Ruby gazed out of the windows upstairs? Had she ever considered the next people who might live in her home? Jessie felt a pang of guilt for never visiting the woman whose home she would now invade.

They rounded the corner of the house, and Randall pulled the car to a stop next to the barn. Jacob hit the door and bounded out before Randall had even stepped out of his side of the car. Jessie watched her brother hop over to the barn.

"What's in there? You got tractors and stuff?"

"Why don't you go take a look? I bought the place with all the stuff in it, so you may find something I don't even know I have." Randall opened the door for Jessie, and she stepped out of the car and into the shade of the house.

Jacob disappeared into the barn.

"Don't worry, he'll be fine." Randall held out his arm for Jessie to take it, and then, instead of walking her to the back door, they made their way around to the front of the house. "Seems to me that the first look you have of your own home should be the parlor, not the kitchen."

Jessie nodded and followed him up the steps. He opened the door for her, and she stepped into the cool room.

Except the dust, it looked like a house out of an old magazine. A davenport with pink cushions stretched across the floor. She touched a large crocheted doily spread across the back. Two smaller ones sat on either side of it, marking the place where each person could sit.

An upholstered chair sat next to the fireplace, facing the davenport. Jessie glanced back at Randall before taking another step. It felt as if they'd just interrupted a conversation taking place between the pieces of furniture. A mantle clock ticked its steady rhythm, and the still warmth reminded her of a dusty museum. Randall gestured for her to take a seat.

"I know this is a lot to take in."

Jessie nodded and gingerly sat on the cushions. The faint scent of rose perfume drifted up and around her. "It's beautiful."

"It needs a woman to care for it." Randall reached for and squeezed Jessie's hand. She did her best to hold her fingers still under the weight of his. She wondered how long it would take for her to grow accustomed to how quick his movements could be.

Randall cleared his throat. "Want to see the rest of the house?"

Words failed her. She nodded again.

"Let's look at the kitchen and then upstairs at the bedrooms."

She let herself be led deeper into the house.

"There's still food here, plenty of it."

The sink, the appliances, they were all new.

Jessie stepped to the icebox and opened it. Cool air pooled around her ankles. "Where did you get the ice?"

"It's a new electric one. The stove too. It seems Old Widow Ruby had a weakness for new kitchen appliances."

Jessie put her hand over her chest and tentatively reached out to turn the knob on the stove. She turned it off again. The cabinets had glass doors, and everything was white except the butter-yellow walls. It was hard to believe that this kitchen had the same basic function as her mother's. Even though the house had been closed up, and was stuffy and warm, Jessie felt like she could finally breathe. Like white introduced a possibility again, like the stark landscape couldn't invade this one perfect place. Randall slid open the window over the sink, and the tiny yellow and white checked curtains fluttered into the room. Jessie could almost smell the non-existent grass.

"Here's what I was talking about. There's still a lot of food left, and whatever we don't have, we could get." Randall tugged at her sleeve and pulled her into the closet. Top to bottom, the shelves were lined with preserves, carefully stacked bags of flour and rice, and other unknown items. Something glinted in the corner. Jessie reached for it—a jar of coins.

"Must have been her household money."

It weighed more than she'd expected. She turned the jar over, trying to count the quarters, the dimes, the pennies. More money rattled around in that jar than she'd ever seen.

"Put it down. Let's go upstairs." Randall leaned closer and whispered the words against her neck. Jessie nodded, her mouth dry.

"I think I should check on Jacob."

"That's probably a good idea." Randall walked over to the kitchen door and pulled it open. "Hey, Jacob," he yelled, "how's it goin' out there?"

His first answer, a rattle and a crash, had Jessie nearly pushing Randall out of the way. But a second later, Jacob appeared with a sagging tool belt strapped around his waist and a too-big hat flopping around his head. "There's some really neat stuff in here. You should come see."

"Maybe in a while, sport."

Jacob skipped back into the barn.

Randall turned, smiling. "I think he's going to be busy for a while. Let's head up."

The mix of excitement, danger, and guilt for being where she knew she shouldn't be made Jessie's head spin. She'd wanted to be alone with him—conspired to be alone with him—but now his age and the reality that he'd already had a wife all came flooding in. She really didn't know him at all.

"What's wrong? Are you feeling ill?" Randall touched her jaw and forced her chin up so she had to look him in the eyes.

"I'm fine."

"You don't look fine."

"I'm..." Jessie couldn't finish her thought.

"Are you nervous about going upstairs with me?"

Jessie didn't want to be honest. He probably thought her a child. She was throwing it all away. This house, her future, her parents' only hope to keep the farm. A slow tear made its way down her cheek. She pulled from his grasp, disgusted that she was such a child.

"If I promise I won't touch you, will that make you feel better? Is that what you want?"

It wasn't what she wanted. She didn't know what she wanted.

"Tell you what, you go take a look upstairs without me. I'll go out and see what kind of trouble Jacob is getting into."

"Are you sure?"

Randall nodded and smiled and made his way out the kitchen door.

★★★

Emma tied one scarf around her hair and another around her nose and mouth. A breeze had picked up since Jessie and Randall left with Jacob.

"Are you sure you want to go out in this?" Henry called from the bed. "It can probably wait."

Emma shook her head. It couldn't wait. She needed to get to the store for a few things in case the wind whipped into a fury overnight. She just hoped Mr. Mitchell would understand and extend their credit a bit more.

"I won't be gone long." Emma shooed Little Henry back into the house and closed the door, ducking her head against the blast of dirt. She shielded her eyes and kept her gaze pinned to the ground. Only a couple of doors away.

The store bell rang her entrance, and old Mr. Mitchell rushed to close the door behind her.

"I almost closed up shop. Didn't figure anyone would want to be out in this. It seems to be picking up pretty strong out there."

Emma nodded. "I had to come by to get a few things and talk about our bill."

"What about your bill?" Mr. Mitchell looked confused.

It wasn't like him to be mean. "You know." She looked at the floor then forced her eyes up to his face. "Henry's back now. Things have changed. He's not better, and now we have hospital bills, but you know Henry, he'll be good for it."

"I don't think you understand. Your bill is all paid up."

"No. My bill here, at the store."

"That's what I mean. Someone in town made a donation to the church, and the pastor came and divided it between the families here. There was enough to pay yours off."

The lines on the plank floor swam closer and then farther away. Emma braced herself against the counter. "Henry won't like taking charity."

"I suppose he don't have much of a choice. You all get back on your feet again, I suppose he could pay back the church. But it seems a shame. Isn't that what the church is for? To help folks when they need help?"

Emma set her basket on the counter. A gust of wind battered the front window with a sandy blast. "I think I'd better hurry."

"Agreed." Mr. Mitchell dropped the typical things in her basket and handed it over. "I'll start a new bill for you, but I don't want you worrying about the old one. You all have enough to do over there."

If her daughter and son hadn't been out in the dust, she might have thought to argue. But she needed to get home and see if they were back yet.

She lifted the scarf back over her face and waited for Mr. Mitchell to round the counter so he could close the door tightly behind her.

"Good luck if this wind don't die down soon. If I can, I'll stop by to see if you need anything."

"Don't worry about us," Emma shouted through the scarf over the sound of the wind. "You take care of yourself. We'll be fine."

The dirt bit into the tiny places of exposed skin on her wrists and around her eyes. She reached up and pulled the scarf higher, trying to breathe shallow, timing each minuscule inhale for every other time her right foot hit the ground. Her porch loomed ahead. She tucked the basket in tight and ran for the door.

CHAPTER TWENTY-TWO

Jessie studied everything: which stairs squeaked, the lazy stain of rust that trailed from the faucet to the drain in the porcelain-coated tub, the colorful quilt pattern on the bed in the guest room. She'd been right. Three bedrooms upstairs, a bathroom—an actual upstairs bathroom with a tub—and a door to the attic. She'd save the attic for later.

Each room had two windows, and they all had screens to keep the moths and flies out. A window seat in the hallway had a bench surrounded by bookshelves filled with dusty volumes. She ran her finger along the titles; most she'd never heard of.

If she married him, and if this house became hers, she could read them all. Jessie sucked in a breath and called for Randall to join her. She'd heard him come back in a while ago.

"You sure?"

"Yes." What had she been thinking? He'd been nothing but a gentleman since meeting her. Even their kisses had been the result of the more reckless side of her nature rather than any pressure from him.

"What do you think? Do you like it?"

"I think this was hers." Jessie stood outside the doorway to the largest room. She'd opened the armoire. The old widow's husband's clothes still hung there. "What are you going to do with all their things?"

"I hoped you'd help me decide."

Jessie stared at the dresser. A square without dust stood out. "What do you suppose sat there?"

"Her jewelry box. Her niece took it. She took a few other things too ... not much, though. I don't think they'd been very close."

"And she didn't take the money from the pantry?"

"I found that later."

The room darkened. Randall noticed the change too. He crossed over to the window and pulled the curtain wide in time to hear the first needle-like sounds of dirt blast the glass.

He turned. "You stay here. I'm going to get Jacob."

Randall took the stairs down two at a time, and Jessie followed as fast as she could. The screen door slammed open, and he disappeared outside. Jessie closed the door and watched out the kitchen window for their return. Standing upstairs in that bedroom, the room that she might soon share with him, she'd almost forgotten Jacob playing out in the barn.

The cloud grew thicker and the wind, angrier. Finally, Randall ducked out of the barn with Jacob in tow, barreling toward the house. Jessie slammed the door and locked it as soon as they were in the house. For a long time, the only sounds were their breathing and grains of dirt pelting the windows.

"I don't think we'll be going anywhere for a while." Randall looked over Jacob's head to Jessie.

A phone sat on the kitchen table. "You suppose that works?" Jessie asked Randall.

He shrugged.

They were alone now. She picked up the receiver, their only connection to anything but the house they now sheltered in, and controlled her shaking fingers enough to dial the only number she knew.

★★★

Lillian and Peter sat at the kitchen table, deep in the stifling grip of the hot, dirty air. Lillian pulled the handkerchief away to test if enough of the dust had settled since Peter ducked in out of the black cloud.

"That one got bad fast."

Peter folded his handkerchief and wiped the dirt from his eyes. With as little movement as possible, he slid it back into his pocket.

Lillian rose and crossed to the stove where she'd set a pot of water to boil. They'd learned not to move fast during a storm. It only stirred up more dust and made breathing near impossible. A thin sheen of dirt floated on the surface. "This is no good anymore." She turned off the stove and left it there to cool. She didn't start another. It would only taste like dirt.

A ring broke through the hissing sound of the cloud. Peter stood to answer it.

"Yes... I see... I'll let them know... Take care of yourself... Don't leave the house... Call back if you need anything." Peter dropped the earpiece back into the cradle.

"Who was that?"

"Randall, Jessie, and her brother are stuck out at the old widow's place."

Lillian hummed a questioning sound.

"I'm guessing he was successful in buying the place from her niece."

"But why would he take Jessie and Jacob?" Lillian didn't like that she'd seen them drive down the street and didn't like it even more that they were still out there together.

Peter frowned and shook his head.

"They're stuck now?"

"I have to let her parents know they are alright and will be holed up until the wind dies down." Peter picked his hat off the stand and pulled it down tight over his head.

"You'll need more than that." Lillian ducked back into the kitchen and came out with a couple flour sacks. One she tied over his hat and under his chin, the other, a damp one, she secured around his face.

A coil of rope hung on a nail next to the door. Peter tied one end in a loop and threw it over his shoulder. The other end he would tie to the front porch. "Give me ten minutes."

"Hurry back."

He nodded and Lillian opened the door to a blast of dirt and debris. The wind had gotten worse. It would be a long night.

***

The electric light hanging over the kitchen table burned through the brown haze filling the room. Jessie lit a candle and stepped into the pantry. She held the light up to the various cans and jars, deciding on what she could cook for their dinner. Canned tomatoes and beans, canned and dried meat, and sacks of flour lined the shelves. She'd never had so many choices and known less what to do.

And the food in the icebox had been replenished with eggs and cheese and a few apples. Where Randall had found the treasures was another mystery.

Everything rattled in the wind: the windows in the panes, a shutter straining on its hinge, her heart in her chest. She shouldn't be here, but the choice had been made for her. Her parents would be distraught. And she could no more satisfy their fears than she could stop the wind.

At least the pastor agreed to relay her message to her mother.

"How's it going in there?" Randall called from the parlor, where he entertained Jacob with tedious talk of cars and the city.

"It's okay." She didn't even know how to answer that question. What did he want to know? Is supper made? No. Is she burning the place down? No. Is she staring blankly at the food everywhere wondering how she got there and if she even wanted to be there and if she didn't want to be there, if she even had a choice? Yes.

That probably wasn't what he was asking. She picked up a bag of flour and stepped out of the pantry.

Randall stepped into the room. He leaned against the wall, crossed one ankle over the other, and smiled. "You are very pretty."

Jessie nearly dropped the small bag of flour.

"I'm sorry. That's too forward." He looked down at his shoes and turned them to see the light glint off their dusty shine. "I just wanted you to know I think you are pretty."

The wind sounded like it could take the roof. Jessie turned her face to the ceiling. "I don't think I'll ever get used to the sound of wind like that without the sound of rain."

"I can take care of you, you know." Randall crossed the room. His nearness trapped her between the counter and his body.

Jessie nodded. He didn't seem so big from a distance. Maybe the city clothes made him look slight, maybe the trick was accomplished by how he walked, but when standing next to him, close enough to feel his heat, the way he towered over her always shocked her. She lifted her hand to his chest and forced a smile. "I know."

"I won't let anything happen to you."

Jessie nodded and looked up to meet his gaze.

He touched her chin and held her there for his kiss.

She liked the feel of his lips on hers, so foreign and so familiar. Closing her eyes, Jessie concentrated on enjoying it rather than worrying about her parents in the storm, or about how this— them in the kitchen together, alone—was probably her parents' biggest fear.

His fingers fell from her chin and brushed her ribcage. Jessie held her breath, not sure what she should do, if anything. After all, she'd wanted this.

He stepped closer. "We should be married soon."

Jessie thrilled at the thought of this being her house, and maybe having enough money to help her father keep the farm. She forced her arms up around his shoulders and drew him nearer. "I think so too." Unexpected tears welled up, and she buried her face in the linen of his shirt before he could notice.

★★★

The dirt blinded him. Peter closed his eyes against the sting and trudged into the street. He couldn't see the Owens' place. He could barely see his own shoes. And instead of finding their gate as he'd expected, he kicked up against the fence, and then had to decide whether he'd landed left or right of the opening.

A stiff gust of wind had him holding his breath and hoping his decision to move left along the dried-out pickets wouldn't lead him to the wrong house. His fingers found the gate then the latch. About fifteen more steps, and he tied the rope to the post near their front door, stumbled up the couple of steps, and pounded on the door.

It swung open immediately. Emma's small hands pulled him in out of the black wind.

"What are you doing? Is someone hurt?" She took a step back as Peter pulled the towel off his face and coughed.

One of the children handed him a glass of water with a sheen of dust floating on top. Peter gladly took it and gulped it down before trying to talk.

"We got a call from Jessie."

"Where are they?" Henry called from across the room. The concern in his voice sounded out of place coming from the stolid farmer.

Already, the air hung heavy with soot. Peter took care not to shake any of the dust from his clothes into their house. He crossed to stand next to Henry's bed. The man struggled to lever up.

"They're at the old widow's place. The winds started after they'd arrived."

Henry let loose a dissatisfied grunt. "We shouldn't have let her go with him."

"We couldn't have known this would happen. And we can't keep her here forever." Emma almost dropped the empty glass Peter had handed back to her.

Henry shook his head. "They doin' fine? They need anything? They don't plan on trying for home in this, do they?"

"They're going to ride the storm out," Peter said. "They have food and water, and it's probably the sturdiest place in town, so they should be okay."

"Don't much like the idea of Jessie with him if this lasts for a while. She's a good girl, but he, well, I'm not so sure."

Emma glanced at her husband, and then at Peter, and set the glass down on the small end table. "He's said he wants to court her."

Henry shot a look at his wife. "And you planned to tell me this when?" He trembled with the effort to fully sit. "Don't you think he's a bit old for her? He's got to be near my age..."

The next few words he sputtered out were masked by grunts of effort to heave himself out of the bed.

Hands on her hips, Emma blocked his way in case he thought to try to swing his legs out of the bed. "She's sixteen now. She knows how to handle herself. And anyway, it doesn't matter how we feel about him. No one is going anywhere in that." She pointed at the shuttered window. "Not you, not me, not him. No one."

Henry exhaled loudly out his nose. A few seconds and a flushed face later, he broke into a fit of coughing that made any arguments moot.

"There's nothing we can do now," she said. "When the wind dies down, they will be on their way home."

★★★

The wind hadn't died down completely, but it had cleared enough to see the road. Jessie stuffed a few extra groceries and some jars of water in a bag she'd found in case the wind had suffocated the drive with tire-grabbing drifts.

"Are you sure you want to head out already?" Randall rinsed a coffee cup in the sink and looked around the room for anything else they'd left out. His confident posture and overwhelmingly domestic stance made Jessie blush.

She frowned. "We don't know if it'll get worse or better. I need to get back home and make sure everything is good there."

The winds during the night had been intense. She and Jacob had shared the bed in the guest room and spent the wakeful night listening to the sound of the roof being nearly torn from the walls. The construction of her parents' house—the single story home with attic bedrooms and a lean-to porch, built when the biggest concerns were getting the crops in, not putting together a home that would last—left a lot of questions as to its ability to withstand winds like last night's. Jessie needed to get home to make sure everyone made it. Sometimes the winds lasted for days, weeks even. Any break in the blasting dirt meant it might be the last reprieve for a while. They needed to take advantage of it.

"Do you see yourself here?" Randall picked up the bag she'd packed and slung it over his shoulder.

Jacob wandered into the room, rubbing sleep from his eyes. "Sounds better out there." He yawned, sat on a kitchen chair, and looked at Randall and the bag of things. "We going to try for home?"

Jessie ruffled his hair. "You betcha. Get your shoes on. There are a couple of leftover biscuits from last night. You can eat one on the way."

He heaved his lanky body out of the chair and left the kitchen to find his shoes. Randall continued watching her, waiting for her answer to his question.

Jessie inhaled deeply. She didn't know what she should feel. Something about Randall unsettled her. She'd spent most of the night trying to figure it out.

One thing she did know—she loved the house, the things in the house, and the land the house occupied. Before the drought, it had been the best in the area, and she didn't doubt it would one day be that again.

She looked at Randall, waiting for her answer. "Yes. I can see us here. I can't see why we wouldn't be happy here."

CHAPTER TWENTY-THREE

It had been more than a week since he'd dropped Jessie off at that hovel she called her home, and Randall hadn't been able to call on her yet. Her parents hadn't been overly welcoming upon their return. What did they expect, anyway? He'd kept Jessie and Jacob safe, in the house he rightfully owned, which, by all accounts, stood stronger and better than any house their parents would be able to provide for them.

He shoved some folders into his attaché case and focused on not slamming the bedroom door on his way out. The banker had called with news. He wanted to meet today. Randall jumped at the chance for a distraction.

"Where you headed?" Justin looked up from the ledgers he continually examined.

Owning a store seemed exceedingly boring. All day long, his brother either wrote numbers down or swept the floor or listened to old women prattle on about things no one cared to hear. At one time, Randall felt a pang of jealousy for his older brother. Now, watching him trudge on through life, it felt more like pity.

"Headed to the city. Need to meet with the banker."

Justin looked up, pulled his glasses off, and rubbed his face. "How's everything out at the old widow's place."

"You mean my place?"

Justin cleared his throat and slid his glasses back onto his nose. "I suppose that is what I meant." His gaze returned to the lines on the paper in front of him.

Randall mumbled he'd be back sometime in the evening and escaped to the dry heat outside. He looked up. The sun had yet to fight its way into the sky. He'd be to town before lunch.

Usually in the summer, he preferred to keep the windows of his car open so it wasn't so blasted hot when he climbed in. Not here, though. Open windows meant a thick coat of dust on everything. Not that the thick coat of dust was much worse than the thin coat, but still, dirt was dirt.

He turned the starter and listened for the engine to rattle to life. He smiled at the sound of the chugging cylinders, gunned the gas twice, and couldn't tamp down the feeling of satisfaction that came with the parting of curtains across the street. Putting the car in gear, he turned around in the middle of the street and drove as fast as he could out of town. Well, as fast as the rutted road allowed.

★★★

Jessie wiped the dirt from the sill in her upstairs bedroom into a pile. They'd spent days scooping bucketful after bucketful, throwing them anyplace but the house. Somehow they'd missed the corner of the windowsill.

No matter what they did, the house couldn't handle the constant battering of the last few years. She looked around the room, at the dried floorboards long sanded free of their varnish and the loose wallpaper with its cracked glue and faded flowers. A year ago, she'd set to peel the wall across from the bed. Halfway through she decided it looked worse for her efforts. She'd never returned to the project. Jessie slammed the sash wide and brushed the small pile away with both hands, wanting to scream at it as it first floated down then back up. She could taste the cloud but could only cough at the grit and dust surrounding her.

"Jessie, you up there?" her mother called from the bottom of the stairs.

Jessie slammed the window closed and sulked over to the top of the stairs. She didn't want to blame her parents; they'd done the best they could. But the thought that she could be done with this if she wanted, that Randall would take her away and to a house that didn't invite the dirt in, made it hard to keep her voice calm. "What do you need?"

"We need to talk to you for a bit."

Jessie listened for the sounds of her brothers and sisters. No other voices floated from the downstairs. They'd been sent out to play. She backed down the steep steps. "What about?"

Her mother made half an effort at a half-sorry smile, and Jessie's stomach took a sick turn.

"Come on in here," her father called from his bed in the front room.

Jessie glanced at her mother, who nodded toward where her father lay. She fought the lead in her feet and made her way to the side of his bed. After a quick pat on the edge of the lumpy mattress, Jessie sat as bid and waited for them to say whatever they might.

Her father cleared his throat. "There's no easy way to say this."

His thinning hair bounced on one side of his head and lay flat on the other. An unfamiliar pallor had crept into his cheeks that no matter how hard she tried, she couldn't remember ever before seeing.

"The medical bills are going to be too much." He coughed into a handkerchief that her mother used to bleach white. Now, rarely did they subject scraps of fabric to whiteners. There were so many other useless things they could spend their time on instead. "We've been able to make it this long without mortgaging the house. Not anymore." He took a deep breath and looked at her mother.

She continued for him. "We talked to the banker. But with the drought as it is, well, there isn't much value to the land. Even if we mortgage it, we'd have enough for the hospital bills but not much left over to buy seed for when this all ends."

A high-pitched ringing started somewhere out in the yard and worked its way inside the house. Jessie shook her head to stop the ringing. "Do you hear that?" She looked up to her mother.

"Hear what?"

"The ringing." Jessie rubbed her hands over her face, and the ringing subsided. "Never mind." She watched as her father shot her mother a concerned look. "What are you saying?"

"We think we will need to join the other families who've worked their way to California. We think we're going to have to leave the farm."

Jessie shot up. "But we've made it like this for three years." She looked out the cloudy window at the pastor's house across the street. "How can you leave now?"

"We don't really have a choice." Her mother crossed to the window and pulled the curtains closed. "There's really nothing we can do." She turned and fisted her hands against her hips. "Besides, there's not even a school here anymore. You need to get an education."

Jessie stood and paced to the door and back. She kicked against the foot of her father's bed. "No, I don't."

"No, you don't what?" Her mother scowled at Jessie's kick and raised her chin to meet Jessie's gaze.

"I don't need to finish school. I could be a farm wife." Jessie did her best to stand tall.

Silence permeated the room. The same silence that had buried everything for the last few years. "You're barely sixteen." Her father fisted his hand against the blankets. Jessie could see his muscles bunch against the thin fabric of his shirt.

"If you're thinkin' about who I think you are, you've got some more thinkin' to do." Ugly red blotches crept into her mother's complexion.

"Why?" Jessie knew the challenge in her question, but with the risk of her parents losing everything, she had to make them think. A new start wouldn't be better. That never actually worked out for anyone. They could be poor here or poor somewhere else. They'd never been anything but poor. It wasn't like it was new for them. At least here there were people they knew. At least here, if she married Randall, she could help them out a bit.

"He has money, Mama," Jessie whispered to the floor, suddenly apologetic for the way she'd spit out her last question.

"I'll not have you farmed out to weasel money out of an unsuspecting husband. We've never taken charity before." Her father pounded his fist against the wall, earning a shower of dust. "I'll be dead before we get along on the back of our daughter."

Jessie took a deep breath and held it, then surprised herself with the next cascade of words. "What if I love him?"

It could be love, couldn't it? She looked at the shocked expression on her father's face. It didn't matter if she loved Randall, anyway. If it wasn't love yet, it would develop. How many old couples talked about marriages of convenience that turned to love?

"What did you say?" Her mother took a step closer. "What happened when you were out at his farm?"

"Nothing." Jessie held up her hands in protest of the thoughts she knew ran through their minds. "He was a perfect gentleman the whole time."

"Has he offered marriage?" Her mother's hand rested on her chest like it had been glued there.

Jessie shrugged. "We've talked about it. He wants to talk to the two of you."

Her father struggled to sit up further, shaking his head. "We're talking about two different things here. First, whether you get married, to him or not, has nothing to do with having to mortgage the farm. That is something that has to be done, and that is what we need to talk about first."

Jessie clamped her mouth closed and nodded.

"We spoke with the banker yesterday. The bank will give us a mortgage, but it will not be enough to sustain us once the drought ends. The other option he thinks might help—a way to avoid going west—is to sell the farm."

Her mother sucked in a quick breath and stared at the floor.

"He knows someone who may purchase it and then rent it back to us. We would farm it for him for however long it takes to buy it back again, with interest."

"Who is the buyer?" Jessie asked. "I can't imagine anyone would want to buy it now." She pointed to the door as if they could all see the barren fields through it. They looked at the door as if they could.

"The banker didn't want to say until he spoke with the buyer."

"Is that what you'll do?" Jessie picked at a string at the edge of her father's quilt. Large and heavy, his legs laid stiff and useless under the cover of the blanket. Part of her couldn't believe what he said. Selling and renting back their farm seemed nothing like the father she grew up watching work the equipment in the fields.

He nodded in answer to her question.

"Why are you telling me?"

"We thought you should know things will be getting better." Her mother took a step nearer and leaned on the foot of the bed.

Both of her parents looked like they'd aged a decade in the last month or so. Jessie brought her hands to her cheeks, wondering if the drought had pulled her weariness to the surface too. "I guess you have to do what you have to do."

Her mother laid her hand on Jessie's shoulder, but Jessie barely registered the touch. She sat still for what seemed to be an appropriate amount of time when faced with the news that her parents were forced to become people she didn't recognize. Then she smiled, stood up, and left the room, grateful they were too distracted to remember the second part of the conversation they were destined to have with her.

When Randall came back from the city, she would talk to him. There must be something he could do. She would tell him she loved him. Even if she didn't now, love would grow. She'd heard of that happening, so it wasn't a lie, really.

★★★

The lunch dishes sat empty, but the man across the table still spoke from an endless conversational bowl. Business had been concluded. Their discussions, ended. Yet the banker sat back, hands hanging restfully from the tiny pockets of his vest, and continued with the stories of childhood memories.

Randall smiled and nodded, hummed in the appropriate places. When the man became distracted by a pretty waitress in a tight skirt, Randall signaled for the check.

The afternoon had been worthwhile, more so than he'd hoped. Unknowingly, the banker had done the work for him with the Owens. They needed to sell, the banker had thought of Randall. He would rent the farm back to them.

With the abandoned farm he picked up for an almost embarrassingly low sum, he now owned three farms.

He would talk to Jessie when he returned. Maybe an after-dinner visit. As the banker prattled on like an old woman, Randall let his mind wander to what he would wear and how he would walk.

And Jessie would say yes. He didn't doubt it. After all, she responded to his kisses. He hadn't planned on finding a wife so young, but her age gave him a distinct advantage: even with the drought, she remained a dreamer. She still had hopes for a good life with a doting husband.

He could give her those things. He'd train her how to entertain, how to greet his business associates, how to be a good wife.

Randall smiled and nodded again as the waitress tore their check from her pad of paper.

"I'll get this." Randall took it from the waitress's hand.

"That's not necessary," the banker protested. "I usually take the bank's clients out, not the other way around."

"You can get it next time." As much as Randall did not look forward to more mundane conversation with the man, the banker did have his uses. And this past week he'd come through with more than Randall had hoped possible.

CHAPTER TWENTY-FOUR

The stars burned brightly in the night sky. No hint of a breeze kicked up any dirt, and Jessie thought if she tried hard enough, maybe she could float away.

Dinner had been quiet. The news, although it completely changed their lives, did nothing to change the needs of the younger ones, so they sat at the table like they did every night. And ate, like they did every night. And cleaned up the dishes with the windows open and the curtains still and the lack of animal noise buzzing loudly through the silence.

The plates clinked against each other as Jessie stacked them in the cupboards, and her parents whispered in the front room. The younger kids had already been tucked into bed.

Jessie closed the cabinet, wrung out the dish rag, and hung it over the edge of the basin. Then she slipped on her shoes, made an excuse that sounded like she would be using the outhouse, and let the door close behind her.

She'd grabbed her faded shawl, and even though heat still radiated from the baked ground, she could feel the night's chill falling from the clear stars overhead. Jessie walked around the back of the house, through a couple of yards, and eventually stood, watching the store's rear entrance.

She didn't wait there long.

Randall, dressed in clothes too fine for the town, stepped down and onto the dirt. Jessie moved into the light. "Hi, Randall."

He stilled and Jessie saw the slow smile spread across his face. "I hoped you'd be out tonight. In fact, I came out to look for you."

Even through her nerves, Jessie felt the surge of pleasure at being wanted.

He motioned for her to follow him. They walked side by side in silence into a dead field and kept on until the houses and stores shrunk in importance.

"We've talked about it before, and I know we haven't known each other long, but things aren't like they used to be. I need a wife to help me take care of the farm, to help me get it ready for when the rains eventually come, to help me sort the things we want to keep from the things we can give away or sell. I can't do it myself." Randall stooped, picked up a rock, and threw it deeper into the nothingness. The starlight shimmered against the dust that rose with the impact. Together, they watched the dust settle.

Jessie weaved her fingers between his and stopped, forcing him to look down into her face.

"I know it's not romantic, and I haven't spoken with your parents, but I'm asking if you will be my wife."

A smile rose from somewhere deep, and Jessie couldn't keep it off her face.

"It's okay to be happy, you know. It's been a long time since anyone around here has been happy." He lifted his free hand to her cheek and brushed it with the back of his knuckles. "We're going to have to change that about this place."

Jessie blinked back tears and marveled that she'd been so hesitant to accept the proposal she knew he entertained. "I would like to marry you."

Randall pulled her close enough to feel the heat come off his body. She hadn't even known she'd been cold until she quelled a quiver and sunk into the warmth that gathered inside his jacket. She rested her head against his chest and listened to the sound of his breath.

Part of her screamed too much. She forced her head to stay where she'd put it, forced herself to match his breathing, to relax, because the other part of her rejoiced at the thought of a house that could keep the dust at bay, and the thought of not being hungry, of offering her siblings sugary sweets, of helping her parents buy back their farm, of being able to breathe again.

★★★

They had to sell the farm. Emma opened her eyes in the still-black morning. She'd slept, here and there, but finding her husband had done nothing. Their future remained as unstable as if he'd stayed missing, and the acid in her stomach ate at her throat all night.

Emma rolled to the side and lifted her body to a sitting position. She rubbed her feet along the already warm wood floor, hoping for the pain of a stray nail. To feel anything would be a change from the numbness of worry and stagnation of no rain. Of course, the boards had already been worn smooth, and Henry would have seen to any stray nails long ago. She stood, ignored the desire to stretch, and stumbled to the kitchen.

The entire house still slept. She shoved kindling into the stove and fanned it until it stoked to life. Movements she never thought about anymore. Three years into the worst of the drought, and she'd learned thinking, considering, wishing, only led to sleepless nights.

Jessie would shortly announce her engagement to Randall to her father. Emma knew it, and she didn't blame the child. At sixteen, she would have been looking for a way out too. And who's to say Jessie's decision to marry wasn't the right one? After all, the house offered more than they ever could. Henry, like most men, would be surprised by his daughter's revelation. Emma snorted out loud and then looked to make sure no one else had already woken. He'd probably forbid it, probably grow angry and sullen.

After a few days, he'd realize how much more she'd have without him, and he'd be depressed. He'd sulk, but get over it.

Emma hoped he wouldn't drag out the forbidding and the anger too long. Life was hard enough without having to worry about a sullen husband.

★★★

"Not a lot has happened over there since Henry came home." Lillian let the curtains fall into place and turned around to face Peter. Years ago, she'd had more to do in the afternoons than spy on neighbors. Now, with no gardens and housework rendered all but useless, the equally dull lives across the street took importance.

"They weren't in church last week either." Peter set the book down that he'd been reading, something about theology and Second Timothy. "Of course, I didn't expect them, with Henry probably needing a fair amount of assistance."

"Randall was there, though."

Peter sucked in his lips and breathed out loudly. "He put twenty dollars in the offering plate again."

Lillian turned back to the window to hide her expression, mostly because she wasn't sure what it would say. And she wasn't sure what it should say.

"He's helping the community. In more ways than Sunday morning offering too. He's buying up a few of the abandoned farms, and donating here and there to help families in need."

"How do you know?" She'd be unsurprised if Randall had shared his giving with Peter. He seemed the kind of man who might feel the need to brag.

"He didn't say anything, if that's what you're getting at."

Lillian crossed her arms over her chest and glared at Peter. It didn't happen often, but she hated it when he could see through her lines of question.

Peter smiled and cocked one eyebrow high. "Justin told me. Randall's been anonymously paying off some of the larger grocery bills."

"Justin is surprised by this?" Lillian sat across from Peter and handed him some looped yarn. He dutifully held his hands out so she could ball up the remainder of the skein she'd used for an afghan.

"I'm not sure. He didn't sound surprised—maybe a bit proud— but if he hadn't been at least a little shocked by his brother's generosity, there wouldn't have been a need to mention it, would there?"

"I suppose not." Lillian concentrated on twisting the strand to continue an even sphere. "I just ... I guess I could understand if he did something. I mean, what does he do?"

"He wants to farm."

Lillian cocked her head to the side and looked at Peter. "But what kind of a person comes to a place that can't be farmed if they want to farm? I understand it's likely a way to amass cheap acreage, but it'd make more sense if he had some other kind of interest. Like if he were a doctor and wanted a slow country lifestyle. Or if he were a mechanic, had saved a bit of money, and wanted to make a go at farming. What did he do before now?"

Peter dropped his yarn-wound hands and looked up at the ceiling before meeting her gaze. "You know, I'm not sure. Justin's never said anything." He lifted his hands again and nudged them against Lillian's, reminding her they were trying to complete a task. "Just said he'd been married and that he'd come into money at his wife's death. That's all I know."

"Emma said she thinks Randall is going to try to marry Jessie."

"Isn't she too young?"

"Sixteen." Lillian shrugged and lifted one brow in a quick sarcastic sweep.

Peter sighed. "Old enough, but not old enough."

Lillian let the silence stretch. She and Peter married after she'd turned twenty. Still young, but she couldn't imagine marrying at sixteen. At sixteen, she'd been more concerned with the newest hairstyles than managing a household. Of course, marrying that young as a minister's wife, where there were social obligations, and marrying into a farmer's lifestyle, where the wife only had to be involved where she chose, meant the comparison wasn't remarkably valid.

"Will you perform a wedding for them?"

Peter's shoulders sagged. "I have no grounds not to."

Lillian frowned. Some parts of being a minister's wife ate at her. Especially when people asked for their involvement when they knew Lillian and Peter had a limited ability to offer assistance, or worse, their input would have a negative consequence.

CHAPTER TWENTY-FIVE

Emma moved Henry's pillows to the wall side of the bed as he hoisted up to a sitting position. She knew sitting upright still caused him some pain, but he'd made it abundantly clear to everyone that he would not be lying down when Randall made the case for Jessie's hand.

And they'd talked about how they would respond and how they should respond. And they'd left Jessie alone to her thoughts—she hadn't even spoken with them of the reason for Randall's visit, hoping that whatever came of the conversation would be the right thing.

Henry sighed, a noise he often made now. Before the drought, he never used to make that sound. Before the winds came and took everything, they used to talk. "What are you thinking?"

Emma shrugged. Her oldest child wanted to marry a man nearly twice her age who had already been married once. On the other hand, Jessie now lived in poverty, and they couldn't even promise her she could finish school. That changed the picture.

She watched Henry, the man she'd loved her whole life, as he shook from the effort it took to sit in a bed. She brushed her fingers along his clean-shaven face and smiled as best she could. "I think we will not have much choice in the matter."

Henry grunted. Helpless in bed, and the man still did not like to think things were ever out of his control.

A knock at the door had them scrambling to smooth out his blankets and open the door.

"Please come in, Mr. Mitchell." Emma gestured toward the chair directly across from Henry.

"Please, call me Randall." He ducked into the room and moved to the offered seat.

Henry stretched his hand out, and Randall grasped it in his. Emma could see the tight grip surprised Henry, but he hid any pain he might have experienced.

"I won't take too much of your time, Mr. and Mrs. Owen." Randall sat down and smoothed his pinstriped pants.

Emma tried to remember the last time she'd seen a pair of pinstriped pants. Or the black and gray two-toned shoes he must have spent hours shining.

Randall cleared his throat and crossed one leg over the other. The small room made it so his knee nearly touched her husband's. Emma wanted to back away for him.

"I know I've only been in town for a short time, but in that time I've had the opportunity to speak with Jessie and get to know her quite well."

Henry's face darkened, and Emma knew he was thinking about the unchaperoned hours Jessie spent with the stranger.

"As you are aware, I'm older than Jessie, and being older, I do not have the time or the desire to proceed with a relationship where marriage is not the goal. I'm sure you've heard that I've purchased the old widow's farm, and honestly, I need a wife to help me run it."

Emma shifted her weight and kept her eyes on her now paling husband. He hadn't sat up for so long since he'd come home, and Emma worried he might become sick with the effort.

"I've reason to believe Jessie would welcome my proposal, and I am seeking your blessing."

Henry nodded and rubbed his hand over his face. "Her mother and I will need to discuss it, of course."

"Of course." Randall stood and extended his hand again to Henry.

Henry took it, this time much weaker for the effort. Emma stepped in and thanked Randall for the visit. She needed to get him out of the house so Henry could lie back down.

Thankfully, he made a hasty exit. Emma rushed to Henry's side, slid his pillows to a more comfortable position, and helped him settle in.

"I don't like that man," Henry said.

"Neither do I." Emma sat next to him on the bed. "But I don't think it matters. If she wants to marry him, who are we to stop her?"

With one, heavy punch, Henry took his frustration out on the bed. "Are you telling me that if things were better, she would still consider marrying him?"

Emma laid her hand over his. "I've no idea. But things aren't better, and they won't be for a very long time. This may be her best chance."

Henry closed his eyes. Emma could see the conversation was finished. There wasn't a conclusion because none of the options were good enough to choose. She walked back to the kitchen, hoping Jessie wouldn't ask what she thought. If poverty had taught her one thing, it was that very few decisions had to be made. The situation would dictate their response at the time, and all efforts spent thinking and planning and worrying never actually paid off, because, like every other day for the past few years, they would do what they had to do to get to tomorrow.

★★★

Henry lay in bed in the front room, useless to everyone, especially his family. Now his oldest daughter might want to marry a sop of a man solely for the reason he had money and Henry did not. He squeezed the edge of the mattress, willing his body to heal and the land to heal and his family to be whole again.

The morning visit was only the first of two. Later that afternoon, the banker would stop by to present the offer from his buyer as well as the numbers in case he and Emma wanted to mortgage the farm without the buyer. If only that were enough.

His hospital bills had bigger numbers than he ever thought possible. Henry smirked. His life, at least when he sustained injuries, held more value than the entire farm. It might have been better for everyone involved if his identity had remained a mystery, and his wife and children were left to wonder what had happened to him. At least they would still own a piece of property and a home.

Emma did the best she could. And she loved him despite the extra burden he now presented to her. They'd fallen in love as children, moved here, built a life with their own children, and now their oldest daughter faced a loveless marriage because a loveless marriage to someone who could promise she wouldn't go hungry held more attraction than a dormant life spent waiting for the sky to open.

"What time will the banker be here?" Emma poked her head out of the kitchen. She was still beautiful and had a smile for him even though he laid in bed, useless to her. The delicate way her hand grasped the doorframe belied her strength, and his chest constricted just a bit knowing how difficult this was for her and that he could do little to ease the transition.

Henry had to pretend to cough so he could rub the moisture building in his eyes. "After three."

Emma stared at him. She knew his weakness, that his presence presented a liability. He looked away, plagued by the guilt that came along with undeserved care and effort and time and love. Undeserved love. He wished she would leave him. That she would take the kids and start fresh.

But instead of leaving him be, she walked to the side of the bed, lowered herself, and stretched out next to him.

She whispered into his ear. "I'd rather live a hundred lives with you stuck in this bed than one without you." She ran her fingers down his arm and pressed her palm in his. "Do not forget that. We need you for far more than the work you can do."

Henry looked toward the wall. He didn't want her to see what her words did to him, a grown man, one who should be providing for her.

"Tell me you know that."

Henry nodded because that was all he trusted himself to do.

★★★

"What did they say?" Jessie poked her head into Randall's car as he put it in park.

Randall chuckled. "Not a lot. But they didn't say no. They said they need to talk about it."

Jessie chewed her lip and crossed one ankle over the other. "What do you think?"

Randall reached up and pulled her chin down with his thumb. "I think you shouldn't chew your lip. It doesn't deserve the torture."

Jessie couldn't keep her blush at bay. She frowned at him.

"What are you doing this afternoon, anyway?"

"Nothing. I'll have to help with dinner but nothing right now."

"I have to be back later, but I've got a few hours to spend. Hop in. We'll go for a drive out to our place."

Jessie thrilled at the thought of a place of her own. She turned her head to look down the street. No one milled about. No one to report her to her parents or to raise questions. Besides, soon she might be a married woman, and then all the questions would stop anyway.

She smiled, ran around the car, and jumped into the passenger seat. The springs under her gave a little bounce to her movements, and Randall laughed.

Jessie stared at him. "I don't think I've heard you laugh before."

Randall reached for her knee and gave it a squeeze. She fought the urge to pull away. Instead, she let his fingers rest for a while longer than they should have.

"I think we all need to do a bit more laughing around here."

He pulled out into the street, and they headed out of town toward the old widow's place. Their place. Her place.

"Do you want to do a bit more looking around the farm?"

"I never did get to see the barns." Jessie paused to think. "Are all the drawers in the bedroom still filled with her things?"

"Didn't you snoop around when we were there before?"

"Nah." Jessie shook her head. "It didn't feel right."

"It's going to be your home now." Randall opened his hand to hold hers. "It's not snooping when it's yours."

Jessie smiled and rested her hand in his. "I suppose not." She watched the brown scenery slip by. "Let's go look at things."

Randall smiled back and turned toward the house, and Jessie waited to feel something, anything, that would hint at the kind of future she might have with him.

CHAPTER TWENTY-SIX

Emma sat next to her husband on the bed, trying to make it seem like they sat on a sofa, but it didn't quite happen. The banker took the chair across from them and spread the papers out on the small table Emma had set up for him to use.

The papers spilled out of the folders, off the small table, to the floor that no matter how many times Emma had swept, still remained dusty. Emma and the banker took turns picking them up and placing them on the worn surface. At one time, the small table had been beautiful. The carvings that danced along the edge were reminders of life before the dry air and dust had worn away the varnish and cracked the wood along the grain. The kitchen table would have been preferable, but Henry couldn't get there. Even if he could have made it into the other room, he certainly couldn't have sat up straight in a kitchen chair for long. But none of this would be happening if he could still make it to the table, if he hadn't been in an accident, if he hadn't been ill.

Emma fought the urge to stand up and scream at the banker that they really were not the people he could see. That if he looked harder, he would see successful farmers with acres of lush wheat so green and bright it hurt to look at them against the impossible blue of the Oklahoma skies she'd grown to love. Instead, she picked up the pen when he pointed to her and looked at the pained expression on Henry's face. The mortgage from the bank would never be enough. They might get the money necessary to make it one or two more drought years, but they'd have nothing to mortgage when planting time came. They'd be sitting on land without the ability to do anything with it. There would be no use owning a farm when they couldn't buy seed or animals to breed.

"I guess it isn't even a question, then." Henry examined the papers as if by will alone he could change the numbers.

"I'm sorry the bank can't offer more right now. I'm sure you can imagine what kind of position the bank is in with so many farms going under right now."

Imagine the bank's position? Emma wanted to scratch the smug, useless words out of the clueless man's mouth. He looked well fed enough. His kids probably weren't facing winter with last year's worn shoes and without anything stocking the pantry. She buried her shaking hand in her skirt and willed herself to calm down. He didn't know. No one did.

Henry set down the pen and stared at the banker's clean hands. "Were you able to find a private buyer?" The words fell from his lips as whispers from the dead. Emma fought the instinct to reach over if only to make sure his heart hadn't already stopped.

"As a matter of fact, I did. And I think you'll be relieved to see his most generous offer."

Henry furrowed his brows and looked up to the banker's relaxed face. "Generous?"

Another pile of papers followed the first, and the banker flipped through the pages until he found the last one containing the financial information. "Here we go."

He set the paper down and slid it the short distance across the table. Henry looked at Emma and then picked up the paper as if he were afraid to get it dirty.

"Is this the correct amount?" Henry pointed to the number at the bottom of the sheet.

The banker broke out into a wide grin. "I thought you might like it."

Emma craned her neck to see the sum that had her husband nearly speechless. She rested her hand over her heart. It would be enough to pay the medical bills, to get them through the next couple of years if the drought persisted, and still have a sufficient amount left to plant when the time came.

"Why..." Emma couldn't think of the appropriate questions.

"I thought it was amazing, too." The banker sat back and lifted one ankle to rest on his knee. "He is also willing to forgo any sort of payment until after your first harvest. At that time, you will pay him back yearly in one lump sum, with interest of course, for however long it takes. He is also willing to negotiate from year to year based on your harvest and on wheat prices."

Henry dropped the paper between them. "Who's the buyer?"

Emma stared at him. The tone of his voice had changed like he already knew an answer he didn't like. On instinct, she slid away. Neither of the men noticed.

"He's recently relocated here; you may know him." The banker smiled as if what would come next was bound to make the deal something they couldn't resist.

Emma stared at the man. How could he be so dull? How could he not see the tension in Henry's twitching muscles? How could he not feel the atmosphere of the room thickening?

Still, the banker plowed on. "A Mr. Randall Mitchell." The banker shuffled through a few more papers, trying to find the one he'd signed. "You see..."

"Get out." Henry's two words carried a warning.

"What?" The banker shot a confused look to Emma as if she might help her ailing husband process things more efficiently. Emma refused to allow her expression to read anything but neutral.

"I said get out." Henry struggled to force his legs into a position that would make standing possible. "Now."

The banker jumped to his feet before Henry could labor to his. He gathered the papers up in messy piles and made his way to the door, mumbling something about returning at a better time. Soon enough, he sped away.

Henry never made it to his feet. Emma rushed over to help him lie back down.

"We will find some other way," Henry said. "And Jessie's answer is no. She will not marry that man."

★★★

Jessie wrapped a silk scarf around her neck and paraded in front of the mirror.

"I like that one," Randall said, flopping onto the bed in what had been the old widow's room.

Jessie flushed at being caught playing dress-up with the old woman's clothes.

"Don't be embarrassed. All of this is ours now. And I don't think I'm going to have much use for a silk scarf."

She couldn't help but laugh at the thought of him in a silk scarf.

"Do her shoes fit you? She had a lot of shoes. If they don't, we can order some for you, but I think we could donate these to some of the people in town."

Jessie slid her foot out of the brown shoes the minister's wife had given her. She couldn't imagine being able to look at a catalog, at all the women dressed fashionably, and then be able to point to the ones she liked, knowing she could have them. She chose a white pair with blue details and delicate laces and slipped her foot inside.

"It's a little roomy. Not so much that a wad of tissue paper in the toe won't fix it." Jessie looked up expectantly. So many shoes lined the closet.

Randall rolled off the bed and sent her a dark look. "No wife of mine will be mashing tissue paper into the toes of her shoes." He scowled and walked closer.

"Of course not." Jessie scrambled to pull them off her feet.

"You will only have the best. That's the way it is."

Jessie nodded and looked at the worn pattern on the rug. She tamped down the sudden panic she felt at his closeness. "I ... I will only wear things that fit." She didn't know what else to say, so she dropped her arms to her side and whispered her apologies.

Randall nodded. "I didn't mean to frighten you. I just want the best for you. You understand that, right?"

"Yes." Jessie forced her head up and looked at Randall. His expression softened at her gaze, and Jessie's heart began to slow the furious hammering against her ribs.

"I think we should get going. Wouldn't want your parents worrying about you, now would we?" He pulled her in for a shockingly hard kiss that had Jessie fighting the urge to pull away.

She didn't, though. She stood her ground. Made herself comfortable with his presence and stayed until she convinced herself she enjoyed the feel of his penetrating kiss.

★★★

Jessie waved at Sidney as they drove past his place. He'd been standing outside, like he always did, frowning at Randall, like he always did.

"That man unnerves me." Randall punched the gas harder than necessary and left a billowing cloud in his wake.

"Sidney?" Jessie sent him a confused look. "What's wrong with him?"

"He's always standing out there, watching when it's none of his business."

Jessie made a dismissive sound and then quickly apologized at the swift intake of breath coming from Randall. "I'm sorry. That's not what I meant. But maybe we should visit him together. I'm sure you'd like him once you get to know him."

Randall nodded, remaining silent. "I'll speak with him. No need for you to worry."

Jessie felt like she should say that she wasn't worried, or offer some kind of information that would make Randall like Sidney, but she couldn't think of what to say. And the sound of the engine conveniently covered the quiet. Maybe after they were married, Randall would talk more, and she would get to know what he liked and didn't like without having to upset him.

Jessie sat back to watch the brown fields of dirt speed by. The day had cooled a few degrees, and the backs of her knees didn't stick to the leather seats of the car. Jessie crossed one leg over the other and felt Randall's gaze slide to her exposed knee. She didn't try to cover it up. Instead, she looked out the window and pretended she didn't notice his attention.

"I remember when this farmland was the prettiest thing I'd ever seen." Jessie let her head fall against the back of the seat and closed her eyes. "I used to play in the long grass. It came up to my chest, and in some places, where the land dipped down, it stood taller than I did." She opened her eyes, and the sun burst into her line of vision. She had to blink it away. "Maybe it's just me, but I think the sun used to have more color. When the flowers bloomed white and lavender, and the green and the blue of the sky shone, when all that existed, the sun seemed the most brilliant spot of yellow. Now it's dull. Hot brown, I guess I would call it."

She glanced at Randall, who watched her intently, and wondered if she'd talked too much.

"But somewhere in the world, it is still green and blue, and the sun still shines yellow."

"Does it?" Jessie sighed. The town loomed ahead, and soon she would have to go into their dull house and talk to her dull parents, and keep her dull siblings entertained with nothing but the piece of brown world they owned.

"Does your father plan on selling the farm?"

"How did you know about that?" Jessie cocked her head to the side and uncrossed her legs. "Did I say something earlier?"

"Just talking with the banker. Your father needs to mortgage the property, but I made a better offer to buy the place."

"What?"

Randall stared at the road ahead. "I said I offered to buy the place and rent it back to him until he could purchase it back. It works for me, us really, because your family's farm connects with the others I've already purchased; and it works for them because they will get more cash than if they mortgaged it back to the bank." He studied the worried look on her face. "Why is that a problem?"

Jessie looked down, the white knuckles of her hand tightly gripping the door handle betraying her concern. "Did you bring up this offer this morning?"

"No. I thought the banker could better handle that."

"So he's talking to them this afternoon. That's the reason for the meeting?" Jessie could feel the panic swelling in her voice.

"What's wrong?"

"My dad is going to be furious. I have to get home."

"What? Why?" Randall slowed the car down. They were almost to Jessie's home.

She needed to get out. "He'll never be okay with that. He's much too proud. Did you think you wouldn't offend him by offering to marry me and then trying to buy his farm? He'll take that as saying you think he's incapable of providing for his family." Jessie could hear the rising tone in her voice but felt helpless to stop it. "I need to get home." She pulled her skirt down to cover her knees as best she could.

"I think you misunderstand my intentions." Randall sounded confused.

How could he be so rich and stupid at the same time? Jessie looked at him like she'd never seen him before. "Do you want to marry me only because you want my family's land?" Her voice shook with the effort it took to ask the question.

Randall stomped on the brake. "Of course not."

"That's what it looks like." Jessie thought back to the sunny kitchen and the rows of bright preserves in every color, the closet full of silk and lace, the pictures on the walls, and the gilded frames and lush carpets. Randall began driving again, slower this time, confusion and determination registering on his features, and Jessie could feel the color slipping away. That night, she'd be in bed next to her sisters, staring at the faded ceiling, thinking of the room she could have had, and apologizing to her sisters while they quietly snored because none of them would be eating the way they could if her father would accept the offer she knew he wouldn't.

"I'm sorry," Jessie said. "My dad's a proud man. He'll be angry. I know it. But that doesn't change anything for me."

Randall closed a hand over her knee and squeezed. "Good. As long as I know where we stand."

Jessie tried to keep her trembling under control. They could lose everything if her father took Randall's attempts to be helpful in the wrong way. Randall did care for her. That meant he had to care for her family, too. He was only doing the right, the expected, thing.

Randall slid his hand up her leg. Jessie stilled at the novel sensation. "You will still marry me? Even if he does not give us his blessing?"

Jessie looked out the window at the houses as they paraded by. Fence posts stood askew, porches hung from rotting frames, rusted windmills and water pumps chugged along, and flower boxes lay heavy and bare, filled with the same black dust invading every other place. They slowed in front of her own hopeless house.

She nodded. She would still marry him. His hand felt nice. That was something. But even if it repulsed her, the chance to invite her sisters to a place with colorful wallpaper and soft rugs, one that didn't feel like it would blow away with every gust of wind, gleamed. The chance to let them grow up in a place that didn't fill with dirt with each hellish black cloud was too much to let fall away just because her father might suffer from a bit of wounded pride.

CHAPTER TWENTY-SEVEN

Saturday morning dawned clear, and Peter breathed in a prayer of gratitude. Every day they woke without the soul-abrading dust whipping against their houses at least let the community pretend the drought didn't have them all by the throat.

Peter walked into the small chapel alone to spend some time in prayer before tomorrow's service. Lillian stayed at home, sweeping, dusting, cleaning windows, like they all did every day. If Peter had been a single man, the cleaning would have stopped a long time ago. It seemed the more she swept out, the more came right back in.

The weeks and months marched on, and Peter's duties had gone from reminding people of their responsibilities as Christians, to emphasizing God's grace as they all faced difficult decisions, to speaking of His forgiveness as they'd fallen prey to the easy comforts of their vices. And now, years deep in drought, he had a congregation of abandoned wives, spent old men, and listless children.

They didn't need to hear of their Christian duties when making it to tomorrow took everything they had. And Peter knew when he spoke of grace, those sitting in the pews spent more time wondering why His grace had been denied their family than they did thinking about His eternal grace.

And even Peter could hardly blame some of the people for falling prey to the simplicity of the blissful relief found in a bottle.

He rubbed his face and dropped down to sit in the front pew. He looked at the dingy ceiling and practiced holding his breath. The town had slowed to the point he felt like he could hold it indefinitely, like his breath existed only as an extension of a life that had already stopped. And maybe it had. Maybe they were all dead, maybe this place didn't even register as a spot on the map anymore. Maybe everything he thought about eternity had been wrong, and they were all dead and roaming in this dry place forever.

Peter whispered a prayer of repentance for his unfaithful thoughts.

Across the street, Jessie had created some kind of ruckus with her parents. Peter and Lillian had listened to the unintelligible shouts from Henry with more worry than curiosity. He'd wanted to step in. Lillian said his interference wouldn't be welcome. She was probably right.

Eventually, the noise stopped. Evening fell. People stayed in the shelter of their homes. The dirt blew about in the occasional dust devil and nothing. Always nothing.

His Bible sat on the pew next to him, but that had changed, too. He'd gone from studying it, attempting to glean meaning from passages that would enlighten the congregation's understanding of God, to opening it to random places and hoping for a word of encouragement. It rarely worked, and when the pathetic strategy didn't, he tried again, entirely defeating the purpose of a deliberate search for serendipitous comfort. When it did work, he questioned the truth in the gratifying words and still tried again. Efforts in futility wasted most of his day. But that, he had in common with his flock. That feeling, they could share.

★★★

Jessie paced upstairs in the midday heat. Her parents had been clear. They would not be selling the farm, and she would not be marrying. Her father said the hospital could waste their time suing him, and if they got the farm, he'd rather it be them than the ... well, she didn't want to think of the way her father had described Randall.

Last night she'd slept on it. Slept on her father's anger. Slept under the roof of a house that held little hope of seeing them through the next day, let alone the next storm. Her father's decision doomed them all.

Mostly her. When would she get another chance to marry someone who had the ability and the desire to help not only her but her family? She didn't have much knowledge about how things worked, but she had enough to understand the value of a dollar and that you didn't turn away help that had been offered. Her father came from a different time, a time when they could afford pride. But pride was a luxury she couldn't assume.

He was confined to bed, for goodness sake.

Jessie pulled an old, dusty bag from a high shelf and stuffed her clothes into it. She wasn't going to let her father sink any chance they had of keeping the farm. After dark, she'd leave. Randall would be outside, just like every other night. And she would tell him they needed to be married right away. Maybe they'd leave tonight. She'd be ready.

★★★

Randall rolled out his maps of the area and cursed. The Owen land stood at the center of everything and buying it was a key to making the whole thing work like he'd wanted.

Mr. Owen had made his decision clear. Randall looked out the window down at the deserted dirt road. Jessie had not. Although more complex than an outright buy, marriage was still a viable option as a way to eventually get the property. But only if she didn't mind going against her father's wishes; only if she still chose to marry him without her parents' blessing. And she would. He had to admit he wouldn't mind seeing the look on her father's face when she did. But for now, the man had slowed his progress.

Randall slammed his palm down on the paper and paused to look at where it had landed. There, in the space between his thumb and forefinger, something new caught his eye: a narrow strip of land, little more than a thick line. Randall opened the top desk drawer and rifled around for his magnifying glass.

The blueprint was hard to make out. He tipped the lamp closer and held the glass over the fuzzy text. He hadn't paid much attention to the little plot of land sandwiched between the other huge farms. But the tiny square bit had one key feature: access, via a small strip, to the old widow's farm. And it served to connect the others he'd already purchased.

Randall sat back and considered his options. He knew nothing about this spot of land, but a quick ride could solve that problem. Light still poured into his western-facing window. He had time.

He grabbed his things quickly and left the store without seeing his brother. In a day or so, he'd be moving to the farmhouse anyway. His brother would have to get used to wondering where he was. And frankly, answering Justin's constant questions had become tedious.

Few roads twisted through the area he needed to search. Randall flattened the map against the seat next to him and headed out of town.

Between downed fences and the lack of landmarks, figuring where one farm ended and another began became a difficult chore. More than once, Randall stopped the car to reevaluate the map. Eventually, he pulled up in front of a decrepit cabin. In the afternoon sun, he studied it for signs of life.

No windows, save the open top half of a Dutch door, adorned the front. Randall waited to see if anyone would appear. After a few seconds, he stepped into the long hot rays of the late afternoon sun.

"Anyone there?"

When no one answered, he shrugged and walked up to the shack, calling out as he went. "It's Mr. Randall Mitchell, from in town. Is anybody there?"

He took the lack of an answer as reason to look into the cabin.

Other than a table, a single chair, and a broken bed frame, the cabin contained nothing. Dirt piled in the corners and covered the planks so heavily that the cabin almost appeared to have a floor of grit and dust rather than wood. It had been abandoned. Randall let his smile spread across his face. This would be much easier than dealing with Old Widow Ruby. And a great deal easier than with Jessie's father.

CHAPTER TWENTY-EIGHT

Jessie waited for the lights in the surrounding houses to go out and the evening sounds to die off. The quiet of the night eventually invaded the Owen house, and after a while, her father's snores fought the overwhelming silence of a landscape devoid of even humming and creaking insects.

They used to hear frogs at night. Frogs and crickets and all sorts of things that flew and chirped. Of course, crickets still hid in the cracks here and there, but the drought had stolen even their desire to expend the energy it took to sing to their mates.

Jessie eased the kitchen door closed behind her and stepped into the yard. The now-familiar night landscape required no lights, even on a night with little offered by the moon. She slung her bag over her shoulder and took the first few steps to Mr. Mitchell's store.

If Randall didn't welcome her after her father's foolish outburst, she didn't know what she would do. Best not to think of it.

Jessie felt around with her feet for the place where the ground pitched down into the neighbor's land. She stumbled over it but regained her footing. He had to still want her, didn't he? She tightened her sweaty grip and pushed ahead.

Her father had said no. No to everything. No to allowing Randall to purchase the land and no to her marrying him. Her mother sat stone-faced next to him, not arguing. Jessie couldn't blame her. Her usually mild father could fiercely stick to an idea once he'd made up his mind. Arguing would only bring frustration.

Jessie reached her hand out to feel for the fence she knew should be somewhere to her left. Her father had left her no choice. Without the money from the sale, they would lose the farm anyway. And she had the chance to marry someone with land and a house and money to see them all through the drought to better days. Denying her that opportunity, when the alternative looked like hunger and homelessness, reeked of nothing but bullheadedness.

And her mother—her mother had done everything she could do to keep everyone fed and clean and healthy, despite the roadblocks her father's pride tossed in their path.

Jessie spun, sure she heard a voice call her name.

"Jessie. Stop." Her mother's soft tones called out from the dark.

Jessie shifted the weight of her bag, unsure if she should listen or move on. She didn't resent her mother. She'd done the best she could. Turning around, Jessie scanned the shadows and waited for her mother to catch up.

Clutching her unbuttoned housecoat, her mother rushed to her side. Her disheveled hair sprang out in all directions, and in the faint light of the moon, she looked both too young to be Jessie's mother and ancient all at once.

"I know what you're doing."

Jessie dropped the bag from her shoulder and let it fall into the dust.

"I know you think you need to marry Randall, and I understand why you want to."

"So why did Dad tell me I couldn't?"

"Would you expect anything less from him? He doesn't think you love him. That the only reasons you would marry Randall are his money and home." Emma glanced toward the house and then back to Jessie. "We don't have a lot, we know, and I feel bad about telling you not to marry Randall. But we do have love. It's the only thing that makes life"—she threw her hands out over the barren landscape—"worth it. Love is free, and marriage lasts a long time."

Emma dropped her arms to her side. "Even that pretty house will get old sometime, and your father knows that then, you will be left with nothing. He can't protect you from much right now, but if he can protect you from a life without love, you can't blame him for trying."

Jessie looked at her bag, slumped on the ground. "If I loved him, I don't think it would matter for Dad. He'd still say no."

Her mother shrugged. "Maybe not." She paused, shifting her weight from one foot to the other then back again before continuing. "Do you love him?"

Jessie felt the trap closing, tightening. If she said she didn't, her mother would do everything she could to make sure Jessie didn't marry. If she said she did, she'd be lying. Jessie glanced at the minister's house, just visible between the shadows of the other buildings. She could go to hell for lying. That much she knew.

But she couldn't imagine another way her family might make it through the next winter—let alone years, if the drought persisted— if someone didn't do something.

"I think so," she half lied.

Jessie's mother's eyes bored into hers. She worried her bottom lip with her teeth and looked up at the sky. "Your father is not going to be happy."

"I know."

"He'll eventually come around. He always does."

Jessie nodded, surprised at her mother's resigned tone.

"You will need my permission to marry, you know."

Jessie broke eye contact, embarrassed by her next words. "Not everywhere."

"I see."

They both looked up, then down, then up and down again.

Her mother spoke first. "It will be easier with my permission."

The fear and dread coursing through Jessie's veins settled into her stomach, making it feel like she'd eaten much more than she should and would be sick any second.

"Are you sure this is what you want?"

Jessie didn't trust herself to answer. Instead, she nodded and hoped her mother would believe.

"Then I will help you. I want you to understand, though, I'm not helping because I think it is right, or because I'm trying to find a financial solution." She took a step nearer, and with a fluttering hand took a lock of Jessie's hair between her fingers. "I remember when you were little."

Despite her efforts, Jessie's eyes threatened to spill over.

She played with the lock of Jessie's hair, running it across her palm then smoothing it over Jessie's shoulder. "I want you to know … no, I need you to know that I am doing this because I want you to have what you want in life. Because I don't want you to ever blame me when times get hard, and because you are old enough to make your own decisions and live with your own regrets. You have the right to your own consequences, be them good or bad, and I won't stand in your way."

The tears spilled down her cheeks, and when her mother turned back to the house and left her standing in the desolate landscape, all she wanted to do was sleep. Sleep until something changed. Sleep until she didn't have any decisions to make. Her deflated rebellion had left her exhausted and wishing only for the simplicity of the bed she shared with her sisters.

She turned back and followed her mother, wishing more than anything, that time would just stop … that she could blink and wake up in a field humming with life. She kicked at the dust, leaving a cloud to rise behind her. She could wish for a lot of things. But it was a waste of time.

★★★

Lillian crept out of bed and outside. Sunday hadn't dawned yet, but she couldn't sleep anymore. Peter had spent half the night praying; she could tell from the sounds of his breathing that he hadn't fallen asleep quickly. And when he didn't sleep, he prayed.

But when his breathing finally steadied, and his fingers twitched against her arm, she knew he'd dropped off.

And then she'd slept in fits, here and there, slumber snatched between thoughts that refused to stop roaming. So now here she stood under a sky ablaze with stars, in her shoes and housecoat, wandering along with her thoughts.

Until a figure darted between the houses.

Lillian slipped back into the shadows and listened for more than her own heartbeat. The silence and dark overwhelmed in a way an overabundance of sound never could. She strained against the nothingness, wanting evidence of more than her own existence in the insulating night. Eventually, the reward came in the shape of Randall.

He paced against the side of the Owen house as if he'd waited too long and grown tired of the trial, so now he wore a path in the dirt out of spite.

His sharp steps carried him in and out of the light, like an old tomcat who'd grown weary of stalking and decided to finally pounce. He bent over to pick up a rock and chuck it into the street. With a small puff of dust, it came to rest on the other side of their gate. Lillian backed up as far as she could.

That he waited for someone was no question. Jessie.

Lillian tightened the belt of her robe and worked up the courage to call out to him, to ask him why he stalked the night, but he turned on his heel, mumbled something she couldn't understand, and walked briskly back toward his brother's store.

The breath Lillian had held rushed out all at once, and at last, weariness coursed through her body.

She stumbled back to bed.

★★★

Emma brushed and scrubbed the children clean. They would go to church without their father again. Although he made progress almost daily, his injuries still kept him confined to the bed in the front room.

Once completely healed, Emma hoped he'd get up again. The way he stared at the wall, as if even it had betrayed him, had her inventing excuses to make him talk.

The hospital bills worried him. His health frustrated him. But the latest hit—that his daughter wanted to marry the man he saw as taking advantage of their situation—might have been more than he could take.

He'd always been so strong.

"Mama, that hurts." Betsy whimpered at Emma's distracted brushing.

"Sorry. Go get your shoes on now."

The little girl scuttled up the stairs.

"Time to go," Emma called up to the other children.

Jessie came down first, done up in her best dress. They hadn't spoken since the previous night, but the nod they shared meant they'd reached some kind of understanding, even if neither of them knew what it might be or where it might lead.

"I'll take Little Henry." Jessie held her arms open to the steps and caught him in midair.

"You know that makes me nervous." Emma didn't like it when they jumped down the stairs like that. "Someone could get hurt, and that's the last thing we need right now."

Jessie smiled her apology and headed out the door without saying goodbye to her father.

The rest of the children fell into place behind Emma, and together they made their way down the dusty road to the sunbaked chapel. Strains of the first hymn floated out the open windows as they approached. Emma gave the slowest children a shove and rushed them up the worn steps and out of the sun. They hurried to their pew and shuffled to places of comfort. As much as possible, anyway, given they wore their Sunday clothes, and most of the children scratched and chafed against the confining fabrics.

At one time, the church had been filled almost to the brim with farmers and their wives, workers and store owners, a doctor and a teacher, and everyone else who made a town a town. Now, the mostly empty pews supported a strange bunch of people who looked like they belonged nowhere. Almost as if they were the few broken flower heads left in the bottom of a basket. The ones no one knew what to do with. Too short, or too bent, or too many petals missing. So they went unnoticed until all the pretty flowers had found their homes in vases, and then sat there, drying.

Randall sat next to his brother, like he did every Sunday. The offering plate passed and he put something in, like he did every Sunday. And at the end of service, he turned and acknowledged Jessie with a look. But the look lingered. Questions she had no ability to discern floated between her daughter and the enigmatic newcomer, and Emma fought a wave of nausea at the impending deception she knew would make Henry furious.

Jessie smiled and waited for Randall to come down the aisle after service. They walked out together. Emma watched as Randall ducked close to her daughter to better hear what Jessie said. Nothing in his actions, nothing in his look gave Emma any reason not to like him.

"What's going on there?" Lillian whispered the question from behind Emma. The church had all but emptied, with only a couple people milling about the entrance.

Emma turned and faced her. There was no reason she shouldn't be honest. "They want to marry."

Lillian's eyes widened a fraction. "What does Henry think?"

Emma shook her head.

"What do you think?"

She took a deep breath. "I think he can offer her everything she could wish for, everything we can't, and I think if I say no I will only be standing in her way." She let out a slow breath. "It doesn't matter what I think. I just want her to be happy, and that's a lot to ask right now."

Lillian shoved her hands in her skirt pockets and looked at the ground. "I saw him out the other night."

Emma's eyebrows rose the tiniest bit. "Who?"

"Randall. He stood outside your house for the longest time."

Emma shook her head. "I can't imagine why," she lied. She knew. Jessie had been sneaking out for some time.

Lillian pulled her hands out of her pockets and took a step toward the door. "I guess I should get going. Hope Henry is on the mend?"

"Better every day. Well, a little." Emma shrugged. "It's slow."

"Let us know if we can help, okay?" Lillian touched Emma's sleeve.

Help? They needed everything and nothing. Emma nodded and stepped out into the sun feeling like even the ground beneath her feet might be the next thing to go missing. They had food, but tasted nothing; ample sun, but nothing grew; and she a husband, but no partner. The list of things they needed had expanded from the simple to the complex, and no one could help with that.

She crossed the dirt road to where Randall and Jessie stood making plans. It was time to do something, to make a decision. Because living like this, without knowing how they would get from day to day, couldn't happen anymore.

And she refused to force Jessie into the same nightmare.

CHAPTER TWENTY-NINE

L illian listened as Peter slammed the front door and toed his shoes off before dropping his Bible on the small hall table and making his way to the kitchen.

"What was that all about?" She lifted a wooden spoon to her lips, testing the lunch broth.

"Sorry, what?"

"You slammed the door."

"Oh. Didn't realize..." Peter's words died off, and he stared out the small kitchen window.

Lillian dropped her spoon on the small plate beside the stove and crossed her arms over her chest. "What's happened?"

Peter shook his head and collapsed into his chair at the table. Mouth clamped closed, he shook his head as if he were having a conversation with someone, but no words came out.

"You know, if you are talking to me, you have to tell me what you're thinking, right?"

"I'm sorry." He scratched his head and rubbed his hands down his face. "I don't even know..."

"Just tell me what happened." Lillian took her place across the table from him and held out her hands.

Peter reached for her fingers, studied her nails, and then played with her wedding ring. "Emma went to town with Randall and Jessie."

"Really?"

"They came back with a marriage license."

Lillian stared at her husband. The drought had aged him in the same strange, dry way it aged everyone else. "What did you say?"

Peter shook his head. "I said I have to pray about it."

Lillian knew what that meant. Yes. It meant he'd pray, and pray hard, but it also meant he didn't know what to do and needed to stall.

Peter looked up. "I don't like him."

Lillian nodded.

"He does everything right: he treats people well, he speaks with folks on Sunday like they were his long-time friends, he's generous, he seems to dote on Jessie, but I can't shake the feeling that I just don't like the man."

"How does Henry feel about his daughter marrying?"

Peter inhaled deeply. "They haven't told him. And they won't until it's over."

"Is that a reason not to marry them?"

Peter shrugged. "It could be. I could use it as one. But I'm not sure if I want to. Randall now owns a good chunk of town. Do I want to alienate him?" He stood and leaned against the counter, looking out the window. "And Henry has never been the most welcoming fellow anyway. What if there's nothing wrong? Is it fine for me to help Henry stand in his daughter's way?"

"But something is wrong?"

"Nothing I know of." Peter opened a cupboard that hung askew and fiddled with the hinge for a few seconds before closing it again. "But if there is and something goes wrong, do I want to make Jessie feel like she can't come to us if she needs something, like she's going against the wishes of the only minister in town and has to be on her own?"

Lillian stood and made her way back to the pot on the stove. "What are you going to do?"

Peter shook his head. "I'm going to sit in the front room and read the paper. That's what I'm going to do."

"When will you speak with them next?"

"After lunch they'll come back to the office." Peter walked out of the room.

Lillian turned back to the pot on the stove and tested the broth once more. She added a dash of salt, gave it another stir, and decided to let it simmer for a while longer to give Peter a few more minutes of quiet.

He wouldn't marry them. She knew that. It might take him a while to come to terms with it. But he never did anything that went against what he felt to be right. That much she could count on.

She looked out the window. Emma might be angry. Jessie and Randall would be angry. She dunked the wooden spoon into the dishwater and scrubbed a stubborn piece of vegetable from the handle. There would be a price to pay. There always was.

★★★

Emma walked in to see Henry sitting at the side of his bed. Papers were strewn about. He peered at the small print, squinting to read the details of the mortgage offered by the bank.

"Oh. It's good to see you up. Do you need anything?" Emma closed the door behind her and stood at the end of his bed.

Henry looked up and smiled. It was the first smile she could remember for quite some time. Her heart skipped a beat and then the nausea of the betrayal she'd helped to perpetrate took over.

"I could use my reading glasses. Not sure where I had those last."

Emma ducked out of the room then returned with his spectacles.

"The terms of this mortgage are not as bad as I'd imagined. We might be able to make it work."

Emma glanced at the pile of papers. "Are you sure?"

"Sure? No. I'm not sure of anything. But I think it's our best shot."

She knew better than to ask him to reconsider selling. And she knew better than to tell him right now that she'd signed for Jessie and Randall to get a marriage license. He'd find out soon enough, anyway.

"I think I'd like to try the crutches today." Henry pointed to the wooden sticks that leaned against the corner next to the door. "It's time for me to do something around here."

"There's not a whole lot to do, you know."

"The gate doesn't latch properly." He pointed out the window. "Kids always slamming the thing."

Emma nodded, guilt plaguing the hope she felt at seeing a shadow of her husband return. "Do you want some coffee or something?"

"That would be fine. Just fine. Oh, and the banker left a message at the store. Justin stopped by to tell me he'd be coming over later this afternoon. I suppose to pick up these papers." Henry held up the few in his hands and smiled again. "You know, we're going to make this work. We'll make it through."

Emma escaped to the kitchen, swallowing against the rising taste of bile.

★★★

Peter sat across from Jessie and Randall. He'd half expected Emma to join them for the meeting, but she hadn't, and now he would have to guess if she supported the marriage or simply didn't want to stand in the way.

Either way, his answer had to be the same. He couldn't marry a couple whose license required parental support while knowing one parent had withheld their blessing.

That he felt thankful for the excuse was another matter entirely.

Randall's smug expression grated on Peter. He prayed for patience and love, but something clung to the well-dressed man sitting across the desk. Nothing Peter could see, almost more of an odor, or an essence ... whatever hung there, whatever it was that made Peter want to close his door and pray.

"I know I'm the only minister in town," Peter began.

Jessie sat back and crossed one knee over the other. Randall edged forward on his chair.

"But I am sorry to say that I don't feel like I can perform a ceremony that would be against your father's wishes."

"You're against the marriage?" Randall stood quickly, the legs of the chair behind him squealing against the floor. "What do I have to do to prove myself to you?"

"Please sit down," Peter said.

"I'd prefer to stand." The man's slicked-back hair had fallen in a chunk to hang over one eye. He pushed it back with a trembling hand.

Peter watched the man pace to the door and back. The hair on the back of Peter's neck rose in warning. He kept his voice as calm as possible, watching Jessie for any hint that she felt in danger.

Her expression remained stoic.

"It has nothing to do with how I feel about you or Jessie. It has to do more with loyalty to Jessie's father. I don't feel comfortable performing a ceremony he rejects while he is stuck in bed sick."

Randall paced back to Jessie's side. "Come on. We don't need this." He grabbed her wrist and pulled her up to stand next to him. "You'll regret this, Reverend."

His grip on Jessie's arm caused her to wince for the smallest fraction of a second. She quickly recovered and nodded her goodbyes to Peter.

Peter watched them leave then found the altar and prayed for her safety.

CHAPTER THIRTY

Jessie shook with the force of her anger. She opened her front door, unsure what to expect.

After meeting with the minister, she'd been upset with her father for his stubbornness, and then with her mother for her meekness, and then with herself for ever believing something could actually work in her favor.

They'd left the church, or rather, she'd been pulled out by Randall just in time to see the banker's car roar away from the front of her house.

Randall had smirked. He'd looked down at Jessie and said her father's objections shouldn't matter much anymore.

Jessie tore her arm away and ran up to the house. Randall didn't follow.

When she stepped in, papers had been tossed everywhere. Her father stood, coughing, his chest laboring to take in enough air. Her mother was trying to pull him back to sit down.

"You will," he pointed to Jessie, "you will not speak with that man again."

"What happened?" Jessie looked for an explanation to register on her mother's face, but she revealed nothing.

"What happened?" She stooped to pick up some of the papers and repeated the question to her father.

His face, blotched red from effort or anger or both, refused to reveal any thought or emotion other than hatred.

"The bank decided to rescind their offer of a mortgage," Jessie's mother finally answered.

The quiet words rang through the room like a gunshot.

"But why?"

"They wouldn't say. But there's little doubt Randall had something to do with it." The sentence came out of her father as something between a sob and a roar.

Jessie took a step nearer, but her mother nodded her away. She needed to give her father space.

She needed space, too.

Walking through the house to the kitchen, Jessie struggled to process what was happening. The kitchen stove sat untended and cold. Dinner hadn't been started. She opened the cupboards. They were still next to bare. And the curtain hanging in the window, the one that used to brag of happiness with its bold floral print and eyelet lace, hung limp and faded from a drooping rod. After seeing the pantry at the old widow's house, after allowing herself to dream the place might someday be hers, the stark emptiness of her parents' kitchen left her breathless. She slammed the door shut. She couldn't breathe.

She stumbled out the kitchen door and stood for a second in the orange late-day sun. How had she been so dull? Had Randall stopped her parents from getting the help they needed at the bank? She wandered through what used to be a backyard, past the rotting clotheslines, past the old shed, and kept going.

Chunks of dirt that used to be rich fields crumbled under her weight. The resulting clouds rose to fill her shoes with the ever-present soot. Jessie didn't care. She kicked through, walking as fast as she could, until the sky turned from pink to lavender and the houses grew to be nothing more than boxes with shimmering eyes, reflecting the setting sun. She should head back. But back to what?

She pushed forward into the nothingness. North. She walked north, wondering how far she'd have to go before she found grass, or a stream, or anything, really. She spun around, looking for anything but the dust she could taste. The dirt coated her skin, and all at once she couldn't stop rubbing and scratching at it.

Scraping at her arms and her legs and her hair, she couldn't get down to just skin. It was like the earth itself wanted her. Finally, she screamed loud enough to hear her own voice reverberate then disappear into the cracked dirt. She sank down to rest on her heels and hugged her knees to her chest.

A huge locust climbed, unaffected by her outburst, up the stalk of a dead weed. The insect's antennae twitched at her nearness. Slowly, it picked up one foot and bent its brown striped leg nearly in half. Jessie touched the insect. It didn't move. She pushed the stupid thing and tried to pull it from the dead plant. It stayed firm. Finally, she stood and brought her foot down hard. The dust rose to swirl around her knees.

And then she walked away.

Farther away from her parents' home. Farther into the nothing. Until she saw the old widow's place rise out of the vast expanse of brown.

It wasn't the old widow's place. The old widow was dead. The sun had just sunk below the horizon. Jessie picked up the pace and headed in that direction.

She'd no idea what role Randall had played in her father's frustrations, and frankly, she didn't care. She doubted he was the kind of person who would go out of his way to harm her father, but even if he did, it was only because her father had been too stubborn to see what was best for his family.

Bullheadedness used to be valuable. At least when it meant you plowed late into the night by the bright electric headlamps on the machines only because you wanted a few extra acres planted. But when the land, the town, and their family had nothing, her father's relentless, hardened approach to anything not his idea put them all in danger.

The windows of the house reflected the lavender and darkening hues of the sky. Jessie paused. Randall's car sat between the house and the barn. He was there.

She took a deep breath, ignored her dust-covered clothes and hair and skin, and marched up the stairs. She would have this decision made, tonight.

★★★

Emma had settled the kids into their beds and then Henry. She'd deftly avoided any questions about Jessie, and instead allowed him the not-so-small comfort of thinking their eldest daughter slept upstairs with the others.

Emma, on the other hand, had no such reassurance.

Jessie had gone off, leaving no clue as to where.

Outside, Emma pumped more water into the pail, sat down on the rickety chair, and sank first one bare foot and then the other into the cool relief. The shadows offered some level of cover, so she hiked her faded skirt up over her knees and leaned back.

The water rippled around her calves. Her ankles ached from the cold, but she didn't care. It felt like life. One spot of life in an expanse of dry nothing.

And now even the false hope of a mortgage had floated out of their reach.

She took a deep breath in and held it. Eyes closed, Emma thought back to when she'd been sixteen, when promise existed, when the world was filled with dew-covered wildflowers, and she had a choice of suitors and a choice of a future.

Jessie had no choice. Not any choices a sixteen-year-old could recognize, anyway. Not with the weight of a hungry future without a home weighing down on her.

The water splashed up the side of the bucket each time Emma shifted her feet. She could hear the water's voice lap against the metal. It was a subtle, reassuring song that should have calmed her, or at the very least, grounded her. But when things were bad, like now, when little hope hung out there, the weariness sank in so deep it couldn't be assuaged by tiny tricks like the sound of water or the scent of butter in a pan. This weariness sank in until those small, rare luxuries simply brought on fitful sleep, plagued with more problems she was hopeless to do anything about.

★★★

Jessie climbed the back steps, dirty, hungry, and angry. She pounded on the door.

Randall opened it slowly and peered out from behind the door. Confusion marred his usually unruffled demeanor. Obviously, he hadn't been expecting her.

"Did you tell the bank not to give my dad a mortgage?" Jessie crossed her arms over her chest and waited on the top stair for his answer.

"Why don't you come in. You look like you've had a rough afternoon."

"Did you?" Jessie didn't budge. She crossed her arms over her chest and clamped her teeth tight, refusing to budge until he at least gave her an answer.

"No. I did offer to purchase the property. I don't know why he refused, but I didn't tell the bank not to give him a mortgage. I can't tell a bank what they should and shouldn't do." Randall opened the door as wide as he could. "Get in here. You can't just stand there all night."

After a frown and a curt nod, Jessie stepped inside what was to be her new home, with Randall just behind her. A bowl of apples sat in the center of the table. Jessie's stomach growled at the smell of the sweet fruit.

Randall frowned at her dirty dress. "Have an apple. I'm going to go upstairs and fill the tub for you. You're going to take a warm bath, put on some clean clothes, and then we can talk."

Jessie dropped to a chair and picked up a blood-red apple. She missed color. Not every day. Not when she walked down the street, or when she scrubbed the laundry, or when she chased Little Henry around the yard. Color was one of those things she only realized she missed when faced with the startling reality of a red apple in her brown world.

She rolled it over in her fingers, searching for any imperfections, wondering how a tree could create something so wonderful. Sinking her teeth into the crispy flesh, her eyelids fell at the burst of moisture. In a matter of minutes, she was searching for a bucket to toss the core into and then eyeing another one in the bowl.

"It's all ready. I've set out towels and a dress I pulled from one of the cabinets up there. Hopefully, it will fit." Randall shifted, and for the first time, Jessie could sense a tinge of awkwardness in his posture as if he didn't know what to expect from her.

"Thank you."

She hadn't planned to bathe here. She hadn't even planned to come here, or knock on the door, or step into the house. Now she would be taking her clothes off and climbing into a tub filled with warm water. Stifling a shiver of pleasure at the thought, she avoided eye contact with Randall and slipped past him and up the stairs. "I'll be back down in a bit." The statement rose in pitch at the end. Almost as if she were asking him for permission.

Randall nodded. "I'll wait in the kitchen. Take as much time as you like."

Jessie nodded, words abandoning her. She lifted her hand to the stair railing and paused.

Randall covered her fingers with his. "I still want to marry you, you know."

She nodded and turned to climb the steps, uneasy with being told, again, what to do, but at the same time grateful that someone cared enough to order her into a bath. Did she want to be free to make her own decisions, or did she want to be taken care of? Or was she still a child, because, truly, she wanted both?

★★★

Jessie eased into the bath. She sucked in a hissing breath at the feel of the hot water. Her clothes laid in a dusty heap on the clean tile floor. If she never put them on again, it would be too soon.

This was it. She was done. The warm water that caressed her body boosted her resolve. Stretching and then relaxing, she sank deeper into the luxurious bath. Her father could demand and rage as long as he wanted, but she didn't need another night of hoping her brothers and sisters wouldn't starve, not when she had a choice.

And there were worse ones.

Jessie picked up a fragrant piece of soap and plunged it into the milky water. Sprigs of lavender were carved into the surface of the bar. She lifted it to her face and inhaled, remembering when things smelled good. Remembering when she smelled good.

She scrubbed the bar roughly down her arm and back up until it worked into a lather. And then she repeated. By the time she finished, every inch of her body had been rubbed raw, and she'd never felt better. A folded towel rested on the nearby window ledge. Jessie grabbed it, stood, and stepped out of the tub and onto the softest rug she'd ever felt. Her clean toes sank against the plush pile. Wriggling them in deeper, Jessie stood there, wrapped in a towel, remembering the feeling of comfort. She exhaled for what felt the first time in years, emptying her lungs completely, and then held it until her body screamed against the lack of oxygen. Only then did she allow herself to take a breath of the humid bathing room mist. Only then did she feel the blood rush back through her veins.

No questions remained in her mind. Tomorrow they would be married. She would insist. Tonight she would sleep in a soft bed with clean quilts. She dropped the towel to pool at her feet and examined her reflection in the mirror. Tomorrow she would be a wife. Tomorrow she would not be the only one to have seen her body. Her stomach rejected the thought, flipped over, and she rushed to the toilet to lose the apple she'd eaten before her bath.

The retching stopped. Jessie stood, rinsed her mouth, slipped on the dress, and folded the towel over the side of the tub. Looser than perfect, the dress still fit. Jessie forced a smile and made her way down the stairs.

She was done. They would go to sleep early, in different rooms, and tomorrow they would leave early for the courthouse.

Her father would just have to get used to the idea.

CHAPTER THIRTY-ONE

The day dawned cloudy. Not the dusty kind of cloudy, but the real clouds kind of cloudy. Lillian opened the curtains wide and looked out onto the street that, for the first time in a long time, did not look like the inside of a dirty old furnace.

She used to look forward to sunny days. Lillian glanced out the window. Rain was doubtful, but the clouds changed the way everything appeared. She smiled. Even that bit of difference made her want to do something, go somewhere.

She glanced over to the pile of sheets she'd planned on washing and frowned. Well, at least she wouldn't be standing in the sun to hang them out.

Lillian pushed the curtains open as far as they would go and tied them back in time to see Emma walk across her yard toward the water pump. Before stooping to fill the bucket, she looked one way down the road and then the other. Finally, not seeing what she wanted, she set the bucket on the stand and grasped the handle. Lillian watched the back of Emma's house, waiting to see at least a couple of the children sprint around, but everything stood quiet.

The teapot whistled, bringing her back to her own home. Lillian rushed to the stove to turn off the burner then glanced out her kitchen window.

A car, Randall's car, sped down the road toward the houses. Lillian could make out the shape of a passenger. Twisting her wrist, Lillian glanced at her watch. It didn't even read seven in the morning. She lifted the teapot off the burner and dropped it on a cool one before rushing to the front window in time to make out Jessie in the passenger seat.

Emma had seen it too.

Through Lillian's windows, the women shared a look—Emma shaking her head to signal she couldn't talk but lifting her eyebrow to let Lillian know she would stop by later to fill her in on what had happened. Peter had already left for his office. Lillian grabbed a scarf, tied it over her unruly hair, slipped on her shoes, and waited for Emma to disappear back into her house before making her way to the chapel.

***

"What do you think they were doing?" Lillian paced to the window that overlooked the stretch of nothing that used to be fields.

Peter frowned and drummed his fingers against the worn wood of his desk. "They're going to get married. No doubt."

"But why would she do that?" Lillian knew the answer; she just didn't want to think about it.

Peter looked up, meeting her gaze. He knew the answer, too. Jessie had no other choice.

He slammed a theology book he'd been studying closed. The sound reverberated through the room. "What good is it to sit here and preach when I can't even offer enough help so that the children of this town don't have to ... well, for lack of another way to put it ... sell themselves to the first person who steps into town with some change in his pocket just so they can have a future?"

"She does have a choice. Everyone has a choice," Lillian countered, taking care to keep her voice soft.

"What choice? Her parents are ruined by medical expenses. By winter, all of them could be going hungry—hungrier than they have been up to now." Peter stood and shelved the book with the others in his library. "Look at this." He pointed to the colorful spines lining the wall. "Look at this. Hundreds of years of knowledge and wisdom, and I can't keep a sixteen-year-old safe."

"Safe from what?"

Peter exhaled loudly. "Randall is not a good man. He acts upright, but he isn't good. I've nothing to base my feelings on... Do you know how his first wife died?"

Lillian's brows shot up. "You're not saying..."

"No. Not really." Peter leaned against the front of his desk. "It's just there's something not right about him.

"I think she became ill."

Peter nodded and frowned. "I really hoped Jessie would reconsider after I explained why I couldn't perform the ceremony."

"Why would she? She's sixteen. Would you have listened when you were sixteen?"

Peter's frown deepened.

"Not only that, but she's carrying the burden for her family. Has it occurred to you if she marries him she has the means to help her parents? If she marries him, her brothers and sisters have a chance of not going hungry?"

"I hate this." Peter studied the floor planks and kicked at a nail that had worked loose.

Lillian leaned next to him and crossed her arms over her chest. "So do I."

"Do you think we should follow them to town?"

"What good would it do?"

"It would at least feel like we're doing something?"

"Has it gotten that bad? That we purposefully do useless things so we can pretend to be of some use?"

Peter snorted. "Maybe it has."

They stared at each other long enough to begin registering the click of the clock on the wall. Finally, Peter looked away.

"What are you going to preach on this week?"

Peter reached out over his large desk. Lillian laced her fingers through his and squeezed. His hands, large for a preacher, confessed of a childhood filled with the outdoors and trouble.

"I honestly have no idea," Peter said.

She looked out to the hovering sky. "Something with hope. That's it, just hope. I don't think we could handle much more."

"I don't think I could handle much more."

★★★

Jessie stood beside Randall while the judge spoke of duty and devotion and all of the other things she thought she should listen to but couldn't quiet her mind long enough to hear.

She said "I do" when her time came, and Randall said his when his time came, and then he slipped a heavy ring on her finger, and the judge ordered them to kiss.

Jessie felt nothing like she'd always imagined she might feel on her wedding day. The butterflies she'd heard of felt more like rocks. And when their lips met, it was for a rough, businesslike, seal-the-deal kind of closing that left her breathless, but not in the way she'd expected.

From ceremony to signatures, the process took less than twenty minutes, and then they spilled out onto the steps of the courthouse in a city she'd rarely ever seen.

"Well, Mrs. Mitchell." Randall smiled down at her, condescension alive in his face. "Would you like to get some lunch?"

Jessie nodded dumbly. She couldn't figure out how a wife should talk to her husband.

"We'll stay the night at a hotel here in town before heading back?"

It was a question. It demanded an answer. Jessie nodded, suddenly feeling far too young to be considering her wedding night.

Cars sped past and then Randall pulled her into the street to cross. She hadn't even had the sense to look before following him. She just trusted he would look for them both. Jessie shook her head. She had to retain some kind of control.

Once on the other side of the street, Randall stopped and reached for her hands. She looked up into his eyes and found the reassurance she'd hoped for.

"It will be alright," Randall spoke softly. And then, cars still buzzing by, he dipped his head and kissed her in the way that made her forget everything but his lips pressed to hers, and in the way that made her want to lean into his strength. Then he pulled away. "You will see. Everything will be wonderful."

Jessie took a deep breath and followed him into the restaurant. Windows lined the wall by the tables and stools lined the lunch counter. Men in suits and in work clothes sat next to each other while a pretty waitress poured steaming coffee into plain cups. Jessie crossed the black-and-white tiles to a table tucked into a corner between a window and the back wall where she could watch the waitresses rush in and out of the kitchen hoisting trays laden with foods of every color and aroma onto their shoulders. Jessie had forgotten how colorful food was. How everything had different scents and textures and that there was a difference between gravy and sauce. Her mouth watered as her memory filled in the flavor of the passing dishes. Outside the window, people whisked by on the street, inches from them, separated only by glass, intent on their own troubles or victories and oblivious to the profound change in her life. She was a wife. Or she would be after tonight. It didn't really count until, well, until...

"Do you know what you want?" Randall flipped the single-page menu full of normal-sounding food.

The items were all words she knew: sandwiches, meats, potatoes, and vegetables. But the list, everything together, the number of choices, seemed to make it impossible to comprehend.

It might as well have been written in a different language for as able as Jessie felt to process it. She shrugged. "I don't know what's good."

"I like the roast beef. Comes with pie too."

Randall's eyes drifted over the menu then to Jessie. She could feel the blush start at her collar and work its way to the top of her head. "Th ... that sounds fine," she stammered.

Randall smiled. "You can relax, you know."

Jessie nodded and soundlessly berated herself for her ignorance. She knew what would happen. She'd seen the animals on the farm. And she'd heard some of the kids talking at school. But she didn't know everything. It made her feel stupid. She glanced at Randall. He looked older now. He'd been married before.

Randall ordered for them both, and they sat back to watch the people stroll by the window. "You know," he turned to Jessie, "I'm looking forward to getting you home. I'm looking forward to making that place ours."

Jessie nodded, biting her bottom lip. The price she'd pay once her father found out, the price her mother would have to pay, she'd no idea. But she'd just secured everyone's future. She stole a quick glance at her husband. Her husband. It couldn't be much of a sacrifice, being his wife. At least he was handsome.

★★★

Justin paced in front of the darkened store windows. His brother had left with the Owen girl, and no one had seen them since.

News traveled fast through the few left in town, and no one doubted the reason the pair had for leaving. Randall had spoken of marrying the girl. Justin slapped his fist onto the counter next to his ledger book. He'd thought he had more time to convince Randall otherwise.

Of course, not for his brother's sake, but for the sake of the girl.

The phone call had come late in the day. Out on the east coast, the police had been looking for him. Said they wanted to ask him a few questions. Justin had pried, of course, and of course, they hadn't given him any information.

And he had no reason to suspect his brother of anything. Randall had been nothing but supportive since he came to town, and from what Justin could see, he'd gone long lengths to treat the Owen girl with the kind of respect she deserved. He frowned. That was, he'd gone long lengths to treat her with respect. If someone asked him, Justin would have to be of the opinion that the kind of respect a sixteen-year-old girl deserved from a man who was nearly thirty was distance and avoidance. Obviously, Randall had other ideas.

But he had always had other ideas.

Justin lowered himself to the bench behind the counter. The store had been closed for hours, but he hadn't been able to leave sight of the telephone. Just in case it rang again. Just in case the Owen girl changed her mind and needed to contact her mother. Just in case.

He pushed his glasses up to balance on his forehead and rubbed his face with both hands. Randall had always been a problem. Had always been the spoiled one. The child born to his mother long past the years she thought she'd be able to conceive. A late-life blessing, she called him.

But a blessing he was not. Justin's father had died when he was young, and Randall's father met the same fate. Only Randall's father died before he was even born.

So he'd been raised by a grieving mother. And Justin, being more than a decade older, hadn't wasted any time leaving home and leaving his mother to deal with his younger brother.

There'd always been questions about the boy. He'd disappear for days on end and come back quiet, more relaxed. Their mother would call Justin, concerned, but then later excuse her concerns as a mother's weakness. Justin would listen and then do nothing.

And now his brother had walked into Justin's life again, and once again, Justin had concerns. He picked up a pencil, twirled it between his fingers, and watched the instrument spin, and then stop, and then spin and stop again. The problem with Randall was the same problem as always: by the time Justin thought he had him figured out, news from somewhere came and changed everything he thought he knew.

The phone call did just that. It changed things. It shifted his mindset from trying to believe his brother had turned around and wanted to do the right thing to suspecting everything again.

If Randall and Jessie had gotten married, they'd be staying in town for the night. Justin knew that much. No sense subjecting the wedding night to an irate father. He dropped the pencil, feeling a little sick at the thought of the Owen girl spending the night with Randall. But her mother had signed off, so what could he do?

And what did the police want with Randall anyway?

CHAPTER THIRTY-TWO

His breathing became regular and steady, and Jessie eased from underneath the covers. Stumbling over his shoes, and the overwhelming mountain of masculine clothes and things, she eventually felt her way to the bathroom, eased the door closed, and slid down the wall to sit on the floor. She didn't bother with the light. Nothing in the dark could compare to the pounding of regret. Jessie hugged her knees to her chest, trying to process what had just happened.

She'd done this to herself. Raising a shaky hand to her hair, she felt for tangles and combed them out with her fingers. She had ignored the warning looks from her mother and the outright demand from her father and had made her choice.

The cool tile felt good. Lowering her legs, she felt every bruise, every inch of soreness that earlier she'd tried to ignore. She was a wife. Most women were wives at some point. She should be able to handle this.

Feeling along the wall, Jessie found the button for the lights and pushed it. From where she sat on the floor, the tiny sconce shades did little to dim the blaze from the bare bulbs. Jessie blinked until her eyes adjusted then pushed up off the floor.

A mirror hung from the wall above the sink. She steeled herself to look, to assess the damage, but when she did, nothing stood out. She turned her face, checking her cheeks and her neck. Stripping off her nightgown, she examined farther down for marks or anything that gave evidence to the way she felt. But nothing stood out. Her own blue eyes appeared as they always did: unexceptional.

She turned the knob on the faucet and splashed water on her face. Cold dripped down her arms and neck, a mixture of relief and punishment. She reached for a washcloth and plunged it under the icy water. Lifting it to her face, she pressed the cloth to her eyes, breathing in the moisture.

It had started gentle. He'd started out gentle. She rubbed the fabric against her closed eyes, trying to wash the images from her memory. She didn't want it. Any of it.

The water pooled into the sink basin. The nearby tub beckoned, but she didn't want to risk waking him. He slept now. Jessie knew her place was beside him. She might never sleep again.

She turned the hot water on to temper the cold and found a bar of soap. Lathering it against the cloth, she rubbed gently around her face, but as the tears fell faster than she could wipe them away, and the soap stung her eyes, she began scrubbing in earnest. First her face, then neck, then arms and chest, and everywhere he'd touched. And finally, the place she wanted to forget, the place she wasn't sure she could ever clean again.

Her knees buckled and Jessie let the cool, hard reassurance of the floor soothe her hot face. She'd let him. She'd let him do those things. Those things that were so much worse than she'd imagined. Her skin burned with shame, thinking of the times they'd spent behind her house when she'd thought she'd wielded some kind of power, when he'd let her think she'd had some kind of control. She'd been a fool.

She swallowed, gritting her teeth against more tears and holding them back until her throat burned with the pressure. Climbing to stand at the sink once again, she looked in the mirror, at her red face, at the stupid child who still stared back. Why she'd thought once married she would suddenly transform into a woman, she'd no idea.

She was wiser, though. Much wiser.

And now she knew the cost. She looked at the door handle. Going back to the room, sleeping next to him, was inevitable. So was watching her family go hungry if she hadn't married him.

Everything had a price. Now she knew the price. She'd live with it. No other choice existed. Shrugging her nightgown back over her head, she pushed the lights off and stood in the dark until her eyes adjusted. Tomorrow she would have a home all her own. A home she could be proud of. A home that would stand up to any storm, with enough rooms for her siblings if necessary.

Tonight she would lie next to her husband. The price. She could pay the price.

★★★

The whole town watched the car ease up to the front of the store and stop. Randall stepped out first and walked around to open the door for Jessie. Emma nearly cried out when she saw her daughter climb the steps. Overnight, she'd become a wife. She was his.

Emma squeezed her eyes closed. She'd have to tell Henry, but suddenly being honest with him paled in comparison to her concern for Jessie. She hadn't shone like a new bride should. Rather, the weight of life hung over her like a cloud. Randall was not the man Jessie had hoped for. Emma wiped away a stray tear. God forgive her. She'd wanted it to be real, for Jessie. For their family. She'd fooled herself into believing he could be what Jessie had hoped.

Jessie hadn't even looked down the street before disappearing into the store. Emma watched the steps long after she'd gone in, wondering what exactly she should do. Slowly, she walked back to her own house, sat next to Henry on his bed, and told him everything she'd done.

★★★

Randall ushered Jessie into his brother's store. She looked beautiful, held her head high, and played the role perfectly.

Last night had been difficult. He knew it would for her. But she'd calmed down quickly and seemed to be settling into her role. It wasn't Randall's fault the marriage bed held less appeal for women than it did for men. In his experience, though, eventually, the woman came around. It just took a while for them to shed the romantic fantasies fed to them by their friends and their dime novels.

"We're going to need a few things," Randall called through the curtain to the back room where he could hear Justin shuffling stock around. "And I thought we should stop by so I can introduce my wife to you."

Justin peered out from behind the curtain. "Some people from out east called for you." He paused and softened his voice. "It's nice to see you, Jessie."

"Thank you, sir," she answered.

Randall cocked his head to the side. "What did they want?"

"Wouldn't say." Justin set down a box he'd carried to the front of the store. "Just that they were looking for you. Wanted to know if I'd seen you."

"What did you say?" Randall tried to keep his expression neutral, but good things never came from people interested enough to call and ask questions.

"I told them you were out of town. They asked when I might expect you back, and I said I didn't know."

"Good."

"Why is that good?"

Justin's superior tone had Randall fighting to keep his breathing even. It was just like his brother to be sticking his nose where it didn't belong.

Randall ignored his question and dropped a few items on the counter. "It being our honeymoon, of course, you will have the courtesy not to send anyone out to our place, at least for a while?"

Justin agreed with one, curt nod. "Of course."

Randall took Jessie's elbow, gathered their supplies with the other hand, and led her out of the store and back to the car.

★★★

Back at the house, Randall opened the door for Jessie then shut the door behind her. They stood together in the kitchen for a long moment.

Randall exhaled loudly. It was a sound that communicated impatience, disdain, and amusement all rolled up together. It also demanded a response. Jessie dropped her small bag on the table and crossed the room to the sink. "What would you like for dinner?" she asked, still unsure what to do with her time in the huge house.

"You decide. I'll be out back." Randall dropped his things onto the table alongside Jessie's and left out the same door they'd entered.

For the first time all day, Jessie took a breath.

Looking around the room, Jessie almost laughed aloud at how the old widow could have never imagined her, the poor girl from in town, standing at her sink and thinking about what to make for dinner. Jessie glanced at the flowered skirt she wore. She'd no idea whose it had been. No idea who had worn it before her. It had to be pinned in at the waist, but Jessie was altogether satisfied with the crisp, fresh fabric. She'd never owned anything like it. Certainly, her mother had never worn anything so nice. Jessie picked up an apron off the hook next to the door, tied it at the back of her waist, and glanced around the room.

First, she would put their things away.

Picking up the bags, she headed up the stairs to the room they would share. The faded, yellow-flowered wallpaper had her smiling despite the giant bed that now seemed far too small. Jessie frowned and dumped the bags on the bed. If she wanted to make the best of the situation, she needed to get some things done. Standing there accomplished nothing. Besides, maybe the first night as his wife wasn't meant to be nice. Maybe tonight would be better.

Unlatching the buckle of his bag, she spread the sides wide and peered in. His things lay in a tangle of clothes and ties and handkerchiefs. She pulled the dirty items out in a bundle and looked around for a basket or a hamper to drop them into. They smelled of pine and mint. Different. Foreign. She held her breath, hoping that when she made the laundry soap, scrubbed them clean, and ironed them she would also be scrubbing the scent of him away.

Finally, she located a basket behind the door. She kicked it closed and shoved the hamper full. Already there were things that needed laundering. She frowned at the wicker container and decided the first thing she needed to do was create a schedule.

After she made dinner.

After she emptied her own bag and figured out where to stow her clothes.

Jessie pulled her things out, threw the dirty ones into the basket, and tried not to consider that her clothes shared a space with his clothes, and none of it seemed right.

She shoved the bags under the bed, near the head so they were hidden. Her possessions in this strange house felt out of place, like none of them belonged. She stood back and examined her reflection in the white-framed mirror. There was a choice—she could either try to make the house hers by displaying the few ugly possessions she had, or she could start new and learn to fit in with the beautiful things that already sat so comfortably in the home.

The latter seemed the better idea. She brushed her hands down her waist and turned to make her way back to the kitchen.

The stocked pantry called to her. Not asking her to cook, necessarily, but more as a brag of abundance. Only two of them in the house and nearly every shelf stood stacked with colorful jars and bags and boxes of dried goods.

There were things she'd never even seen, let alone knew how to cook.

She pulled a can of meat from the shelf—beef, the label read—and set it aside. It came in a gravy, so that saved time. Bins at her feet boasted their items with painted carvings cut into the hinged wooden doors. Jessie calculated how long it had been since the old widow had lived in the home. It didn't take too long for onions or potatoes to sprout. She steeled herself for the sight of climbing roots or the odor of rot and lifted the lid to a happy surprise of fresh produce. Plucking two large potatoes from the bin, she stuffed them into her oversized apron pockets and made her way back to the stove. The pans were piled neatly on the shelf above, and when the meat finally bubbled, and the potatoes boiled, she rushed back to the pantry to pluck a can of peaches from the shelf.

By the time Randall came back in, Jessie had set the table, and she was just pulling the sugared biscuits from the oven. "Oh, good. I was just going to call for you."

Randall hummed and toed off his shoes. "Bunch of machinery in the barn needs working on. Anyone around here see to that kind of thing?"

"Steel might. The owner of the gas station. He's getting on in years, but he might be able to help." She looked at Randall, who clearly wanted her to continue. "And then there's any of the other farmers. Most of them have been working on the machines since they were kids. They should be able to help." The pan she'd been holding started heating through the towel she'd grabbed it with. She set it down on the stove to let them cool.

"What'd you make?"

"Beef with gravy and potatoes." Jessie took his plate from the table and scooped a large helping of the cut and buttered potatoes. Then she ladled a glob of the beef and gravy mixture.

"That's beef?" Randall stared unconvinced at his plate.

Jessie stilled. "It's what was in the pantry."

He looked at it like she'd offered the chicken scraps to him. "Don't you like beef and gravy?"

Jessie could feel his gaze on her face. She forced her eyes up to meet his. "I ... I'm sorry. I can make something different."

Randall shook his head but didn't bother to clear the frown from his brows. "There's meat in the refrigerator. This stuff isn't really fit for people."

"I ... I hadn't thought to look in there." Jessie fought back tears. Her first meal, and he didn't want it. Was there anything she'd be able to do?

"I'm sorry," Randall offered. He patted his knee, signaling Jessie to have a seat there.

She tried to act naturally, to rid her spine of the stiffness, but when his hands ran up her back and settled onto the bare skin of her nape, she couldn't stop the brittle trembling. "Don't worry, sweet. I'm sure there are some cookbooks around here. You're probably not used to cooking fresh food. That will change."

The words flew by in a tumble right past his fingers as they worked her apron knot free. Jessie concentrated on controlling her breathing. In and out. Slower. In. Hold it. Out.

"Little bird. You don't have to be afraid."

Jessie chewed the inside of her bottom lip until she tasted blood. "I ... I'm not afraid." Her heartbeat roared in her eardrums. It was a wonder she could hear his words at all. "Do you want something different for dinner?"

"Those biscuits smell nice. What do you say we skip dinner and have dessert? That way we can head upstairs early. It's been a long day."

Nodding stiffly, Jessie returned to the stove and pulled two bowls from the counter where they'd been left to dry. She tried not to clank the bowls together as she set the biscuits into the bottom and spooned canned peaches over them, but her shaking hands and the deathly still of the airless room made it impossible.

With the bowls placed in front of them both, she forced down a bit of the cool peach and tender biscuit. But nothing had flavor sitting across from him. She squeezed her eyes closed and swallowed what had become an impossibly large ball of dough in her throat.

"This is delicious," Randall offered. "Now, if we can only teach you to cook real food."

CHAPTER THIRTY-THREE

Emma ushered the children from the house. The range of emotions as Henry processed both her and Jessie's deception had been unlike anything she'd ever seen. The flash of white-faced anger faded quickly. Emma knew it would. Henry never could hold a grudge. Sorrow quickly replaced the flash of anger and then the tears fell.

That's when Emma made sure even the smallest of the children played outside.

Turned away from the room, Henry lay on the bed, unable to stop the broken, shuddering, silent sobs.

"Can I get you anything?" Emma asked quietly. She stood behind him in the front room, looking down at his thin form huddled under the sheet.

He didn't respond. Emma sat for a minute, then stood, then sat again, unable to decide what, if anything, could possibly breach Henry's sadness. Finally, she made her way into the kitchen to fix a cup of coffee and sank into the chair next to the kitchen table, the one where she'd spent endless summers peeling and snipping and preserving food for the winter. The chair where she'd sat to brush the children's hair and tie their shoes, when they could better afford them.

She leaned forward and rested her forehead on the bare table, trying to work out how they could even keep the house, let alone the furniture. They'd been separated from their families back east so long, she didn't even know the names of her cousin's children anymore. They couldn't go back there. Not with five children of their own.

She wiped away an audacious tear and took in a deep breath. At least, in all this, Jessie wouldn't go hungry. At least she had a chance.

Randall might not be the best man—he might not have been the man they'd hoped for their daughter—but what could they hope for now? A strong farmer? There weren't even any farms to be had, let alone young men running them. She swiped her fingers across the table, leaving a line in the fine coating of dust. Even most of their topsoil had abandoned the panhandle.

But Jessie wouldn't go hungry. And right now, that was probably the best any of them could hope for.

She didn't regret her decision to give Jessie what she wanted. Not for a minute. A lot of women dealt with difficult husbands. Jessie had certainly found herself one of those. But the payoff of not being hungry held a lot of value right now.

Emma loved Henry fiercely—she had since they were young. And her reward was to watch her children become homeless. She lifted her arms to the table and dropped her head into the cradle of her hands.

Well, not one of them, at least. Maybe Jessie had been right. Maybe she would love her husband, and he would love her back. Maybe her reward for being brave would be a house full of healthy, thriving children.

Emma sat up and wiped a stray tear. At least, she hoped so.

★★★

Lillian wiped down the last pew and stood to measure her success. The sun's rays were only beginning to make shapes on the wood floor. It would still be a while until people arrived. She tossed the oiled rag onto a bench sitting at the back of Peter's office. "I wonder who'll be at service today."

Peter frowned. "I wonder who I want to see at service today."

Ever since he'd tried to visit with Henry, Lillian had watched Peter go from angry to sad and back again so many times, she never knew which he'd be feeling from one moment to the next. Henry hadn't wanted to speak. It was as if the man had given up.

And who could blame him?

Lillian scooted the rag over and sat on the bench. Her pressed yellow skirt, her favorite, flared at her knees. Her mother had sent new stockings in her last package. Lillian longed to wear them but decided on the old pair with small runs instead. New stockings were a luxury no one in town could afford, and when she put them on, even if they were a gift, guilt accompanied the delightfully smooth, new-stocking feel.

So she folded them and tucked them into her drawer. They would wait for better days.

Peter squared the loose pages of his sermon and tucked them into his worn Bible.

"Do you think they'll come today?" Lillian didn't have to add the new couple's name. It was all either of them—most of the town for that matter—had discussed for days.

"I'm sure they will." Peter frowned. "I know everyone needs the Lord, but when it's obvious that someone comes to church for reasons other than meeting Him, it's harder to..." Peter let the sentence die off. He frowned and looked up at Lillian.

"I know," she said.

"I didn't expect this. Any of this."

"I know that too."

"When we came here, I suspected life could be hard for us." He stood and walked over to the window. Crossing his arms over his chest, he took a deep breath and shook his head. "We both knew it. When we came here, I expected we might have to eat oatmeal for two meals a day. I felt prepared for worn clothes and hymnals that fell apart."

"But..." Lillian let the sentence die off, hoping he would keep talking.

"But I had no idea how helpless I would feel watching others deal with how impossible this all is."

Lillian stood and walked over to Peter. She waited for him to open his arms, then laid her head against his chest.

He reached around her, closing her in. His words rumbled against her ear. "Not having enough is one thing. Anyone can do that. People are strong, they can endure. But not having enough for a sustained time, an indefinite time, well, I watch them and pray for them, but it feels like something inside of me is dying. Like my soul is slowly leaking out."

Lillian closed her eyes and listened to his breathing, willing strength into him.

"How do I encourage them when the only choices they have are bad ones? I'm supposed to be the shepherd, but other than deliver food every once in a while, or pray at a bedside, there's nothing I can do. There's nowhere I can lead them. This is as good as it gets. People we love are forced into bad decisions. And I can do my job. I can love them and watch them eventually succumb under the weight of their choices, or I can rail at them about their choices and then we get to watch them suffer, or chase them away from a church that expects more than is humanly possible from anyone. Either way, I'm guilty." He let out a harsh laugh. "I am, I have, as few choices as anyone else."

Lillian lifted her head. "Don't you see, though? None of it is humanly possible. None of this. We live and we die. Not even that is in our power. We can't control any of it."

Peter squeezed her a little tighter, then let his hands drift to rest at her waist.

"What are you going to preach on this morning?"

"The only thing we have left. Grace."

***

Jessie sat in the car until Randall walked around and opened the door for her. He'd parked in the road in front of the church, and Jessie's face burned with the burden of other people's stares.

"Everyone is looking," she said as she stepped out onto the hard-packed dirt.

"Let them stare." Randall smiled and placed Jessie's hand in the crook of his arm.

Together they made their way up the stairs and to the front of the church. The service began as she settled into the pew so far away from the one her mother claimed.

When they'd walked in, she hadn't met her eyes, but she could feel her mother's gaze on the back of her neck. They hadn't spoken since she'd left—Randall seemed to always keep her busy—and now she wore new clothes and sat with a different family. She stole a glance at Mr. Mitchell—Justin, he kept reminding her to call him. For some reason, Randall had done everything he could to avoid town and his brother for the past few days. Jessie had tried to talk to him about it, but it seemed to make him angry, so she'd given up on trying to reason out why her husband acted the way he did. After all, she had a hard enough time just figuring out what he did with his days when they weren't together.

She picked up the hymnal from underneath her seat and flipped to the first numbers scrawled on the board. The pastor led out and people joined as they could.

No one in town had what could be considered a trained voice. Except Randall. His smooth tones rang out over the rest. Jessie mentally tamped down a surge of pride she hadn't earned.

The congregation sang the three hymns and sat down. Jessie arranged her new skirts so that the ruffles flared in loose waves and rested on the back of her calves. She fought the urge to rub one leg against the other to enjoy the smooth feel of her new stockings.

The pastor preached. She tried not to look at him too much; after all, he had refused to marry them because of her bullheaded father. And even though Jessie still liked their pastor—he'd always been so nice—Randall had little nice to say about him. The sound of jingling change announced the offering plate, and Jessie was glad to see Randall dropped money in as he handed it back to the usher.

The sermon droned on and Jessie closed her eyes, seeing her siblings in her mind, the way they probably wriggled uncomfortably in their Sunday clothes. Her arms ached to hold Little Henry. Randall stared straight ahead, head high and listening to what the minister had to say.

Life with him was tolerable. As long as she did what he asked, she had little to complain about. From what she could see, being married felt a lot like living with her family. You did what you were told and everything went smoothly. You didn't, and there was a price to be paid.

It hadn't taken her long to learn the price: silence or a flash of anger. She hated the patronizing smile he gave her at dinner every night when she watched him take his first bite, hoping more than anything, that her biscuits pleased him. They never did, but she'd been reading the old widow's cookbooks, and she'd made some improvements.

When the time came to farm the land, when the rains returned and they could plant, things would be better. No wife wanted to stare at her husband pacing listlessly because he had nothing to do.

Not that Randall didn't keep busy. He'd go into town, or he'd spend time making small adjustments to the machinery. Start it and then stop it again to make sure it still worked. Sometimes he left to meet with the banker, and sometimes he came home late. Those were her favorite days because she would leave his dinner to keep warm in the oven and then pretend to be sleeping when he came upstairs.

Yes, when he worked in the fields for sixteen hours a day, she could maybe sneak over and talk to her mother, or even invite her brothers and sisters to stay an afternoon.

For now, though, he took up a lot of space.

Jessie glanced up to the pastor as he bowed his head in prayer, glimpsed Justin, then bowed her head too.

Justin's expression had grown graver every time she saw him. Maybe he didn't understand Randall like she did. Over dinner, Randall had told her how he and his brother didn't grow up together much because of the difference in their ages. But they were all family now. Jessie looked at her hands folded in her lap and adjusted her fingers so they folded the other way. It felt strange. Just like sitting in the wrong pew.

But strange didn't mean bad. And this new life wasn't all bad. Strange meant strange, and it would stay strange until she got used to it. Then new strange things would happen, and they would make this pew and her seat next to Randall seem normal and good and comforting rather than unsettling.

Randall hated it when she fidgeted. She did her best to stay still until the end of the prayer then followed him back out of the church without speaking to anyone else. He liked it better that way. He liked her to keep focused on his needs. After all, she was his wife now, and it was only right. Jessie glanced back after Randall settled her in the car and smiled out the window at her mother.

This was how it should be. She needed to learn to be a wife. Then, when she had her house in order, the way Randall liked it, then maybe she could invite her mother to visit.

Jessie looked down at her hands folded in her lap. She hadn't anticipated missing her mother as much as she did.

CHAPTER THIRTY-FOUR

Justin frowned as his brother drove out of town on a cloud of black dust. The other folks leaving church covered their mouths and noses or stepped back into the building. He shook his head. Before Randall came to town, people respected the Mitchell name. Now, Justin couldn't understand how anyone could come to the conclusion their family deserved respect after the stunt his brother had pulled with the Owen girl.

Woman, he supposed. But sitting next to the pair of them made it so that lunch no longer seemed necessary or welcome. Justin shrugged apologetically to the now dustier crowd huddled by the church entrance. How his brother could get to nearly thirty and not realize that people around here didn't consider being dirty a desired price to pay for the privilege of watching him roar out of town, he didn't know.

But then, there were a lot of things he didn't know.

Like why so many phone calls came in from out east. People looking for him. People wanting him to answer a few questions.

Justin began to suspect Randall's move west, to a place almost wiped off the map, had been born less of a desire to connect with family and make a place for himself, and more of a need to disappear.

The Sunday crowd dispersed, and Justin crossed the street back to his store. He could call on Randall, maybe let him know people were still phoning for him.

Or he could wait to see how everything panned out without his interference.

It was definitely the safer option. Justin closed the door and waved to Mrs. Owen and her children as they passed before pulling the shade and blocking out the raging afternoon sun.

★★★

The fancy car rumbled by for the second time that day. Sidney crossed his arms and frowned at the trail of dust. Back and forth every day. No one needed to be that busy and still get nothing done. Not like there were fields to plow or a harvest to bring in. No. Just back and forth, fancy clothes in a fancy car, doing nothing but driving around to impress folks with no desire to be impressed.

Someone should tell the boy he'd landed in the wrong spot. No one here cared the least bit if he had seams pressed into his trousers.

Sidney didn't like that man. Even more than he didn't like the banker.

He kicked up on his chair, balancing on the back two legs. He'd stay for a while there, at least until the sun levered down to get in his eyes. Then he'd move.

But he liked the spot. He'd discovered something about that particular place only after the old widow died and the city boy moved in with the Owen girl. Why her parents allowed such a thing, well, Sidney had no idea, but it must have been something the girl wanted right bad. The Owens were good people, and good people didn't mix with folks who weren't good people. And that kind of mixing, well, nothing seemed right about that.

But what he'd discovered about the spot had him staying there. Wasn't much around he could be useful with, but if her parents weren't going to protect the girl from the likes of that city boy, and the opportunity presented itself, Sidney supposed he could. And with his chair tipped just so, and his neck turned at the comfortable angle that let him rest his head against the dried window sill, well, at that perfect spot, he could hear when that fancy boy started hollerin'.

He never liked men who hollered. A lot of men do, but he never did, and his pa never did, and his grandpa hadn't either. In his family, it was the women hollering, but only when the young ones deserved it, or when dinner was getting cold 'cause no one minded the bell. But men. Men didn't need to holler. God made them bigger, gave them an advantage 'cause when they came into the room, the fact they were taller and took up more air made folks listen. Sidney flicked a bug off his stained and faded denim overalls. So men who needed to yell to get heard, well they were just men who didn't have the confidence or the brains to think they'd be heard without having to look the fool.

He never remembered hearing his neighbors before. Of course, they had been quiet folks. Sidney let the front legs of his chair drop back down to the dirt. It must be something about the ground now, about the grass that had gone missing, and no animals; something about all that must have worked to make sound travel, like it did from a boat over a lake to the folks on shore. At least between their two houses.

So he listened. He waited to hear their car doors close and strained to figure when they might have stepped into the house. Sidney kicked up again to lean his chair back and listen to however that sound moved. He waited.

Some folks didn't seem to be able to see the bad that had planted itself right in front of them. Even if it introduced itself and wore pressed pants and drove a fancy car. Some people couldn't see what could happen.

But it was okay, because even if they couldn't see, in this spot, he could hear the trouble coming.

★★★

Lillian dropped her napkin on the table and slid her plate to the side. She'd grown tired of watching Peter push his potatoes around, tired of the silence, tired of coming home from church every Sunday and watching him deal with the questions of why they were there, and what they could do.

It used to be enough that the services went well, that his sermons went off without a hitch, and that the old women left with encouraging words and the old men nodded their thanks. It used to be enough for him to come home with her and pull the Sunday dinner from the oven, and then leave the dishes on the counter and nap until the sun poured in at an angle steep enough to tell them they were encroaching on the border between time spent restoratively and being plain old lazy. It used to be enough. And she used to be enough.

But she had no more ability to make it rain than anyone else, and for all the frustrations of not being able to offer his flock anything of value, his guilt at not being able to help them in any meaningful way, of not being able to make things better, Lillian knew it would all disappear with the simple addition of water.

Life was only possible with water. But none of them had known the quality of their lives—the kind of lives worth living, the kind where people could walk with their heads high, make decisions, know they had some power over their future—depended on that water.

Without water, all they could do was repeat the torture of trying just to watch their efforts dry up and blow away. Day to day living became a game of endurance, not necessarily against the sun and its withering rays, but against the hard-set reality that nothing they did really mattered. When the consequences of decisions, either good or bad, were far less powerful than the everyday trudging, meaning in anything was hard to find.

And that's where they were. Lillian watched her husband move from straining against the lack of opportunity, to making decisions based only on whether or not it was right or wrong, to mucking in the filth of the shifting reality of right and wrong. When consequences didn't exist anymore, and children's tummies rumbled no matter what a parent did, then meaning became secondary to nothing. It ceased to exist.

★★★

At a knock on the door, both Lillian and Peter jumped. They stood together and walked to the front of the house. Without bothering to peer through the window first, Peter opened the door to Justin standing on his stoop.

"Do you mind if I come in for a minute?" Justin held a folded paper in his hands.

Peter glanced down at the wrinkled sheet then stepped over to make room for him. "Come on in."

"Would you like something to drink?" Lillian watched Justin fidget with the folded piece of paper. She knew before he answered that no dust-covered water would be necessary. He was in a hurry, and he needed to speak with her husband.

"No. No, I'm fine. I just need to talk to you." The comment had been directed at Peter.

"I'll be in the kitchen if you need anything." Lillian smiled and left the room quickly. Whatever had happened, Justin looked like he needed help. Lillian closed the door then pressed her ear against the warm wood, more to see if she could hear than to find out what exactly was being said. Either way, she knew as soon as Peter had the chance, he'd tell her the reason for Justin's visit. She made out the sounds of papers rustling and the rumble of men's voices before she stepped back to the counter to set the cover on the butter dish. Quietly, she washed their plates and silverware and listened for any sign that Justin might be leaving or that they might need something from her. Once finished, she leaned against the counter and glanced up out of the window.

The sky had been blue. All day. The clear kind of blue that looked like the travel posters that hung in some of the businesses in town. The kind of blue where if she held her hand up to cover the drifts of dirt and leaning, empty fence posts, she could almost smell fresh-cut hay.

She squinted, studying the distance.

A mountain rose there, just barely. A line on the horizon. It was hard to tell at that distance if it was the echo of some strange shadow or if the afternoon sun was playing tricks. Mirage lines wavered there in the distance, obscuring her view. Lillian rubbed her eyes. Clarity on the sunburned landscape was elusive.

She dried her hands on the dishtowel and looked again. She'd seen something like that before, when she'd been on a train ride with her parents. They'd been traveling west, and she'd watched the mountains change from a hazy lavender line into towering cliffs in a matter of hours.

But this line wasn't purple, and they were nowhere near the mountains.

Lillian dropped the dishtowel and looked around the kitchen. Peter. And Justin. She shoved her feet into her worn shoes. They had to warn the people what was coming.

CHAPTER THIRTY-FIVE

Jessie stirred the soup as quietly as possible and checked the clock on the wall. Randall hated a late lunch.

He'd retired to the parlor, and she'd breathed in relief. He would leave her alone for now. Setting the wooden spoon to the side of the stove, she covered the pot and set out two bowls and two spoons. As a child, she'd dreamed of one day setting more bowls out, of one day watching her children climb up the chairs and sit at the table, waiting for her to serve them. A foolish dream. She glanced at the door between the kitchen and the parlor and wished she knew someone who could help her figure out how to make that not happen. Jessie could deal with his moods, with never getting anything just right, with the stares and the understanding that somehow she'd disappointed him, but the thought of a child growing up like that—she shook her head and straightened the spoon so it rested precisely on the napkin—the thought of her children growing up like that made her pray for a barren womb. She already hadn't met his expectations, and he rarely looked at her without exasperated exhaustion. The sleeve of her shirt inched up, revealing the reddened skin she hoped wouldn't bruise. What was one more failure?

★★★

A crash woke Sidney. He opened his eyes a crack and listened for the shouts he knew would come.

And they did. Much worse than before. And then a scream.

He dropped the front legs of his chair, uncrossed his arms, and stood. The scream came from the old widow's house. Sidney planted one foot in front of the other and crossed the empty road.

Another scream. Crying. At their mailbox, he broke into a run.

★★★

"I think you need to take a look outside." Lillian shrugged her apology to Justin for interrupting their discussion.

"What's going on?" Peter stood and looked around the room as if he could see the problem from where they'd been sitting.

"Outside." Lillian was already at the front door, holding it open and pointing down the road.

Justin and Peter crowded next to her.

"Over there. Look at the horizon."

"Lord help us," Justin said.

Peter grabbed his hat and handed Justin his. "We need to warn as many people as possible. That's going to hit hard."

Lillian tied a scarf around her head. "How long do you think we have?"

"No saying." Justin buttoned his collar and tucked his shirt in tighter. "Twenty minutes, a half hour maybe. It depends on how fast the wind is moving. Heaven knows there's nothing in the way to slow it down."

Lillian looked at Peter. "I'll move west, you two go east. Meet you back here in ten minutes?"

Peter paused then nodded hesitantly. "I don't like you going out in this." He dropped a quick, hard kiss on her forehead and Justin looked away. "Be careful."

Lillian nodded and ducked out in front of the men. Peter pulled the door closed tight behind them. There was no wind. The sun baked down as it had all day, and the sky boasted the same impossible blue. Lillian turned in the middle of the street to see how far the lumbering black blizzard had spread. It went as far as she could see.

She took off running to Emma's first, barking orders for the children to get in out of the yard.

★★★

Sidney couldn't remember the last time he'd run anywhere, and he felt it. He slowed and stopped for a second to catch his breath. Dropping his hands to his knees, he bent over and sucked in as much air as he could. Crashes still rang out from the house. Sidney was almost as angry about the lack of care for the old widow's things as he was frightened for the girl who had been foolish enough to live there with that man.

He glanced to the left and stopped.

A black wall billowed in an undulating line at the horizon.

Sidney broke back into a run toward the neat house, his legs pumping as fast as he could as the sun beat down against his head.

He hit the front door with enough force that he was surprised he hadn't knocked it from its hinges.

Randall opened it and was met with Sidney's fist.

★★★

He flew and landed, sprawled out at Jessie's feet. She stared at Sidney.

"Miss, there's a mighty big storm brewin' to the west." Sidney pointed to the western wall as if Jessie would be able to see through it.

She didn't have to.

"Heard a ruckus from this sod." Sidney kicked the hand of the semi-conscious man at his feet. "Heard the yellin'. You shouldn't be here with him."

Jessie didn't try to stop the one huge tear that spilled from her right eye. It hurt when she blinked. "I thought ... I thought he would kill me..." She couldn't tear her gaze from her crumpled husband. He'd been mean. She brought her hand to her face, feeling the damage from his fists.

"You sit down." Sidney stooped to help Randall up. "I'll figure out what to do with him."

Randall shook his head as if he could rid himself of the aftereffects of the punch. He groaned and, now sitting, took a wobbly upward swing at Sidney. Still standing, Jessie backed away and sucked in a breath. Her expanding ribs screamed out. She pressed her hand against her side and watched the realization hit Sidney.

"He hurt you there, too?"

Jessie didn't respond. Sidney sent a dark look to the man struggling to get off the floor.

Randall stared back with dead eyes. "Get out of my house," he hissed out through his clenched teeth.

Sidney crossed his arms and didn't bother to say he planned to do nothing of the sort. A train couldn't have moved the man.

Randall's neck blotched an angry red. "Fine. I'll be coming back with the police. You can't come into someone's house and attack them." He looked at Jessie. "Let's go," he ordered.

The seething words hit Jessie as if they'd come from far away. "I ... I..." she stammered.

"She won't be goin' anywhere with you." Sidney took one step to the right, blocking Randall's path to Jessie.

"You'll come with me now." Randall held out his hand and stared past Sidney.

Jessie bit her bottom lip and looked around the room for somewhere to escape. She said the only thing that came to her mind. "There's a storm coming."

Randall sneered at her. "I'll be back with the police."

"You do that." Sidney frowned, clearly waiting for Randall to move on his own effort.

Jessie watched her husband walk out the door and slam it so hard the pictures on the wall rattled. Sidney walked over, and with one motion, locked the door behind him.

Then he walked into the kitchen and did the same.

Step by step Jessie followed him through the house.

She looked out the window and saw the swollen, rolling black cloud. She glanced back to Sidney. "Is he going to be okay?"

She looked down to where Randall unsuccessfully attempted to start his car. The grinding engine noise made its way through the glass of the kitchen window.

"He's got the barns or the cellar. He's a grown man. He can find someplace to go. He ain't gettin' back in here, though. Not with you." Sidney frowned at Jessie.

"Engine won't turn over." She pointed out the window.

Sidney shrugged. "Too bad."

Jessie touched her side again. She looked up to see Randall glance at her through the window, shout something, and then take off running to town. "He's going to try to reach the town before the storm hits."

"His choice."

Jessie shifted her gaze to the growing, heaving monster on the western horizon. "We have to get ready." She quickly opened the pantry and grabbed a basket of clean rags and a tub of oil. "Dip these and lay them in the window sills and tuck them in every crack around the doors you can find." She piled the dry rags in his arms. "Hurry. And close the blinds as you go."

Sidney nodded and followed her directions.

Jessie stopped and reached out to touch his arm. "Thank you. I..."

Sidney smiled. "No need, miss."

CHAPTER THIRTY-SIX

The three of them met in the street outside Peter and Lillian's house as the first gust of wind slammed into the town. They ducked against the force of it and ran inside, holding the door so the wind wouldn't take it off the hinges.

"I think you're going to be here for a while." Peter raised his voice so he could be heard over the noise of the wind and the debris it carried.

"Thank you." Justin chuckled, once. "Don't think I'd like to try to make it home right now."

Lillian pulled back the curtain. The roiling black wall towered overhead. To the east, the sun still baked the dry ground. To the west, the cloud, black as night, dominated as far as they could see. "How tall do you think it is?" Lillian craned her neck to try to see the top of the wall of dirt.

"We need to get things buttoned up." Peter began oiling rags and handing them to Lillian and Justin. They both nodded and spread out, stuffing rags in the corners of windowsills and jamming them against door thresholds.

"My store is going to be a mess when I get back." Justin frowned. His understanding of the damage his store would undergo was difficult for Lillian and Peter to watch.

And then the first blast.

The wall of dirt hit the house with enough force to suck the air from the building. Lillian took a step nearer to Peter, listening to the crashing upstairs as the wind battered the roof and then threatened to take it off completely. Thick black settled into the room, and Lillian could hear Peter strike a match against the box. The flame flickered to dusty life. With shaking hands, Peter lit the lantern at the center of the table. The house shuddered.

Justin walked to the window. The sound of static electricity scratched down the sides of the house. Lillian reached up to smooth the hairs at the back of her neck. The old timbers rattled and groaned against the force of the dirt carried by the wind.

Lillian and Peter grasped hands and sat together on the davenport while Justin eased into the facing chair. Hungry for light, they all stared at the flame as it struggled to illuminate the dirt-laden air. This would not be a short-lived storm. Lillian squeezed Peter's hand, reminding them both that they were safe for now, and then let go. The dry air rushed between them, sucking up the little moisture that had been preserved where their palms met. Standing, Lillian felt her way into the kitchen and returned with three damp flour sacks. Justin nodded in gratitude, fighting back a cough, and took the wet cloth from Lillian. They tied them over their faces and sat back to wait for the black wind to stop.

★★★

More than an hour passed before Peter leaned in close to ask Lillian if she'd gotten to everyone.

"I think so. I stopped at the Owens' first. All their kids made it in."

Peter nodded his understanding. It was still difficult to hear, but the wind had gone from brutal, roof-threatening gusts to more of a steady battering. Lillian's eyes fell to the papers Justin had brought over, still lying on the end table. Justin nodded permission for her to take a look.

Lillian opened the first letter and smoothed it across her knees. It was a notice for Randall to appear before the police so he could answer questions about his first wife's death. Lillian glanced at Peter, who had his expressions firmly under control. Justin nodded for her to keep looking.

In an envelope underneath were newspaper clippings. She leaned into the light to shuffle through the collection of speculations regarding a socialite's illness and death. And then the headline that read she'd been poisoned.

Lillian looked up to Justin and he nodded. The socialite was Randall's first wife.

She felt her stomach churn as she shifted to the next paper. It was notice of a warrant for Randall's arrest for the murder of his first wife.

She gathered the papers and set them on the table. The thin newsprint fluttered with the dust-carrying drafts that, despite their best efforts, still managed to snake into the house.

"How did you get these?" Lillian practically shouted to Justin.

"I found them in his things."

She nodded. No explanation was needed for why he'd searched through his brother's belongings. There wasn't a person in town who didn't wonder what had brought the unsettling man their way.

"Do you think he's guilty?" Peter questioned.

"I've no doubt he is." Justin leaned his elbows on his knees then dropped his head into his hands.

Lillian stood and crossed to the window. She pulled the shade over. Dark had settled over the town. Every once in a while, the wind slowed, and she could see to the front gate. It had been ripped open. She couldn't tell if it was still attached.

She waited for the next lull so she could locate the gate.

Instead, the shadow of a man appeared then disappeared again.

Lillian watched more intently, waving Peter over to join her at the window. "Watch right there." She pointed to where the front gate should have stood.

Justin joined them, and Lillian pulled the shade all the way open. Seconds stretched to minutes, and then the man appeared again.

"That's Randall," Justin said. He took a step back. "I can tell by the way he moves." He looked first to Peter, and then Lillian, and then back to Peter again.

"He won't make it to your store." Lillian rubbed her hands on her apron and paced behind the men, Peter's deep breath-turned-cough reverberating next to her.

Justin turned from the window and pulled the shade closed. "He's a murderer. I can't ask you to risk your lives for him. It's dangerous to go out there in the first place, and I think it's even more dangerous to have him in here. As soon as he knows we know, there's no telling what he may do."

"I can't just leave him out there," Peter said.

"If I can, you can." Justin stepped back and shook his head. "He's not right. Never has been. I don't think there's anything wrong with letting him and God work this out."

Lillian watched her husband. The flicker of the lantern glowed against the side of his face, on his jaw, and the sheen of his forehead. Suddenly, the room felt like an oven. *Let him and God work this out,* Justin had said.

But Lillian knew better.

She knew Peter would understand the fact that she saw Randall out in the street as just that—as God working it out. God had already intervened. Peter's duty was already mapped out, because as a shepherd, he had no choice but to protect. His job was to do what was right.

Peter's muscles bunched under his shirt as if he steeled himself to receive a schoolyard punch to the gut. There was no question of the choice he'd make. Lillian just hoped the consequences were few and mild.

Peter grabbed his hat. "I'm going out there to get him. He can stay in the cellar until this is over. Then we'll hand him over to the authorities."

Justin shifted the damp cloth over his face and tied it as tight as he could. "You're not going out alone. I'll open the cellar and get it ready."

"You won't go anywhere unless you're tied off." Lillian reached into the closet for the ropes and handed one to each man. They nodded, tied the ropes around their waists, and she closed the door behind them, praying they would return safely.

★★★

Jessie rolled over and listened to the silence.

It had been three days since the wall of dirt had hit the house, three days of dark, of noise, and of talking with Sidney. She reached up under her nightgown and felt for the lump on her ribs. It still hurt, but nothing like it had that first day.

She closed her eyes and breathed out.

Now she would have to face Randall, wherever he'd gone off to. And then he'd come home.

The unwelcome silence only told her that the life she'd chosen was still waiting outside the walls of the house.

"Miss, you up?" Sidney called up the stairs.

Jessie groaned and rolled over. "I'll be down in a minute."

She glanced at the window with the shades still pulled. Light pierced through the minuscule moth-eaten holes. Jessie tried not to cry.

While the last three days had been filled with pain and worry that the house might tumble down around both her and Sidney, she'd never felt safer.

And she couldn't help it, but she loved the little, perfect house.

She walked barefoot across the dusty floor and slipped off her nightgown before buttoning on her dress. "How much of a mess do I have?" she called through the door.

She could hear Sidney chuckle all the way from the kitchen. She stepped into the hall to the welcome scent of bacon and biscuits.

"You may want to eat breakfast before we answer that question," Sidney called back.

Jessie looked at the dust built up against every piece of woodwork, in between the stair railings, and over the carpet. Sidney had opened the windows, and now, with the sunlight streaming in, everything had taken on the same color as the dirt outside. Even the pattern on the rugs had disappeared.

Luckily, Old Widow Ruby had a vacuum. Hopefully, it still worked.

Jessie walked into the kitchen in time to see Sidney loading up a plate with bacon. "I know the dirt is bad, and I know what's happened to you is real bad, but I must say, I haven't eaten like this since I can remember."

Jessie smiled and sat down.

They ate in silence. Jessie liked that about Sidney. He didn't need to fill up the space with noise. But it wasn't until the plate had been cleaned and Jessie had washed all the dishes that she got up the courage to ask if there'd been any sign of Randall.

"No. Looked around this morning a bit. Nothing."

Jessie nodded. They would need to get to town to ask if anyone knew anything about her husband's whereabouts and to check on her parents. When she hadn't been praying out of fear of Randall coming back with every thump at the door, she'd been praying her parents' house would hold up to the winds. She glanced around the kitchen. Dust covered everything, and cleaning would take days. But it would wait. All of it could wait.

"You think you may be able to figure out what's wrong with the car?"

"Nothing. Already been out there. It started right up."

Jessie took a deep breath. "We should go for a ride, then."

CHAPTER THIRTY-SEVEN

The quiet woke Peter with a start. He sat up and squinted against the light. Lillian had opened the shades and already had the sashes open wide.

"Nice of you to wake up." Lillian sent a wry smile Peter's way. He snorted, kicked his legs over the side of the bed, and then stopped.

"Has anyone checked on Randall yet?"

"Justin did this morning. He's gone."

Peter stood and reached for his robe. He shoved his arms in and tied it at the waist before slipping on his house shoes. "What do you mean, gone?" Peter made a face at the feel of dirt crammed around his toes and decided bare feet were preferable.

"I mean, Justin woke up earlier, went around to the cellar door, and it had been broken open from the inside."

Peter sat back down, causing a cloud of dust to rise into the room again.

Lillian frowned at him and went back to wiping down the dresser.

"How long ago does Justin think he left?" He stood again and tore off the robe, instead, reaching for his trousers. "We need to start looking for him."

"Justin returned to the store to see if Randall's there. If not, he's going to drive out to the old widow's house." Lillian shrugged. "Other than that, what else can we do?"

"If he were smart, he'd have left town." Peter paused. "And what time is it? Why didn't you wake me earlier?"

"Justin already called the police. It's only 7:30 and there's nothing you can do anyway."

"If he escaped during the storm, he may need help, wherever he is."

Lillian dropped the rag on the dresser and crossed her arms over her chest. "He doesn't deserve that kind of effort. He's a murderer. And no one in this town would be heartbroken to never see him again."

Peter shrugged into his shirt and buttoned it at the cuffs. "We'll let the police sort that out. Right now, he's still a person." He tucked his shirt into his pants. "And don't you think Jessie may want to know what has happened to her husband?"

Lillian frowned and picked up the rag again. "I'm going to do the best I can with this mess, and when it gets a little later, I'll stop by to see how the Owens are getting along." She paused. "What if Randall went back to the old widow's house? Would Jessie be safe?"

Peter bent and tied his shoes. "Justin doesn't think so."

★★★

Jessie and Sidney drove slowly into town and made a jerky stop in front of her parents' home. All except one corner of the roof was still on, and her brothers and sisters were outside picking up trash that had blown in with the storm.

Jessie jumped out of the car, but the stabbing in her ribs did short work of reminding her of her injury. She walked to the house and stepped in the gaping door.

"Mama?"

Her father's bed was empty, with the mattress folded up against the wall, and dust had piled into every corner of the room. They would have to take it out in buckets. In only a short time, she'd forgotten what it had been like to live through a dust storm in the broken old home.

"Papa?" She made her way into the kitchen. That's when she saw them both, sitting at the table. Her father turned slowly and stood. His movements were stunted, but he'd been getting better. By the time he reached Jessie, her mother already had her arms around her.

"Oh, thank God," her mother whispered into her hair.

Her father crushed them both against his chest.

And that's when it happened. When Jessie couldn't do it anymore.

The room spun, and the pain in her chest radiated down her legs. Her knees gave way, but her parents held her up.

"Look at you. Did the storm do this?" Emma put her hand under Jessie's chin and forced her face into the light of the window. Tears streamed down her cheeks, wetting the blue and black and green that colored both eyes and the angry red welt that ran from her chin to her ear.

"I'll kill him." Jessie's father didn't give her time to answer.

Her mother forced Jessie to look into her eyes. She questioned her silently, and Jessie answered with a nod.

Her father squeezed her tighter, and Jessie let out a squeak of pain.

"Got her in the ribs, too." Sidney ducked into the room. "Don't think they're busted, but she's gonna be sore for a while."

Her father loosened his hold. "Where is he now?" He directed the question at Sidney.

"Not sure. Kicked him out of the house right before the storm started."

"You okay here for a while?" Her father looked at Emma and grabbed his crutches. "I'm going to go talk to the old Mr. Mitchell. See if he knows where his brother is."

Her mother looked around at the weeks' worth of work they had to do and shrugged.

"You know, ma'am," Sidney said, "Jessie's got herself a pretty nice place out of town now. It would hold all you just fine. And I know she could use some help cleaning it up a bit. Why don't I take you and the children back out there? Mr. Owen can deal with whatever needs dealing with here. I don't think Randall will be showing his face around here for a while."

Jessie's mother took stock of the room and then looked back at her daughter. "Let's get the kids together and take a drive. It would be good for us all."

***

Justin had dumped every drawer in Randall's room and emptied the closet before he'd had the thought to check the attic access. He pulled the panel off and then tugged Randall's travel trunk out from the dark space. One hit with the claw of the hammer to each of the locks did the job, and now he knelt in the middle of the floor rifling through mounds of papers.

And stacks of cash. And jewelry.

The store bell brought him back to the present. Justin walked slowly down the stairs. Mr. Owen stood in the center of the store, relying heavily on his crutches.

"I need to know where your brother is."

Justin pulled the counter bench out and signaled for Mr. Owen to sit.

"I don't have time. I need to find him."

Justin furrowed his brow and made no attempt to skirt around his own question. If there was one thing he could count on with Mr. Owen, it was a direct conversation. "Why do you need to find him? What did he do?"

Mr. Owen's eyebrows rose slightly. "He beat my little girl."

Justin closed his eyes and dropped his forehead to his hands. He should have never let his brother come back, should have never believed him. "I'm sorry. I'm so sorry. Is she okay?"

"She's busted up, but she should heal. Where is he?"

"I've no idea."

Peter walked into the store and Justin waved him over.

"Good to see you, Henry." Peter clapped the man on the back. "Did your family make it through alright?"

Henry looked at Justin, and Justin nodded toward Peter. He motioned to an empty bench.

"You'd better sit down too, Pastor."

★★★

Peter and Justin walked Henry to his house, but on finding no one home and a note explaining Sidney had accompanied them to the old widow's place, they decided to climb into Peter's truck and start searching for Randall.

"He couldn't have gotten far," Peter said as they settled Henry into the passenger's side.

Peter glanced back to see Justin seated in the bed of the truck and took off.

They planned to first go out to the old widow's place to check on the rest of Henry's family and then start searching from there.

"How long you had this truck?" Henry asked. "It sounds like it still runs pretty good."

"Been a while. Lots of miles, but it's never given me much trouble except for the occasional flat."

Henry nodded and dangled his arm out the window. "Emma says you wouldn't marry them."

Peter hummed his agreement and looked at the man seated next to him.

Henry avoided eye contact by paying keen attention to the road.

"Didn't seem right without your permission."

"Thank you for that."

"Didn't do much good." Peter frowned. "Wish I could have done more."

"He beat her, you know." Henry looked at Peter, watching for his reaction.

Peter took in a deep breath. "I didn't know. Like I said before, I sure wish I could've done more to stop that from happening. Poor thing."

"You did what you could. You did the right thing. That's good enough. In these times, sometimes the right thing is a little harder to see."

Peter slowed to a stop outside the old widow's house. "We'll help you in then Justin and I will start the search."

Henry nodded. "Pastor?"

"Yes?"

"Maybe it'd be best if you don't bring Randall to where I am."

"Wouldn't dream of it. You all have dealt with enough today."

★★★

Peter and Justin had stopped by nearly every farm within walking distance, and no one had seen anything of Randall.

"Do you suppose someone might have picked him up?" Justin kept his eyes glued to the side of the road. It looked like a wasteland.

The drifts had all shifted, and Peter had to watch where he was going. "Nothing is where it was the last time I took this route. If everything can be different and the same at the same time, I think this is it." Peter frowned and wiped some of the dust off the inside of the windshield with his sleeve. "Lillian ought to be happy about this." He held up his arm so Justin could see the dark stain.

"Wait. Stop."

The car had barely slowed when Justin opened the door and jumped from his seat. He ran back and off the road a bit, punching through drifts of loose dirt and kicking up a cloud of his own.

Peter backed the truck up, following him, and stopped when the store owner bent to examine something on the ground. Justin waved him over.

Peter let the engine rattle to a halt. And then he walked over to where all but Randall's legs and his fancy shoes had been buried by the wind.

CHAPTER THIRTY-EIGHT

The Sunday morning service had gone as usual, except now Jessie sat where she belonged—with her family—and Justin decided to join them. Lillian couldn't help but smile at their full chapel. For some reason, the death of the most disliked man in town had brought the people together.

She decided not to dwell on it too long.

The police had come to investigate, and they'd informed Justin of the warrant and their belief that Randall had poisoned his first wife. The three of them—Peter, Lillian, and Justin—had watched the police follow the van with his body out of town as if it were some sort of macabre parade.

After that, no one knew what to do.

So they walked around town, let their greetings stretch into invites for morning coffee, inquired as to the wellness of their neighbors, and then waited for sincere answers. The grandmothers in town made casseroles from whatever they had for the new, young widow—more out of celebration and wordless apology than out of any sense of shared sorrow.

And now Lillian sat next to Peter in the truck with a pound cake in her lap on their way to a potluck dinner at Old Widow Ruby's place. But no one called it Old Widow Ruby's place anymore. Now it was the Owen farm.

Peter slowed the truck as he maneuvered around new drifts of dirt. "I wonder when it will rain again."

Lillian balanced the cake with one hand and tucked a stray strand of hair behind her ear. Peter had preached that morning on grace, like he usually did, except this time he sounded like he believed it. "Your sermon was nice this morning." She looked at Peter, and for the first time in a while, he resembled her husband. The worry that had collected around his eyes and the tense lift of his shoulders were gone. For a second, he glanced her way then smiled.

"It's the same kind of sermon I usually preach."

"I know." The fence posts continued to whiz by. Eventually, Sidney's windmill came into view, and Peter slowed the truck to turn down into the Owens' drive.

"Did you know that the town will meet next week about hiring a teacher for the upcoming year?"

Lillian lifted her brows in surprise. "Where's the money coming from?"

"Not sure yet. I think a lot of the families will pitch in what they can. I suspect Jessie will help as much as she can with the money she's been left." Peter pressed the brake and came to a stop amid a number of other rickety old vehicles. "There's talk that some of the mothers in town could take turns teaching."

"I could help with that."

"I thought you may."

Lillian looked up at the neat house. Visitors' shadows drifted from one room to the next. "I never expected it to be so hard."

Peter nodded. "It's not over. There's still no rain, there'll be no crops this fall, and possibly no planting next spring. People are still hungry, machinery is still rusting, and we are still waiting."

"But that's not all we're doing."

Peter laughed. "It sure feels like it."

Lillian shook her head. "We're waiting with them. That's why we're here. We're here to wait with them, to stand next to them even when things get bad. We can't change it, but we can share it.

And that's all anyone needs, someone who will share even the bad times. It's hard because it's the most we can do, but it feels like the least."

Peter reached over and twisted his fingers between Lillian's. He lifted her hand to his lips and kissed the back of her knuckles. "If we're here to stand by in the bad times, then let's not miss the good ones, okay?"

Lillian nodded and looked up to the house to where Jessie stood on the porch, waving them in.